Also by Joan London
and available in Picador:

Gilgamesh

THE JOAN NEW LONDON DARK AGE

Joan London

PICADOR
Pan Macmillan Australia

Sister Ships first published 1986 by Fremantle Arts Centre Press
Letter to Constantine first published 1993 by Fremantle Arts Centre Press
'The Photographer' first published in *Risks* (1996), edited by Brenda Walker,
published by Fremantle Arts Centre Press
'The New Dark Age' first published in *Best Australian Stories 2002* (2002), edited
by Peter Craven, published by Black Inc.

The photographs included in Joan London's story, 'The Photographer', are by
John Joseph Dwyer (1869–1928). The photographs are 'Miss A Farrar' and
'Mr E Allum, 1908', and are from the Museum of the Goldfields, Kalgoorlie.

This combined edition published 2004 in Picador
by Pan Macmillan Australia Pty Limited
St Martins Tower, 31 Market Street, Sydney

A CIP catalogue record for this book is available from the
National Library of Australia

ISBN 0 330 36487 1

Typeset in 13/15 pt Perpetua by Post Pre-press Group
Printed in Australia by McPherson's Printing Group

Papers used by Pan Macmillan Australia Pty Limited are natural, recyclable
products made from wood grown in sustainable forests. The manufacturing
processes conform to the environmental regulations of the country of origin.

CONTENTS

from
SISTER SHIPS

SISTER SHIPS

1.

Kaye Garrett is late again. She has rushed into the cabin in her bikini and thrown her wet towel on my bunk.

'Have I got time for a ciggie?' she asks, lighting up anyway though she knows we are First Sitting. Then she gets down to work. She circles her eyes with a sort of white lipstick and dots biscuit-coloured lotion onto the compass points of her face. I take this opportunity to slip her towel onto the floor.

'I don't know why you go to all this trouble,' Bar Holland calls down from the top bunk. 'The people on this ship are only interested in food and sexual intercourse.'

'Oh?' says Kaye Garrett. 'Why do you say that?' Her eyes are open very wide in the mirror but she's not looking at us. With a little black brush she is grooming the wing of her lashes. Does she know that as she does this her mouth springs open like a fish?

'Observation,' Bar Holland says. I hear her yawning. 'I haven't put it to the test.'

The dinner chimes crackle over the P.A. Doors

slam up and down the corridor and a great wave of people calling out and jingling keys seems to rush past our cabin. I stand up. I have been ready for ages.

Kaye rips off her bikini and reaches into the wardrobe. 'Oh Hull.' She's turning to me, she's holding my pink shirt. 'Oh Hully, would you mind, could I please . . .?'

I take a breath. I've practised this. I was going to say, in a light, pleasant voice, 'Actually Kaye, I'd thought of wearing that myself tomorrow.' But when she stands in front of me like this, naked, watching me, as if she's testing me, I don't know where to look . . .

There is a quick knock and the door swings open. Kaye screams and clutches my shirt to her.

'Sorry ladeez, so sorry ladeez.' It is Taki, our cabin steward, with an armful of towels. He backs out, groping to close the door behind him.

'Bloody Taki,' Kaye says. She's buttoning up my shirt.

'Hot Greek blood,' calls down Bar.

'He must have thought we'd gone to dinner,' I say. 'We *are* late.' In the mornings I find him waiting outside the door with his mop and duster. I say, 'I'm sorry. The other girls are still slee-ping.' I put my head on my hands to mime a pillow. He nods and smiles. He understands.

'Oh yeah?' says Kaye. 'He's always barging in.' She's pulling on a black skirt, tucking in my shirt. The pink shirt is part of an ensemble my mother and I bought after my last day at school. 'For deck games,' my

4

mother said. Sometimes I think about the Trip as my mother planned it. It is like another ship travelling alongside this one, with all its passengers on deck waving in a friendly sort of way. There are bound to be some awfully nice types amongst them, my parents had a ball on their Trip Out, they are waving but getting hard to see now, the animal throb and grind of this ship is leaving them behind.

The lights flicker in the narrow corridors. We stagger a little as the ship sways. Voices are rising in the bars, 'Aloha' and 'Chelsea', where the early drinkers have settled in. As our heels clatter up the stairs two stewards hiss from a doorway: 'Psst! I love you!' We look straight ahead but we giggle. Don't they know that with us their case is hopeless?

We part at the doors of the dining-room. Kaye Garrett sort of glides in past us, gone for the night.

'I'll meet you here afterwards,' I say to Bar Holland. If I don't say this she is quite likely to wander off in her absent-minded way, and then I am alone for the whole evening. '*Here*, okay?'

'Okay,' she says. She brings her book with her. She sits at a table with a big family. Quite often they are sea-sick and only the father is there. He is glad of a bit of peace and quiet, Bar says. He's quite happy if she reads between courses.

My table is for four, on the far side of the dining-room. I take my usual seat, next to the German man.

I say Good Evening to him, I have never caught his name. He wears a white suit to dinner and has a short white beard. He's about my father's age: it is his eleventh sea voyage. This is all I know about him.

'We thought you were going to miss out on the soup,' Marie says from across the table. She is a secretary from Wollongong. 'Still not to worry, we've only just got ours as usual.' Marie is frustrated by the service on this ship, especially at the table. 'It's the same old story,' she told me, 'the quiet ones get overlooked.'

'Hi,' says Eric, who sits next to her.

'Try and catch the waiter's eye,' Marie advises me, 'when he goes to that big table.'

But I don't want any soup. I am trying to think of something to say to Eric.

'How did you go at deck-tennis this afternoon?'

He laughs. 'I got a thrashing. I'm out of the tournament. I think I'm going to have to invent deck-cricket. Maybe I'd make a better fist of that.'

I laugh, understandingly. I know that Eric plays cricket in summer, swims all year round, likes early Blues and opera, grew up on a farm in northern New South Wales, has just finished his second year of Law. I know because over two weeks' meals I have asked him. The trouble is, I'm running out of questions. He asks me questions too sometimes, often the same questions. I've told him three times now that I've just done my matric, that I'm going to stay with relatives in England.

'Get a load of that would you,' Marie says. 'That big

table. On to the main course already and we haven't even ordered the entrée!'

'I met another girl from Perth today,' Eric says to me. His nose is sunburnt, a big nose, he isn't really good-looking. But the first time he came to our table and smiled and pulled Marie's chair out for her, I thought: He's *nice*. 'A blonde girl, Barbara.'

'Oh, Bar Holland. She went to school with me. She shares my cabin.'

'She seems like quite an original.'

'Yes. Well I didn't really get to know her before this trip. We were in different classes . . .'

'You can't have any secrets when you share a cabin, I can tell you,' Marie says.

'Do you share a cabin?' I ask the German man after a while. It seems so terribly rude not to say anything to him for the whole meal.

'I am alone,' the German man replies. 'I prefer.'

'I think I would too.' I give a little laugh. 'Not that I've got any secrets.'

'Ah,' says the German man. 'Without secrets nothing is possible.'

'What *is* your cabin number by the way?' Eric asks me.

'There she is,' I say to Bar Holland. We are taking our after-dinner stroll around A Deck.

'Who?'

'*Kaye*. It looks like it's Officers' Night tonight.'

'Chelsea' is dimly lit, but the pink shirt, the white

uniforms around it, glow in the light from behind the bar.

'I suppose it's a good way to learn Greek,' I say, climbing up the ladder onto Boat Deck behind Bar Holland. There is a railing at the front of Boat Deck, past the funnels, where we always stand. It is as high and far as you can go.

I want to talk about Kaye Garrett with Bar, but something holds me back. 'All that make-up,' I want to say, 'do you think she looks *hard*? Do you think she looks older than seventeen? I think swearing is unfeminine. Does she swear in front of men? What is sex-appeal anyway? She's got lots of nice clothes herself, I don't know why she . . .'

It is quieter up here, we are further away from the engine, you can even hear the crisp breaking of the wake, white in the black sea. The wind blows back Bar Holland's beach-white hair from her long, stern chin. Her eyelashes are white too, so that her stare beyond the ship seems unblinking. I wish that I was like Bar Holland, my mind on higher things.

'Think I'll go down and read,' she says.

'Yes,' I say, 'I *must* finish my letter.'

Music has started up in the ballroom. The soft thud of the drum, the even ripple of the piano. '*Leesten,*' the singer's voice crackles as he adjusts the microphone, '*do you want to know a see-gret?*'

Corridor by corridor we descend the ship.

We went to the ballroom once, on our first night aboard. Kaye was with us then. We sat at a table by the dance-floor and ordered drinks. 'To us,' Kaye said. The band, in midnight-blue tuxedos, winked and bowed at us. There was a solo on the electric guitar, the theme song from 'Bonanza'. A middle-aged couple danced a professional tango under the swirling gold hexagons of the dome in the middle of the ceiling.

'Oh my God,' Kaye Garrett said, 'This is *dire*.'

But after a while the ballroom filled with people, Second Sitting people. The band took off their coats. The dance-floor thronged, lights dimmed, shadows raced around the walls. A white uniform bowed before Kaye. She got up slowly, her face was severe over his shoulder as they circled the floor. Bar Holland and I sipped our drinks, islanded amongst empty tables and chairs. Bar Holland stood up.

'I'm going,' she said. 'I'm bored.'

We made a great show of fanning ourselves on the deck, of gasping for fresh air.

'Who do you write all these letters to?' Bar Holland's bunk creaks above me as she changes position, sighs, flicks pages. I look at my watch. 9.30. We have made our descent too early. But there's no going back. That would be against our code, our anti-ship stance. And I've already rollered up my hair.

'Oh – my parents mainly,' I say.

'S'pose I ought to drop the folks a line,' says Bar. 'But what do you say? "I am eating, sleeping and reading. Fondest regards".'

'I'm sure they'd like to know how you are.'

The bunk thumps, Bar Holland's legs wave past me. She crouch-lands on the floor. 'They know I'm alive,' she says. 'The rest is just – role play.'

'But your parents – well, they feel for you,' I say from the shadows of my bunk.

'Do they?' She is walking up and down the cabin breast-stroking the air. 'How do you know what you feel if you just keep on spouting off your lines?' Her voice trails off, she yawns. 'Anyway,' she mutters, 'I don't seem to go in for *feelings*.'

There's a knock at the door. I shrink back clutching my rollers. Bar Holland opens it an inch. Her blouse at the back is hanging out of her skirt. Her hair is fizzed into a little crown from lying down.

'Oh it's you,' she says. She sounds almost angry. 'Oh all right, why not.' She reaches for her key on the dressing-table.

It's Eric.

2.

You should see me now, I write, *lying back next to the swimming pool!* I pause. This is more or less the case. It was a relief to see this empty deckchair as I picked my way through all those brown oily bodies. 'Yes dear, come and join me,' the old lady in the next chair said. She's asleep now. We're not all that far from the pool. *The weather is perfect, everybody is here.* I waved to Kaye Garrett but she didn't see me. She's amongst a very lively crowd of people. Marie waves though, from under her big sun-hat, while another girl rubs cream into her shoulders. Even the German man is standing by the railing, looking at something through binoculars. *Bar Holland's in the pool, having a swimming lesson!* Eric kneels by the side of the pool while Bar thrashes her way up and back to him. When she emerges, spouting water, hair plastered over her eyes. Eric leans right down to her to demonstrate a stroke. *Luckily I have the cabin to myself a lot these days. I am teaching English to our steward. He brings me his photos and I point and say 'brother-in-law', 'grandmother' etc. He is very grateful.* His knock is so gentle it might be just another note in the rattle and hum of the cabin. The cool dark cabin. I shut my eyes against the white glare of the deck. *Actually it's getting very hot out here, I can't last much longer. I don't think I'm ever going to finish this letter!*

The funny thing is, I can't see my parents any more. I mean I can't see their faces. I see them as silhouettes moving round the rooms at home, dark figures against light coming through doors and windows. I see light coming onto the kitchen table, onto the knives and forks in their set places, but the room is empty. I see the pool of light under their bedroom door. Voices . . . *join in* . . . *people of her own age . . . the Garrett girl has got a berth* . . .

I see my father's big frame blocking the light of the hall as he comes in from checking the letter-box. The jingle of small change in his pockets has a disappointed sound.

———————

'Do *you* speak French too?' Eric asks me at lunch.

'No.'

'That's a pity. We could have put in a bit of practice over *déjeuner*.' He is buttering his roll lavishly, smiling to himself.

'Bar Holland got the French prize at school,' I say. It is Cold Cuts for lunch again today. I choose a small slice of Luncheon Meat. 'And then of course this scholarship to Paris.'

'Well she's got a real challenge on her hands now,' Eric says. 'She's going to have me speaking French by the time we get to Southampton.'

'Ah ha,' says the German man, his voice cracking out, crusty. We all turn to him. 'That is the best way to learn a language. The language off love.' His head shakes up and down over his plate. I can't tell if he's laughing. We all bend back over our plates.

'Bar will do it if anyone can,' I say. I reach for the Worcestershire sauce and shake it over my meat. 'Not only is she terribly intelligent, she is a very hard worker.' I take my time, making a little package for my fork. 'At school she had no time for anything else. No sport, no social life. It was work work work.' The ship dips, the bright water in the porthole behind Eric flashes on, flashes off. The words keep coming. 'She was sort of famous for it.'

'My cabin mate Nan and I,' Marie begins, 'we can't understand a word our steward says to us. Speaka da English *please*, I say to him . . .' I can hear Eric scraping back his chair, but Marie has caught my eye and won't let go. 'Wouldn't you think they'd try and get an English-speaking crew?'

'If you'll excuse me,' Eric says.

I put down my knife and fork. I can't eat the Cold Cuts. They taste of the ship's refrigerator, they taste as if they have soaked up all the smells of the ship. The ship itself is like a giant refrigerator. If you turned it off you would smell its staleness, its collective odours from a thousand lives in cold storage.

That the knock does come, at the same time as yesterday, makes it seem like an appointment. I too have my rendezvous. I don't leave him to use his key, but open the door myself.

His eyes are waiting for me. No mop, no towels. He's not pretending this time that he has work to do. I recognise the red plastic cover of his photo album.

More photos? That cheerful teaching voice. But it helps, to get me to the bunk, turn on the little spotlight over the pillow, pat a place for him.

Seester, nai-phew, brudder-in-lo. It is touching to see this manly hand, black hair crawling from the cuff over the fingers, stabbing so patiently.

Very good. Pounding blood seems to fill up my eyes. I peer at stoic faces clustered up the front steps of a house. A bare twiggy tree by the balcony. I point. *Brr. Cold.*

Cold? He slides an arm around me. *You are cold?*

No no. The photo. Must be winter. His thighs nudge mine, narrow and hard, like gateposts. *When it's winter in Greece, it's summer in Aus . . .* I am falling back.

You good girl. His breath is warm in my ear. *The most good girl on the sheep.*

Best. The best girl. But I . . . But my voice is small again as he covers my face with little popping kisses. Our knees rise as the bunk creaks. He lurches on top of me and flicks his tongue wetly into my ear, kisses my neck, squeezes my breasts. All this is, I know, to be expected. He is quite systematic, in a hasty way. He seems to be in a hurry.

So this is what it's like. A full close-up of a scalp. He's heavy. My legs are flattened off the edge of the bunk. There's saliva on my chin, but my arms are pinned to the elbow. I roll my eyes and catch sight of Bar Holland's big bottle-green school bloomers slung to dry over the towel-rail. It is rather clinical, I decide, like being in a dentist's chair. The same helplessness, the same need to remind yourself there is no reason to feel embarrassed. His hand is steadily ruching up my skirt. *You should see me now . . .*

'No.' I push at his shoulder. 'Please.'

He lifts his head. 'No?'

He is up like a shot, tucking in his shirt, looking round for his photo album.

'I'm sorry. I didn't mean . . .' I have broken a rule, I know. I have *led him on.*

He smiles down at me. He shrugs.

'Leetle girl.'

He ducks for a moment at the mirror on his way out and, using two hands, smooths back his hair.

3.

We are getting into colder waters now. The swimming pool is covered with a net. There are whole decks where the wind sweeps down and the spray leaps up to startle only empty deckchairs. The sea and sky have joined forces, huge, murky and untrustworthy.

'Dirty old day,' the old lady from the deckchair mutters as we pass. Her head is bandaged in a scarf as if she has the mumps. We seldom pass without a nod or comment, we fellow deck-bravers, who've taken over now the brown bodies have deserted, the blind man and his wife, the mad boy counting his steps, the Indian couple, her peacock skirts brushing against wet railings, the tired-looking father from Bar Holland's table, the German man in a black, high-shouldered coat.

Inside it's different too. The rattle and sway of the ship fighting its way seems to diminish the music and the voices. The bars are cosy and crowded, all day people huddle by salt-misted windows, shrieking as their glasses slide and slop across the tables. There is a sense of closing-in, an end coming.

I see Bar Holland and Eric everywhere. If I pop my head into the Lounge, looking for a private corner, they will be there, frowning over chess. In the Writing

Room, where I might sit, but never write, they are sharing a desk, whispering. I see them emerging from the Cinema, Greek Dancing Classes, the Purser's Office. Will they think I'm spying on them? They do not see me, they are too involved in a sort of permanent private debate. Bar Holland's bumpy suitcase, her pile of dog-eared paperbacks remain untouched in the cabin. Her bunk with its virgin turned-down sheet is a still-life. She is more tousled than ever, but exercise has given a sheen to the pale planes of her chin and forehead. She wears, day and night, a big sweater of Eric's.

Now that I spend so much time out of the cabin, I see a lot. I leave the cabin early, well before breakfast. I see girls with set faces weaving their way in evening clothes up dark corridors. During one of my long mornings on the deck, I see two husbands start a fight between the funnels, with little puffs of punches, stumbling feet. One night I see Kaye Garrett bent over the railing, being sick. I recognise her by the luminous fuzz of my pale-blue angora sweater. She tucks strings of hair behind her ears and zig-zags haughtily back to the bar.

If I see a uniform coming, I have my escape routes. I know my way around the secrets of the ship. I skirt roped-off passages, fortress doors, steep metal stairways marked STRICTLY CREW ONLY. I pass clattering kitchens, doors sucked closed on blackness, tiny decks just above the water where dark men smoke and laugh.

Sometimes it's unavoidable. I have to keep walking. I drop my eyes and watch my feet pass theirs. There is always a whisper, a hiss, a laugh. Once I heard it. *Leetle girl*.

I say it over and over to myself through sucked teeth. I suppose I'm hoping that, like an orange, humiliation can be sucked dry.

One night Eric is late for dinner.

'Will I order the soup for him anyway so as not to hold us up?' Marie asks me and the German man.

'This is not like Eric,' she says a little later.

We eat our soup. We order and munch away silently at our Fried Schnapper à la Saint-Germaine. We are about to tackle our Bon Fillet à l'Anglais with Ribbon Potatoes when Marie spots him. By turning in my chair and following the direction of her faintly shaking finger I can see him too, wedged in next to a pillar far across the dining-room. A fork stabs the air in front of him. A blonde head subsides behind the pillar.

'We've been deserted!' says Marie. She leans over and takes Eric's bread roll, pops it in her bag. 'Aren't I awful?' she says to me. 'Nan and I get starving after Bingo.'

Like Marie and the German man I eat steadily, right through to the Sherry Trifle and Selected Cheeses, and leave my plate bare.

When the P.A. announces that at twenty-one hours and ten minutes precisely we will be passing our Sister Ship, I climb the ladder to the old place on Boat Deck. The sky is star-dazzled. Nobody else seems to be around.

A row of lights comes suddenly out of darkness and rushes towards us. I can feel our own pace now as the Sister Ship takes shape, slides her long glittering flank beside us. The two ships snort at one another like animals from the same litter, mournful bellows across the frothing wakes. Rockets spray out from between the answering sets of funnels. I glimpse long shelves of decks under swinging lights, hear scraps of frantic music. Tiny figures lift their hands: I have lifted mine, like a salute. Then they are gone.

I sleep a great deal. I dream. I dream I am sitting at the table with Marie and the German man. The waiter puts before me a big plate of bones. Large, angular bones, freshly butchered, tufted with meat and cold white fat. I am unable to stop myself attacking the bones. I gnaw, dribble and crunch: as I throw one over my shoulder I reach for another. I shut my eyes and groan with satisfaction. Marie and the German man watch me. Marie shakes her head, sorrowful. 'You are very greedy,' she says.

One morning the wild black decks are forbidden to the passengers. But it's the dangerous hour below, when stewards come out with sheets and keys. I slip through Reading Rooms, Cocktail Lounges, the deserted bars. I come to the ballroom. On the stage the piano is open and the German man is playing. I take a seat at one of the empty tables across the floor.

At first I watch the German man. He has gathered his long private face together as if he is regretful about something. He makes mistakes, stumbles, only just makes it over a hill of notes, but he never stops, his fingers push on, bite down.

Then I pick up a pattern in the notes. Just as I wait for it again it breaks up, scatters, comes together differently. It seems to me the music has a voice that knows more than I ever will, that leads me on, further, further, and at the last minute shows me where it is the pattern really lies.

The German man throws his hands into his lap and swivels on his stool. He shows no surprise at seeing me.

'I play very badly,' he says, shaking his head, though to me he seems flushed and exhilarated. 'I do not practise for a long time.'

'I wish I could play like that.'

'The Hammierclavier. First and second movements.' He gets out a handkerchief and slowly wipes his face. 'It is just like anything else. At first it is technical and then the meaning starts to come as you learn the piece.'

As I get up to go he says, 'You should hear it played – right – one day.'

'Yes, I will try,' I say.

———

'I've put on that much weight,' Marie sighs over soup. 'Still not to worry, I'll probably have to starve in London.'

Our destination is very close now. Suitcases block the corridors. There are flustered queues outside the Purser's Office. Addresses are exchanged in bars rowdy with farewell. The waiters slap down our plates. The menus are stained and repetitive. I take two sips of my Creme Milanese, crumble my roll.

'You're not pregnant are you?' Marie says with a wink at the German man. 'I bet you wouldn't be the only one.'

The German man eats on as if he hasn't heard.

'The trouble with you is,' she says a little later, leaning over to me, 'You're a worrier. You mightn't think it, but I'm a worrier too.'

I have noticed that lines spray out from Marie's eyes and mouth and tendons strain in her neck when she peers at other tables.

'That's why I'm on this trip. You've got to get out of yourself, mix in.'

I don't dare look at the German man.

'I tell you what,' Marie goes on, 'Nan and I are going to the Fancy Dress Ball tonight. It's the farewell do. Why don't you come along, make it a three?

'I will think up a cozzie for us,' she says with a wink. 'Leave it to me.

'Tonight at eight-thirty then, my cabin,' she says.

The German man looks at his watch, stands up, nods to us.

'I'll be glad to see the end of him,' Marie says, as we watch his square white back leave the dining-room. 'There's something about him . . . you know?'

She reaches over and takes his orange.

Kaye Garrett is sitting cross-legged on her bunk, writing. I have not seen her for days. I ask her if she's going to the Fancy Dress Ball.

'You've got to be joking.'

She doesn't look as if she's going anywhere. She is wearing just a T-shirt, bending through her bare knees to an exercise book and ashtray on the coverlet.

I sit down on my bunk. 'What are you writing?'

'My diary.' She doesn't stop. Her hair is scraped back into a pony-tail. She is left-handed. She writes very fast, her hand looping like a child's.

After a while she looks up. Her face is scrubbed of make-up, her skin looks damp and porous, there are dark circles under her eyes. This is how she used to look, last year. Her house was right near the school, by the river. She would stalk into the classroom late, breathing morning steam. While she stuffed her beret into her pocket, her eyes travelled the desks, as if she was counting something up. Or looking for something.

'I'm trying to sort out where I stand,' she says. 'I'm in the shit all over the ship. Greek men are terribly possessive, Hull.'

She bends to write. I can just hear the scratch of her pen. It has a companionable sound.

'Maybe I won't go to that ball,' I say.

'You've got to do what you want *I* think.'

She is still writing when I get up to go.

'Bye Hully,' she says, quite gently.

It is strange to leave Kaye Garrett behind me. Through the corridors I think of her bent head against the shadows of the cabin, and the scratch of her pen, writing.

I can hear the rustling even as I knock on Marie's door.

'Oh there you are,' she says, pulling me inside. She is wrapped neck to foot in white crepe paper. 'Put your arms up! Come on! We're going to miss the Grand Parade.' She starts to wind white paper around me too, so that we both crackle like bonfires. 'Pins Nan!' she calls. 'This is the little lass I've been telling you about, the one from Perth.'

Nan is not in costume. I recognise her as the girl who's often with Marie, the one with the long neck and the red-rimmed eyes as if she's just been crying. She smiles at me through little childish teeth.

'Don't move,' Marie hisses through pins.

'What are we?'

'Guess!' She waves two cylinders of black crepe paper at me. Each has an uneven white cross glued to it. 'Our crowning glory,' she says, 'Oh what a hoot!'

Nan wedges one onto my head while Marie adjusts hers in the mirror. They press down over our eyebrows. We look at one another with pained, spaniel-hooded eyes.

'Sister Ships,' says Marie. 'These are our Funnels. Aren't I clever?'

She slings a whistle on a string around my neck. 'Your foghorn. The idea is, in the Grand Parade we sort of run past each other blowing our whistles.

'Come on,' she says, looking at my face, 'don't go and chicken out on me like Nan. It's only for laughs. You can reimburse me for the paper and pins etc tomorrow.'

We totter up the stairs. The wind catches us as we cross the deck to the ballroom and we rustle like an army of bars. We clutch our funnels. 'They're going to die when they see us,' Marie whispers.

We enter the ballroom to a burst of cheering and wolf-whistles. But the crowd has their backs to us. As we crane, funnels lurching, the band strikes up, the lights dim, the crowd moves off onto the floor. Marie does not waste time on regrets.

'Now is our chance,' she says over her shoulder, swerving a course through dancing couples. She piles bags and coats onto a vacated table, drags the chairs right to the edge of the floor.

'Excuse me, excuse me,' she says, pulling a third chair from under a flailing hand, and sitting down on it.

'I learnt the hard way on this ship believe me,' she says, as Nan and I slide down next to her. 'Nobody's going to lift a finger for you.' She hails a waiter. 'What'll be your pleasure, girls? Going to join me in an Athens' Special?'

I am glad Marie is not too disappointed about missing

the Grand Parade. She seems to be thoroughly enjoying herself, peering at the costumes as they pass on the dance-floor. There are a lot of men dressed up as women, even pregnant women, with signs like SUZY WENT WONG and I SHOULD HAVE DANCED ALL NIGHT pinned on their backs. 'Oh get a load of this one,' Marie cries, slapping my knee. It is a man in a nightie and a necklace of gin bottles. He is called OFFI-CERS MESS. 'Oh there'll be some red faces here tonight.' She has to wipe her eyes.

The band launches into 'I Did It My Way'. For this the lead singer undoes the buttons on his shirt. It is very hot and stuffy. We have drunk our Athens' Specials. Marie sends Nan off to get some more.

An Arab headdress bows before me.

'Go on,' Marie nudges me. 'It's Dennis from Bingo.'

Dennis and I sway together for a while with linked, clammy hands.

'The band is very *thing* tonight isn't it?' he says.

'Yes.' I can't see his face, he's wearing dark glasses, like a sheikh.

'I got this Arab outfit in Aden. What are you supposed to be? Nurses? The Ku Klux Klan?'

'Sister Ships.'

'What?' The band is very loud.

'*Sister Ships.*'

'Oh ha ha, well don't let it worry you,' he says. I don't think he can hear me. He takes me back to my seat and asks Nan to dance. As they bump past I hear him say to her, 'The band is very *thing* tonight isn't it?'

The band plays 'The Girl From Ipanema' and people start to clap and move to the edge of the dance floor. Marie and I sip our drinks and peer through the crowd. The professional dance couple are at it again, under the swirling gold dome. Up and down they pass one another, back and forward, flashing smiles over their shoulders, they turn at the same moment, up and down again, it's a sort of prowl, back and forward . . . it makes me dizzy.

I blink and blink at the couple and it is suddenly clear to me that they are my parents. They are in disguise of course, like all of us: they have been on board all the time! It's their movements that give them away. The way they hold their backs so straight and know their steps so well, everything's planned . . . though there's something rather fixed about their smiles, they're not quite real, the way their arms flare out from the elbow at the same time reminds me of puppets . . .

'Your shout,' Marie is saying, pushing her glass at me. Her funnel has slipped over one eye.

I stand up with the glasses, keeping an eye on my parents. I edge around the dance-floor towards the bar. It is very important that they don't see me, make me join in. I have come this far without them now.

The ship lurches. I have to watch my steps very carefully, but I keep the gold dome swirling in the corner of my eye.

I look up and I see him. The German man, standing by the ballroom door. He is wearing not only his white suit, but also white gloves with which he holds his drink. On his head are fixed two large white ears.

I come and stand before him.

He bows. I see that his ears are two ship serviettes, like the ones that sit on our table, stiff white cones pulled into peaks. I glimpse the thin wire to which they are attached, circling his head.

The ship lurches the other way. He puts down his drink. He inclines his head very slightly towards the door.

'Ready?' he says. I could swear his ears twitch.

I am rustling down a long corridor. My funnel has fallen off, my crepe paper rips and drags behind me.

I am sure I saw something white flash around that corner.

NEW YEAR

1.

They are in the middle of a heatwave. All across the city people are doing unusual things. Walking into fountains, sleeping on the beach, holding conversations under a sprinkler . . . 'It's the heat': don't the Arabs have a wind, Rowena is trying to think of the name of it, a desert wind, so hot that a man is excused for killing his wife while it is blowing?

Harry and Rowena are having dinner with the Hutchisons. This is not unusual, since they live in the Hutchisons' house and share most meals with them: but it's New Year's Eve and here they are on the terrace, legs looped over chairs, opening their second bottle of wine. Festive yet resigned, like workers choosing to drink together after a hard day. The Hutchisons have chosen to stay home with Harry and Rowena tonight. This is what is unusual.

This is what Rowena thinks, stirring Harry's chicken stock in the kitchen. The kitchen is a glassed-in verandah three steps up from the terrace. Tonight it is a little box lit up with heat. Grease glistens in beads behind the stove. Oily fingers seem to have smeared everything, handles, cookery books, jars of herbs. Vine leaves over the terrace drape around the windows, limp and still, dropped hands.

The chicken stock is for pilau, Harry's speciality. Later Rowena, who doesn't have a speciality, will make a fruit salad. It's their turn to cook tonight.

Although Rowena likes watching stock, its slow rich bubble, she knows it does not really need stirring. She is really listening out for her baby Tom. If she can get to him quickly when he wakes – he wakes a great deal – she might be able to settle him back to sleep. Meanwhile she gives a few busy taps to the saucepan with the side of the spoon.

'The person who really needs a drink,' Hutch calls out, 'is Rowena.'

Lately Rowena has suspected a consensus in the house about her, about maternal over-commitment. Her case has been discussed, heads shaken . . . coming down the kitchen steps now as this person is not quite real to her. She feels a fruitless swinging to her arms, she is breasting dark air. She sits down quickly.

'This is very civilised,' Harry is saying. He has just taken off his T-shirt and he stretches out, rubbing the fan of black hair that spouts up over his waistband.

'Hardly civilised,' Hutch says, 'taking off your clothes.' He has a way of drawing out the Australian accent that makes everything he says sound measured and judicious.

'Let's face it,' Harry says, 'we're a hedonist culture.

On a night like this we ought to take off the lot.' His hand hovers for a moment over the front stud of his jeans.

'D'you hear what your husband's proposing?' Hutch turns to Rowena. She has no answer. She never has an answer for Hutch.

'Diane has more of the hedonist spirit,' says Harry. Diane is wearing a sarong hitched up and looped around her neck like a miniature toga.

'Oh for heaven's sake,' says Diane, rearranging her legs. 'It's *hot*.'

'Or is she just going with the au-naturel flow of our household?' Hutch says to Harry.

'I'll drink to that,' says Harry. Across the table his torso is white amongst the shadows of the terrace. Winter white. Like her own hands around her glass. It had stopped being winter when they first arrived here from the beach house. They had stood beside their car in the mild city air, pale, in coats, as if they had come a long way . . .

'What are you looking at?' Harry's voice is low across the table.

'My hands.'

'What's *wrong* with your hands?' Harry mutters. But a steady droning is rising from the house. Their eyes lift and meet. Tom.

'Already?' Diane says. 'He's incredible.'

'He fell asleep early,' Rowena says on her way back up the steps. 'It's the heat . . .' But who would understand the logic and rhythm of Tom's day? Who would want to? She takes her glass with her.

'How about some music,' Hutch is saying.

'It's your *turn*,' Diane says.

2.

In that house music was kept going like a tribal fire. Whoever came home first went straight to the living-room and put on music. The speakers were lugged up and down the hall on long cords, following the action. When they left again Rowena let the music die. There were many arrivals and departures. The Hutchisons were both studying part-time. After work they went to lectures and tutorials, also to films and concerts.

On the weekends they were careful to keep the sound well stoked. Music nudged away each moment, bit at the fringes of thought. Open the bedroom door and you swam wordless into it. The first nights they were here Rowena went walking. Up the empty street. Turn the corner. Drawn curtains at the end of driveways silhouetted with shrubs. Silence. Block after block of it. The beat of the music met her again on the home stretch. Their house looked party bright. She sat on the front steps and leaned her head against a column. It had caught the music's pulse inside it. She watched the light behind the roofs of the houses across the road. There was nowhere else to go.

Now as Tom sucks, his head seems to pump back and forward against her, in time. Their room is another

piece of the verandah, a partitioned cavern. Curtain-
less, it is dark all day, shadowed by the house next door,
but at night the neighbours' bathroom light beacons
through the louvres and everything, the cartons from
the beach house stacked around the walls, Harry's shirt
dangling from the door frame, the roundness of Tom's
head, is outlined in this dull radiance.

Last night, lying like this on the mattress, she had
said to Harry: 'How much longer are we going to stay
here?'

Harry had just shut his book, put out the light and
turned over: there was a sense of purpose about everything he did these days, even to going to sleep. He
turned onto his back and unfolded one finger, two, as
if they had been waiting to spring open.

'We're still paying off the bookshop.' He had to
whisper. Behind the wall next to them were the
Hutchisons, also in bed. 'We could never afford to live
like this so close to the city.' End of point two: he
closed his hand into a fist over their sheet.

'I could live in a tiny flat,' Rowena said. Whispering
was provisional, it was like taking off your shoes and
tiptoeing around each other. 'I could live in a room. If
we were alone.'

'We're always alone,' Harry said.

Tom sucks and, elbow up, she sips her wine.

————————

3.

The light is on under the vines of the terrace but nobody is there. Moths bang against the light bulb and fall among the glasses on the table. Somebody has watered the ferns and they rustle and drip around the steps. Intermission. This happens sometimes. Everybody will suddenly desert on private missions, to read the newspaper, make a phone call, slump across a bed . . . The light is on in the kitchen too. Harry is cooking.

He looks up as Rowena comes up the steps, his chin lifted, eyes gathered together to hold in the tears. But it will do for a greeting, it is so familiar. Onions. He turns back to his chopping board. Steam rises, oil sizzles ready, his strokes are neat and sure. Harry cooks with a sense of ceremony. Step by step, a beautiful patient logic towards a known destination: no panicky improvisations, no peering at the recipe wishing it would tell you more.

He is singing, a beat behind and lower than the larger voice that fills the room beyond them.

> 'Still crazy,
> Still crazy,
> After all these years . . .'

Harry singing, onions frying: Rowena stands for a moment in the doorway. He has always sung, to car radios, in supermarkets and restaurants, easily, knowing the words, 'Yesterday', 'O Sole Mio', 'You Are So Beautiful', as if in tune with a fellow experience.

'Want some help?'
He never says he does.

The Hutchisons' house is old, one day they are going
to knock it down. Meanwhile they have hung mounted
posters of things like sneakers and Coca-Cola bottles
on the stucco walls. Leads and aerials loop between
picture railings. The mantel pieces are cluttered with
jokey plunder: KEEP LEFT and NO SMOKING signs,
a Chinese demon kite, a Snoopy mug half full of small
change. But the rooms remain dark and sedate; tonight
each is a cell of hot still air. The two visions of the
house don't match, they are overlaid like illusionist
sheets, demand something of you . . . a trick of wit,
Rowena feels, and she would see it as a style.

The front door is open, the steps of the porch are
still warm. Rowena lights a cigarette. She has taken up
smoking again.

'Are these for real?' she had asked Hutch, pointing
at the NO SMOKING signs.

'Why else would they be there?' Hutch said.

Why else did Rowena, finding an old packet of cigarettes in Harry's winter jacket, take one out and
smoke it? The air before her lifted and shook. She took
another one. This time it tasted more real, the house
seemed to retreat behind the fraying coil of smoke.
She bought her own packet. She enjoyed the crackle as
she opened it, the precision of the cylinders stacked as
close as bullets. She took to carrying a packet in the

pouch pocket of her overalls. At odd moments, out-side the house, she smoked them.

Just as she lights up now, Hutch breaks through the darkness at the side of the house, pulling a hose. In the other hand he carries his glass of wine. He doesn't seem to see her, but if she wasn't there would he stroll across the lawn like this, taking sips as he plants the sprinkler near her and turns on the tap? He suddenly sinks beside her.

'Very contemplative,' he says. 'You're always very contemplative, Rowena.'

The sprinkler's arms have corralled them against the porch. Water patters at their feet. Hutch is always setting up these little moments with her and she always comes away feeling she has failed a test.

'The madonna,' Hutch says. 'I take it that's what you want to be.'

His voice has dropped, his blond head is bowed towards her. Rowena hunches her shoulders. She will not look at him.

'Dinner,' she says, waving her arms vaguely, getting up. 'Must help Harry.' Her voice is husky, out of prac-tice. She throws her cigarette into the garden and then remembers it is his garden and makes a little useless dive mid-air. She closes her eyes for a moment on her way back up the hall. She should have stamped the butt out at his feet, raised her eyebrows, stalked off . . . Why? Because he would have liked that? In this house value is given to performance.

Just as Harry places the big platter of yellow rice on the terrace table, Tom wakes. A loud outraged howl this time.

'Oh God,' Diane says. 'How do you bear it?'

Harry serves, and Rowena hands out plates.

'Maybe I'm just not the type,' Diane goes on. She picks up her fork with her narrow freckled hand, looks around the table. She often has this moment of animation when a plate of food is put in front of her, Rowena has noticed. 'Why do people *do* this to themselves d'you think?'

'Because they don't know what they're letting themselves in for,' Harry says.

Hutch stands up, turning and turning at the corkscrew embedded in the bottle between his legs. They all watch, wait for the triumphant Pop! 'Tight one,' Hutch says, chasing sweat across his forehead in a kind of salute.

Tom's cry is urgent. Rowena drains her glass, reaches over and takes a forkful of pilau from the platter. She won't be back for a while.

'All I know is,' Diane says, turning to her plate, 'nobody could ever make me miss my meal.'

'Go on,' Harry says to Rowena. 'We'll leave you some.'

4.

One night Harry came home very late to the beach house. It was so black outside you could imagine that he might never find them again, the frail house could disappear into a shifting fold of the dunes . . . He would have phoned, if of course there was a phone . . . it was becoming bloody impossible . . . he swayed slightly above her and Tom in the bed. He'd been drinking with Hutch and his wife, he'd been thinking . . . The Hutchisons said, come and live with them, they're interested in sharing . . . No the Hutchisons have no children. But a child shouldn't make any difference, they said.

Harry seemed to have forgotten that he used to say that too.

There are photos — here, kept close beside the bed — of the time that they first brought Tom home to the beach house. In this bright darkness the black and white leap out at you as if in moonlight. They are good photos of Rowena because she has at last stopped looking at the camera. She is smiling, she can't stop smiling, looking at Tom in her arms. Her hair, which reaches to her elbows, is now tucked back out of the way. She's wearing overalls, but you can see that her breasts are enormous. In the background a ti-tree brushes against asbestos. That's the beach house.

The photos of Harry with Tom are slightly out of focus. Rowena took them. There was no one else around to take them all together, *en famille*. The blurring gives the impression of a high wind. Harry is bending over Tom in his pram as if he's sheltering him.

He is frowning in a comic-father way. The ti-tree appears to be in violent action, caught up in a storm. But you can see that the cigarette Harry holds behind him is still alight.

The bathroom of the beach house was separate, a quick dash from the back door. When one of them wanted a shower the other had to be there to feed the chip heater. The heater roared, the pipes shuddered, draughts rushed in through the warped door. Spiders rocked their cradles of dead blowflies in amongst the steam.

Bent over the heater one morning she thought she heard Harry groan.

'What's the matter?'

He stood still. He was wearing her shower cap. Water ran on and on, clung to the tip of his nose, the panels of black hair on his shoulders, his chest, above his penis, swirled about his feet. He looked straight ahead, through water.

He didn't go to the shop that morning. He went to bed. He stayed there for nine days. It wouldn't matter, nobody came anyway, he said. (Second-hand books! Out there! You must be crazy, everyone had said when he set up the shop.) He slept for twelve hours at a time.

Tom cried and cried. She walked him up and down the verandah, around the peripheries of the house. It might be after midday before she could get dressed.

When he slept she lay on the couch with him in the crook of her arm, like a book.

Sand crept in under the doors. Mice scrabbled, but she could not bear to set the traps. Every living creature reminded her of Tom. The fridge went empty. From time to time she found herself before the open kitchen cupboard eating nuts and raisins fist after fist. She trod carefully past Harry's door. It seemed to take her whole being just to keep Tom alive.

When Harry was awake she sat on the end of the gritty bed, feeding Tom.

'Do something different!' Harry said, sitting up, smoking, watching her with glittering eyes. 'Is this all you ever do? Surprise me! Surprise me sometimes why don't you.'

(He didn't remember saying any of this, later on.)

A storm passed quickly on the beach front. You saw it coming, a mist wiping out the horizon ruled across the windows, whiteness on whiteness, while somewhere a blind flapped, louvres rattled, trees grew furtive. The voice outside took over, the house was hollowed into darkness, din, like a loss of consciousness: five minutes and it was over, a bird sang, the radio spoke again.

Harry got a job with the Government. In the mornings the car steamed as he encouraged Tom to wave bye-bye. It would be well after dark by the time he got back from the city. He made friends with someone called Hutchison, his age, but a senior administrator in the department. He stopped taking a packed lunch. He gave up smoking.

In the late afternoon the wind dropped and Rowena and Tom went walking. Down the carefully curved roads, some still gravel, named 'Pleasant Drive' or 'Linden Way'. It was all allotments, waiting to become numbered houses in a suburb; flowers grew among scrub and hillocks, tough, close-clustered, with a medicinal perfume that scented the dunes. When she picked them she could feel the shadow of clouds moving across the sunlight on her bent back.

At this hour retired couples came out like moths and walked arm in arm towards the glow settling over the sea. The rattle of the pram echoed behind them. They turned to smile at her from their end of the road.

The beach itself was unspectacular, edged with seaweed and miniature limestone cliffs. The winter sea was milk-turquoise, a great bowl in sluggish motion.

The sun glares low over the horizon, shows its power, the sea is a silver reflection, the road gleams, dances with struck flint, Rowena has to half shut her eyes. The wind presses against her, against her eyes and mouth so that she is smiling, blinded over the pram, and yes, she is happy, in some way about as happy as she can be.

The wine has spread through her.

Tom's head is slumped back like a drunk's, around

it the dim bedroom, the house, the music, the lit heads on the terrace spin out in a circle.

5.

It is as hot outside as in.

'*Good* evening!' Hutch calls out as Rowena stands blinking on the steps. 'I was just volunteering to go and wake you up.' He pulls out a chair for her with his foot.

'There's plenty left,' Harry says, waving his hand over the table. It doesn't look appetising. Amongst the spilled glasses, the plates scattered with grains of rice and chicken bones, moths are dragging in circles, grounded in pools of amber oil.

'Aren't you hot in those overalls?' Diane asks. Her legs are spread, she is fanning herself with a sandal.

'Take 'em off,' shouts Harry.

Their faces under the light look yellowish and greasy. Their eyes have almost disappeared.

'Wine,' Harry says, searching for a glass for her. 'Wonderful wine.' His mouth is faintly rimmed with black.

'Eases the pressure of family life,' says Hutch.

Rowena starts collecting plates.

'Just relax,' Hutch says.

'Moths,' Rowena says. She sees Tom's head lolling, a dark spot on their bed where she has left him.

Rowena is making fruit salad. Watermelon, rock-
melon, grapes, peaches, passionfruit, mangoes, plums:
she has taken them out of their stained brown paper
bags and lined them up on the bench. Whether to make
it minimal and chic, just the melon and grapes say, or
to throw in everything . . . Rowena has an idea, she
has seen a picture somewhere, the watermelon carved
like a bowl, the fruits spilling out of it . . .

The big knife has made her bold, slicing through
cheeks of pink flesh . . . it comes away from the rinds
with a sucking sound . . . take it all off . . . and then
chop, chop into children's blocks, pink, all shades of
pink, orange, tawny . . . The music throbs, Rowena
chops, she is hot, she has never felt so hot. The kitchen
is so crowded, its bin is overflowing, the benches are
covered with plates, scraps, fruit . . . she has to work
on a chopping board balanced on a chair, crouching, so
that the buckles of her overalls bite into her, she can
hardly move or breathe . . .

It is so simple. It works with the speed of a good idea.
To unbuckle. Unpeel. To step out of the overalls, kick at
them, and feel that trusty roughness, thigh against
thigh. She gathers up rinds, pips, peel, and dumps them
in the sink. Why stop there? Already she is moving easily, the T-shirt slips easily up her spine, cooling it,
releasing her head. It's as if a breeze is suddenly blowing
all over her body. She's in a hurry now. A glass splinters
outside and there's laughter. *Wait*. Her breasts come
loping out of their milk-stiffened cups, she could almost
fear for them as she bends over her knife . . . the final

touches . . . pants, you need two hands and they're over your knees, binding them, but — you just step out of them . . . She's wading in her own clothes, hands plunged up to the wrists in fruit, mixing it, the passion-fruit sprays out as she squeezes its upturned pouch . . . She washes her hands.

Here is Rowena, descending a staircase, her bowl held out before her, while somewhere over towards the city there is a rude outbreak of car horns. New Year. She is only aware of the whiteness beneath her, this company of globes and triangles, trusting them with her own grave progress.

And the faces looking up at her are frozen, their mouths are frozen open as if they cannot open wide enough for the laughter, they are stamping their feet, clutching their chairs with laughter, like uncles who have had one of their own tricks played on them. Tears run down Harry's face. Hutch claps.

Something white flies by and catches on the vines. Clothing? Actions bring results . . . but she is beginning to feel a drop, a fatal fading of interest. She has already been delivered of one miracle. She is tired. She places the watermelon bowl on the table in front of Harry.

'Here you are,' she says.

THE GIRLS LOVE
EACH OTHER

The girls love each other these days. That's what I told Beth last week. She'd just got back from Bali and we were having one of our catch-up sessions: Beth comes into the salon at eight and we talk our heads off while I give her a shampoo and brush-up before work. By half past there's cold coffee and cigarette ash and photos all over the bench. We're always frantic — that's our word — but it's our only time to really talk since Beth moved in with Douglas, and I've got Morveen at home most of the time. With friends.

That's what I was trying to talk about with Beth. That was my news. After she'd shown me her tan (she was worried she was *too* dark), and given me my carving and the batik for Morveen and gone on about all the tourists who'd been after Mardi's body and even hers — I told her that I was sharing my house with *three* unemployed teenage girls.

'Jan, you're too easy-going,' Beth said, for about the thousandth time. Two weeks alone with Mardi (her daughter, Morveen's age) had been enough for her, thank you, though they'd had their good times too, some good talks. I started to say that yes, so had we, it was interesting in a way.

'Actually,' Beth went on, bending her head away from the blower, 'it's not the girls so much I mind, it's all the boyfriends hanging round.'

'There're no boyfriends,' I said. I was standing over Beth, layering up her left side, she's got lovely hair, coarse, blonde, shapes up beautifully. Then I found myself saying it, as if it had been on my mind all the time: 'The girls love each other these days.'

There was just that moment when Beth looked up and caught my eye waiting in the mirror, and looked down again. Ticking back over ten years like I'd been doing.

'First I've heard of it,' she said.

Morveen and Mardi practically share a birthday – they're both Leos – but it took Beth and me quite a time to give up on pretending they were friends. They learned ballet and tap together until Morveen just wouldn't get into the car one day. And in the school holidays Beth and I would take a day off and drag the girls round town to lunch and a matinee. 'Go on your own,' they told us in the end. Then by the time Mardi was fourteen you'd have thought she was twenty: she's working out at Channel 9 now and the trip to Bali was the prize for the Beach Queen heat last year.

Morveen's like me, no show pony, she doesn't even try. But up to now there's always been this little thing between Beth and me, that our girls were in the same race, only Morveen was shy and young for her age.

I suddenly remembered how different Beth and I were. How when we used to work together at Max's she wouldn't talk to any of the clients she thought were 'weirdos', and called old Max 'the poofter' behind his back. And how she just doesn't say anything about Morveen going on the dole when she could have got a place in the Teachers' College. Morveen had said she wanted a break to think things over, and I know what she means. I'd wanted that too once, and then when Johnny my son left, I'd *had* to have it – Morveen's had a lot to handle, one way or another. There are some things Beth doesn't understand.

'You know,' I started, though I didn't know what I was going to say. But Beth jumped up, she had to rush, she was frantic, she had to be in Perth by nine (she's a cosmetic rep these days) and Douglas had asked all these people over for drinks that night.

'Sure you won't come?' she asked, patting her hair in the mirror. 'Bring Bradley? How is he these days?'

'I haven't seen him for a while,' I said, 'since the girls came.'

'Take care,' she said (it's one of Douglas's expressions). We kissed each other at the door.

Friday is our busy day at the salon, but every time I turned on the blower I was taken back to what I'd said to Beth. I thought about the girls. How they just seemed to appear in my life, sitting round the kitchen table. I'd been to a movie with Bradley: we nearly fell over a couple of duffle bags in the hall. Then we saw these three cropped heads turning towards us at the kitchen door. Morveen had a little glittery catch in her eyes that she gets when she's pleased about something.

It turned out that Steph is a sort of cousin by friendship. Lily Carson, her grandmother, was my mother's best friend. I just remember Lily before she moved to Sydney, but something about Steph's neat sharp face and her quick way of talking reminded me of her.

'Yeah, everyone says that,' Steph said. It seemed that Linda, Steph's friend, who's got a soft baby face and smokes a lot, had been having hassles with the Youth Hostel. They'd been telling Morveen about it. They wondered if . . . So I said they could have Johnny's room.

Bradley didn't stay long. It didn't feel right somehow, to go into the lounge with the whisky and close the sliding doors like we usually do. He stood up and straightened his jacket and said: 'Goodnight . . . girls.'

'Night,' they said, hardly looking at him.

At the door he said: 'Be careful, Janet. Don't let them take advantage of you.' We didn't make any plans for the next weekend.

It soon became clear that the last thing those girls wanted was to take advantage of a fellow woman. They decided that since I was the worker they would do all the shopping and cooking and washing-up.

'That's how a co-operative works,' Linda explained to me.

'In some circumstances,' I said, 'it's also called marriage.'

'We're not asking you for sexual favours,' Steph said with a little smile.

But it worked out pretty well. In fact shopping and cooking seemed to be all they did do.

'It's such lovely weather,' I said, 'and you've hardly seen anything of Perth.'

'Depends what you're interested in,' Steph said. She smiled at Morveen and me. She's got a lovely smile.

Some nights they borrowed my old Torana and went to hear some music in a pub or see a film in Fremantle. Mostly they sat around talking. On nights that we were all at home I seemed to be expected to join in. I must say there was something about the way Steph gave you all her attention, with big nods at everything you'd say, that really got you going. I'd never heard Morveen talk as much either.

Steph tackled me about my job. How did I feel, she asked, that as a hairdresser, I basically 'exploited the beauty trip' that men laid on women? I said that most of my clients at 'Janette's' were older women coming in for a trim or a perm. 'Nobody wants hair down to their ankles,' I said.

'Come on Jan, I'm talking about fashion.'

'Look at you three, that's a fashion isn't it? Who cuts your hair anyway?'

'It's not fashion, it's anti-fashion. It's cut by a friend in Sydney who's dropped out of the straight hair-dressing scene.'

'And it *feels* good,' put in Linda.

'So does my hair,' I said. 'And I can blow-dry it in a few minutes.'

'Whether you know it or not,' Steph said, 'you wear it like that to attract men.'

'Yeah,' said Morveen.

'Well who are you trying to attract with your hair-dos then?' I said. 'Each other?'

They seemed to think this was a huge joke. Linda started to clap and knocked her drink over Steph's record.

'By the way,' Steph said, grabbing the record off Linda and wiping it without looking at her, 'I need a trim. You wouldn't . . .?'

'No I wouldn't,' I said.

It was good for Morveen and me, having the others there. It was a relief not to come home and find her sleeping with five apple-cores beside her bed. Or hear the fridge door open and close all evening while she ate as if she had to save her life.

When had I last heard her hum like she did when she was cooking the co-operative meals? I guess it was when she was a kid and she'd come in after Johnny had taken her for a ride on his bike. She's never been one for smiling much – all chins and frowns as a baby – but when we'd all been talking and it was getting late, she had this sort of sleepy soft look about her, and she'd rest her head on the nearest shoulder. When it was mine I wanted to stop talking, everything, and put my arms around her, but I'm not that silly.

I found out that all this time she'd never liked her name.

· 'It was your grandmother's name,' I said. 'It's Welsh.'

'So?' she said. 'I don't like it. *Mor — veen*.' She beat her fist on the table in time and glared at me. 'Mor — veen — Jones.' Bang, bang, bang.

'I never thought of it like that,' I said. Lennie had wanted it, and then it had become part of a different sound, 'Johnny and Morveen,' the sound that kept me going.

But the next time I came home I heard Steph say quite casually as she put on a record, 'Do you know this one, Veen?' From then on it was 'Veen this' and 'Veen that'. No one said a word about it.

The story of my marriage went down very well. They sat there shaking their heads through the saga of Lennie and his disappearing act. Linda jumped up and started massaging my neck. Not that their own family histories sounded much better. Though I must say it surprised me that a son of old Lily Carson would be a 'mental wife-beater' and an 'alcoholic capitalist exploiter'. His wife's only sin seemed to be that she 'freshened up before hubby came home.' I don't suppose I came off any better when I'd gone to work.

Then the last Saturday before they went, I was lying out the back in my bikini, soaking up the lovely late summer sun. Even my face, though Beth's told me off about that often enough. I still get a kick out of my backyard after all those years in the flat. It's just a big

square of brown grass sloping down to an old peppermint tree by the fence.

Then I heard the crying. It was coming from Johnny's
room on the back verandah. Not just crying, but an
awful rising wail that seemed to curl around my stomach. I picked it out, like you do with little children, as
Linda's voice. I sat up and everything went blurry. I
heard the other two run in to her. She screamed 'You!'
There was talking, and the crying dropped away.

It was all over in a minute. I lay down again but my
stomach kept on tightening. I could see our washing
dancing at me on the line, the girls' big clown clothes
flapping against my uniforms and panty-hose and bras.
After a while I made my way inside. I just kept thinking, I don't know, I don't know anything.

I took the girls out to the bus station on Saturday afternoon, as soon as I got home from work. The
co-operative had been winding down that last week,
the girls had gone out a lot more. I was glad, I was
tired: even at work I seemed to be hearing their young
voices all day, back and forth with mine.

They didn't talk much in the car. Every time I'd say
something to Morveen next to me, she'd say 'What?'
She kept looking out the window, humming.

At the bus station Steph fished out their tickets
from the little purse she wears looped around her
waist, and Linda queued with their bags. There seemed
to be a rhythm going round between them all. I

watched Steph, standing there with her head just nodding and one foot tapping away in its old tennis shoe. I thought, she's so sure. She's dangerous.

They stood waiting for the call then, the three of them, with their arms around one another. When it was time to go there were big serious hugs all round.

'Jan, thank you,' Linda said through tears. I watched them darting off behind the other passengers, like children. When I turned, I found that Morveen had already set off. I saw her striding ahead of me towards the car.

It seemed so quiet at home that afternoon, you could hear the peppermint tree tossing about in the wind. Morveen went straight to her room. I couldn't settle to anything. I put a few things back to their old places in the kitchen. In the end I jumped in the shower. Then Morveen stuck her head round the door and said: 'It's the big B for you on the phone.'

Bradley's voice seemed to come from another world. I stood there watching the mist spread out from my hot toes over the polished boards. He was trying to let me know how busy he'd been these past weeks.

'Are you all right?' he asked.

'I've missed you.'

There was a pause. Then very gruff he said:

'Pick you up at eight then – sweetie.'

Morveen came into the hall.

'Are you going out tonight?' The same old question.

'Yes,' I said. 'Are you?

'I'm not into socialising, just for the sake of it.'

'Some of us actually enjoy a man's company from time to time. Drinking and talking like you've been doing every night.'

'We had real talk. But Bradley's a shithead. They've all been shitheads, you know that.'

'Don't you think,' I said at last, 'that there're any good men around?'

'Well one thing's for sure,' she said, walking off. 'I don't need them.'

I headed outside then and sat on the front steps, still in my dressing gown. There are no houses in front of us, just a lovely stretch of sky over the railway line. The street lights had come on and the evening traffic was starting up. I watched the cars, joined up by head-lights, filing towards the subway.

Saturday nights. The city. Morveen always hated me going out in the old days. She'd scream and scream so Johnny'd have to take her for a ride around the block while Beth and I drove off. 'She's just jealous,' Beth would say, accelerating. 'You deserve a bit of fun.'

Morveen hated me talking on the phone too, those long sessions picking up the pieces after all the fun. Every two minutes one of us would have to break off to hiss and slap and bribe with biscuits, just to stay on that life-line, just to say: 'Do you know what that bas-tard said to me?'

And now here was Morveen saying she could do

without all that. You could hardly blame her. I think her view's lopsided: she thinks mine is. We're opposite each other like a pair of scales. But for a long time my side carried the weights. Maybe Morveen was pushed out of balance, right from the start.

I *had* learnt some things. Not enough for Morveen now, not enough to even up. But I learned to pay my own way. In the beginning, when I married Lennie Jones, I thought that from then on I'd be taken care of. Even afterwards, when I was alone, I had my sheikh dream. I'd be walking to the bus-stop after work (Jan, you get along now, Max'd always say, dead on five, I'd spend all year wondering what I could buy him for Christmas), two buses I needed to get the kids home, and I'd think that if a big fat sheikh pulled up beside me in a limousine, I'd just crawl right in. 'Come on kids,' I'd say. 'We're going to live in a harem. Won't that be fun?'

Beth came along and she taught me: you always pay your own way. Now I didn't ask for much, just my own place, and a chat with Beth, and Bradley turning up from time to time.

Bradley's a shithead. Well I know what she means. You think he's good-looking, so clean and well-cut, till you get up close and there's something missing in his face, he has to practise looking you in the eye. And practise having what he calls his 'R and R': he fits me in between badminton and bushwalks, and then cuts everything short to get a good night's sleep. He can't cope otherwise, he says. Well, that's how he is.

So why do I bother? Just sometimes, out of the blue, driving home late, or having breakfast, once when we were standing in a queue, I start to tease him, I can't stop myself, I'm laughing like nothing matters any more. And he bends his head to me (he's very tall) and calls me a terrible girl, and keeps looking at me sideways in a shy, pleased way . . . So I hang in there, while the weeks build up again between us, work and the telephone, dinner and a show. Waiting for those real times again.

Morveen was sitting beside me in the dark.

'Jan. I'm going to Sydney.'

'When?' The stars seemed tiny above the lights on the road.

'As soon as I can get my act together.'

'What'll you do there?'

'Live with the others. They've got a big place, there's six of them.'

'Six girls,' I said.

'I'll look for work of course. I'm not going to bludge forever.'

'Six girls, in a house. Don't you think that's a bit . . . narrow?'

'People come and go a lot, Steph says. Anyway, what are you trying to say?'

'I dunno love. It's not my way I guess.' *You pay for your choices*, I wanted to say.

Morveen had put her arm around me.

'Mum, why don't you come over when I'm settled and have a holiday? We'd have a good time I know. We could look for Johnny . . . Steph and Linda reckon you should.'

'Thanks love. I'll think about it.'

Morveen jumped up soon and went inside. She couldn't keep still for long that night.

I felt very tired out there. Too tired to get ready for Bradley. It was getting cold.

The phone rang. Beth.

'I know this is an awful time to ring,' she said as usual. 'It's just that I'm feeling so *flat*.'

'That makes two of us.'

Then she was off. Douglas hadn't come home yet, he was on his high horse, he said she drank too much when she was with his friends. Who were so boring anyway . . .

'Honestly Jan, sometimes I miss the old days. When you and I used to hit the town. I think I'm a romantic at heart.'

Also her tan was peeling, and Mardi was off looking for a flat. 'God knows what she'll get up to then,' she said.

In the kitchen Morveen had switched on the light and the radio. I smelt scrambled eggs and I felt like a glass of wine. This was something that seemed to stretch right back to Mum and Lily Carson. A kind of talk. I'd been speaking it for years now at the back of all the heads of those faces in the mirror.

'Hold on a sec, Beth,' I said. I whipped into the kitchen and filled up a glass from the cask with a wink at Morveen.

'Anyway, how's things with you?' Beth asked. You always have to remind her that you've got a life ticking away there too. 'How're Morveen and the girls?'

'The girls have gone back to Sydney,' I said, 'and Morveen's going to go over there too.' I took a deep sip while Beth went on about how they all leave us and how we'd probably end up in a Home together.

'Morveen wants me to come over for a holiday.'

'Yeah?' said Beth, listening.

'I dunno, I'd have to get someone in at the salon, and it might put Bradley out a bit, and I'm tired, there doesn't seem much point . . .'

'Well hang it all,' Beth said, out of the silence. 'Hang it all, why don't you go?'

ENOUGH ROPE

Every now and then an energy builds up in me and I know that it's time to visit Michael. Quite suddenly everything, the set of rooms I move through, the see-saw glare and darkness as I pass outside and in, the glint of the dam down on the boundary, becomes the background to a dream.

I rush the boys off to the school-bus and throw my packed bag into the car. Ian just watches me. But we've finished seeding and I haven't visited my mother for a long time.

As soon as I reach the metropolitan area I ring Michael at the school where he is teaching.

'Oh hello,' he says. I can hear the faint, endless barracking of children in a playground. 'Tonight? Yes, fine, see you then.' He could be making an appointment with an anxious parent.

I always arrive rather windswept on Michael's doorstep. This is a tradition. It is not windy on the quiet streets of Lakeside Estate where Michael has lived since his marriage. But he used to live on the top floor of a block of flats with a cosmopolitan's-eye view of Perth. In those days, when the boys were very young, I was always late. I would stand for a moment in the cold tunnels of city air and study the careful schoolteacher script of *M. Makevis* beside the door.

I still wear an air of haste and escape now, dodging among the hanging baskets on Michael's discreet front porch. It is a form of apology. I juggle with my bottles in their damp paper sleeves – beer, wine or champagne, I try to vary them so as not to look too predictable.

'Bon soir,' says Michael, while his door-chimes are still pealing. This greeting is again a tradition. Years ago at teachers' college, we liked to season our exchanges with 'adieu' and 'merci bien' and 'c'est pas mal tu sais'. Unlike the French however, we do not kiss on meeting. It leaves, has always left, a tiny gap, during which Michael takes my bottles into the kitchen and I try to decide where to sit.

There is something deliberate about Michael's clatter in the kitchen.

'Is Lauren home?' I call across the bar.

'She's rehearsing.' He brings in our drinks. 'She's got a recital next week.'

She wasn't home the last time I visited either.

'Your house is looking great,' I say, though in this dimmed light I can't notice any change. Couches seem to grow out of the pale carpet. The smoky glass of the coffee table is still unsmudged and bare. It stretches between us, shin to shin. His are crossed, in pale jeans.

'We finished the music room last week.' He puts

down his drink. 'Would you like to have a look?'

For the first time he leads me into the private part of his house. An old sensation of conspiracy unfolds as I follow him down a corridor. We used to stifle laughter in my mother's kitchen once, making coffee late at night. Something about the cannisters' diminuendo from big FLOUR to little TEA . . .

'. . . but the view'll improve when the trees have grown,' he is saying. We are crossing a little courtyard. I glimpse a plastic washing basket, an upturned mop, ordinary domesticity. 'She always hated me listening when she practised.' He smiles at this over his shoulder as he unlocks the door.

The music room smells new, of pine and cement. Lauren's baby grand stands sleek and black in the middle of the room. There is an old couch under a bare window. Michael stays by the door.

'I bet Lauren's in here all the time,' I say, opening the piano.

'Not a great deal yet.' His hand is on the light switch, ready to go. 'She's very involved with this Bach group. Out nearly every night. Though she's got a friend, a flautist, who comes over in the day sometimes to play duets.'

He locks the door again as we go out.

'How are the boys?'

This is better. We are on sure ground here. For Michael this is no routine enquiry. They are restless, I say, and too rough with each other at the moment. Ian says they need pulling into line. My voice is hesitant. I think they're bored at school.

Michael nods. He starts talking about his class. The theme this term is the planets: the space-ship they're building is becoming more complex than he can always understand. It incorporates the school computer. The boys in his class are working really well together since they started this project.

I say I do not think Miss MacPherson at the Yardoo Primary goes in for the space age. 'I wish *you* taught the boys.' I think I say this every time I see him. And he just gives the same half smile and goes on talking. Of course. Even as a student Michael had his own ideas. I listened, but ended up going with the stream: *don't let the little bastards get you down.*

I think about the time I brought the boys here to see Michael. As usual we were staying with my mother.

'You certainly have your hands full,' my mother always says.

Michael had taped the World Cup soccer final ready for them on his video. He showed them how to make a milkshake.

'Wow this place is like that T.V. commercial,' I heard them tell him in the kitchen. They swivelled on his bar-stools and tried their jokes on him.

'Can we go to Michael's?' they still ask me when we're driving to the city.

Michael is still talking. This year he has been posted to a school in a wealthy middle-class area. The kids are great – Michael always says this about his classes, they're *his* kids now – but there are different sorts of problems. Some of the parents push their children, ask Michael when he'll be giving the class real work to do.

'Have I told you this already?'

'No no, go on.' I can watch him as I used to when he talked. In winter his face is so pale it's almost luminous. 'Milkface': that's what the kids called him when he first came to Australia. He stood on the edge of the playground in his shorts made by his mother and saw that no one else wore shorts below the knee. He told me that once.

'Things are changing,' he is saying. 'I think the children are the only ones who can keep up.' Now he's cupped his palm and balanced his empty glass on it. 'But you have to trust them, you have to let them go a bit . . .' He flicks his glass with his other hand and strikes a precarious note.

Michael and Lauren have no children. This has never surprised me although they've been married for some years. Perhaps it's because I always think of Lauren as being very young. She must be in her late twenties now, but the last time I saw her she was as thin and childlike as ever. She has a little flat white face, with eyes and nose and mouth crowded together, and a bush of crinkly brown hair springing back from her forehead.

I couldn't say that I really know Lauren. When

Michael wrote to tell me he was married, I arrived at the new house with champagne and a wedding present. Michael met me juggling a glass of dissolving disprin. Lauren had a headache, she was going to bed. She sat in a dressing-gown on the arm of his chair while he opened the present.

'Thanks very much,' she said as she got up to leave.

She was very gifted, Michael explained in a low voice. Her mother had pushed her, practice six hours a day, no friends, talent quests, frilly dresses. It was amazing she still wanted to play at all. She was very strong really, knew what she wanted. He was helping her work towards that.

Yes, I'd said then, looking around me. Lakeside Estate. Full-page, colour supplement, *Where your dreams become realities.* We drank a toast to his marriage, smiling but not finding much to say.

I've never told Michael about the time I saw him and Lauren at the lake. We were down for the Show, I'd taken the boys there to let off steam. They disappeared, I sat in the car to look at people. It was a wet and windy Sunday afternoon. Some sort of a club, or an office on picnic, was playing a rather bossy game of cricket with an outfield of girlfriends slouching among the eskies. I saw them suddenly, weaving their way through the players. Their familiarity, Michael's leather jacket, Lauren's hunched shoulders and blowing woolly hair, materialised for me as if I'd been expecting them.

I saw Lauren break away, veer towards the lake,

stand looking down with her hands in the pockets of her parka. Michael followed, said something to her, set off towards the kiosk. He walked right near my car on his way back to her. I saw that he was holding two ice-creams. His head was bent and he had a little smile on his face. You've got your hands full Michael, I caught myself thinking.

Tonight Michael and I are shifting fast from second gear into third. We haven't got this far past the rituals for a long time. Michael's given up on getting drinks for us from his bar. He's put a bottle of wine and the whisky on the table between us. Through it I discover an aquarium view of my blind stockinged feet.

Better make this my last, I think into my wine. Or second last. But already I'm feeling that gathering of cheer that means it could be too late for limits. Recently I've been rather pushing the limits, all around the district. *You* certainly enjoyed yourself, people tell me later. The end of every social occasion has been a blank. When I come to, I'm alone in a qui-etly throbbing car. Ian is outside, opening our gate in the moonlight. He gets back in the car, I shut my eyes, the car lurches forward, then throbs to itself again. I open my eyes. Ian is closing the gate. Limits.

I don't want Michael to know this. I don't want him to have to escort me reeling to the car. Or worse. Throwing up into his native garden. There's a lot I don't want him to know about me. My triviality. My laziness. How much I weigh. Our relationship, as I've often told myself, is characterised by a beautiful restraint.

Although tonight Michael himself is not holding back, I notice. As he leans forward to pour himself another whisky, a strand of hair falls across his forehead. He leaves it there. He rips open a packet of peanuts and makes an avalanche of them into a bowl. Both of us ladle up peanuts and munch in an absent-minded way.

'You know Michael,' I say, 'there isn't one sign of Lauren in this room.'

He looks at me.

'Ah yes.' My remark hangs between us. 'Ah yes. My waiting room.'

'Oh I don't mean . . .'

'My waiting room. Where I *wait*.' There's that little smile again that creases up his eyes.

'Lauren's rehearsing . . .'

'Ah yes.' I don't recognise the new cut of his tone. It goes with the smile, '*And* Lauren cannot drive. Therefore the flautist must give her a lift. The Polish flautist.'

This time I say nothing.

'And I wait.' He says this to me as if I might accuse him of something.

Michael and I can't sit and face each other any more. Michael has wandered off somewhere. But first he's put on some soft jazz, as if to keep me company.

I'm sorry, I say across this room where I don't belong. I've never known what Michael wanted of me. Even if that meant keeping away.

What now? I lean back, shut my eyes, waiting. But my centre of gravity seems to have moved to my left ear. I slide my cheek down into the rough surface of Michael's couch. With one eye I survey a tweed horizon. I see the colours of the native garden growing across this suburban block. Grey sand laps the feet of a raw brown fence. Dull green nursery saplings shake their name-tags beside gravel paths. He says their names to himself as he passes. One day they will wave a private shelter around his house, her music room.

How do I know about waiting?

Once Michael and I sat in a cafe, saying goodbye. We had both just graduated. Michael was leaving for Europe the next day. I didn't know where I was going.

It was January, but it had been a day of freak tropical rain. Cars swished by outside in a luxuriant greenish twilight. The jukebox was playing bouzouki music, the cafe-owner smiled at us. We'd often sat here, it was one of the few places in this city with any atmosphere, we said. But this time Michael kept checking his watch. He showed me his ticket and stowed it away again with careful fingers.

'I'd better get you home. I'd better get myself home. My last night and all that.' He smiled at me for our old shared bondage. I did not respond. Our widowed mothers sat on opposite sides of the city. His mother wore black, served sweet black coffee in tiny cups, spoke in another language. But about the same things, Michael said. Probed and warned, chased up lineages. We had been encircled. But he was getting away.

I couldn't look at him. This new, harder presence, no longer attending me, was suddenly proof of its own value. I felt him at the edge of my shoulder, at the tips of my fingers, at arm's length where I had been so careful to keep him. Quiet, pale Michael Makevis.

'Wait!' I said outside the cafe. I was scrabbling in strange desperation for my sunglasses. It had stopped raining, the footpath glared, the air was again thin and bright.

The hallway at home was stuffy.

'That you love?' I chose not to answer. I could still hear his car at the end of our road.

'Let-ter!' She must be lying down because of the heat . . . There was a manila envelope waiting for me under the jardiniere. O.H.M.S. My posting had come. Grades 3 and 4, Yardoo Primary.

It is raining now, steady winter rain beating on the hollow of Michael's house. The sound has been creeping up on me ever since the music died. The button glows red on the stereo. Salt dribbles from the empty peanut packet onto the glass table. No Michael.

I leap up from the couch, and hobbling on my

numbed left foot as if I'm tethered, open the front door. My car still sits askew on the verge, its wheels streaked with wet country dust. The air is very cold. Stamping my foot to life, I shut the door.

I move swiftly now through every room of Michael's house, opening and closing doors, snapping lights on and off. The rooms are smaller than you think back here. I note in passing an intense disorder. Unmade beds in two rooms. I move on. It is not until I come to the end of the corridor that I know he must be in the music room.

I don't switch on the light. He is sitting on the couch under the window. I go across to him.

He says: 'It's worse when it rains. It's like the whole planet's poisoned.'

Back in the house a phone starts ringing. Lauren? My mother? It doesn't matter. I am moving quite by instinct now.

TRAVELLING

There were four of them who had arrived in Luang Prabang that day, and now hung around the entrance of the Royal Air Lao office in light rain, waiting for a man called Ted Akhito. As far as they could make out (here Ruth for once had made the enquiries, her matric French promoted by Galen), this Ted was a Japanese English teacher who rented rooms to travellers on the second floor. Probably C.I.A. Who wasn't? An introverted, sleuthing silence fell among them, not helped by the rain.

Travellers were scarce in Laos that year, and they seemed to be sticking together, linked by a sort of professional pride. On the traveller's scale of values, Laos had an off-beat, quietly dangerous chic. Vietnam had lost its glamour even for the foolhardy, but in those days, Laos, with war flickering through its jungles so you had to town-hop in a battered DC3, and sleep in the curfew to the distant sound of planes and even gunfire, still had that nice edge of controllable adventure.

In Ban-Houei-Sai, the little border town on the Laotian side of the Mekong, shopkeepers had refused to serve them, and the one cafe that would give them a meal had been full of armed soldiers and beefy American men in laundered mufti. *The place is crawling with C.I.A.*, Galen wrote to a friend back in Australia (he liked to write on-the-spot accounts in cafes), *it's probably only a matter of time before the borders are closed*. There was that Shangri-la savour of a soon-to-be-lost frontier.

But last night in Ban-Houei-Sai, while Ruth was dousing herself in a mandi bath, an unseen watcher had laughed at her from behind the window bars. There are peeping Toms everywhere, as Galen said, but there was something about the sureness and scorn of that laugh, its pause, its continuation, as she had clutched a sarong about her pink body and fled down the curfew-darkened corridors of the hotel, that she related to war. She wasn't sure that they had any right to be in this country at all.

It was nearly dark when Ted Akhito arrived, under a dripping umbrella. They followed him up a staircase that opened, loft-like, into a large rectangular room with shuttered windows at either end. It was bare except for the rows of bamboo mats along the walls.

'Five hundred kip a night,' said Ted Akhito, looking at his watch. He was young, as young as they were, dressed in Westernised tropical whites. There was no question of bargaining about the price.

'I must go now. I have a class. I'll be back later to check things out. Curfew is at ten o'clock.' He spoke excellent English without an accent, except he said 'class' like an American. What was he doing in Luang Prabang? Yes, almost certainly C.I.A.

Mats were already being claimed while he was talking.

'Here?' said Ruth to Galen. There were two mats together near the staircase. That tiny panic, like schooldays, when the gym teacher would say, 'Find yourself a spot,' and you'd jostle and circle to be at the back, near a friend. Galen shrugged. She took the mat that would be furthest from Bob, the Englishman, who as usual was hovering to see what Galen would do.

The Canadian was already striding up and down the room, looking out the windows.

'Wonder where you can get a meal in this town,' he said.

'Wouldn't mind a cup of tea,' said Bob. He was always ready to attach himself to a superior energy.

Galen was flicking through his *Student's Guide to South-East Asia*. 'Got the name of a cafe here somewhere,' he said.

There was a general movement to the stairs.

'Hold on,' Bob was muttering, arm-deep in his rucksack. 'I've lost my mac.'

Ruth hurried to join Galen, who with Canada was already at the bottom of the stairs.

Luang Prabang's wet empty streets did not seem under siege. The *Student's Guide* was pre-war, but the Melody Café still existed by the river, a dimly-lit little cave scattered with a handful of their own kind. A hang-out. Like the German Dairy in Chieng-Mai, or the Thai Song Greet in Bangkok. Made you realise that the trail had been well and truly blazed before you. Look at the menu. Along with all the usual rice and noodles, you could get roles and jam for breakfast, bolled eggs, stek fry, bananas milkshek. They wouldn't be quite the real thing of course, they were hybrid dishes cooked up for nostalgic Western palates.

'I'm gonna have me a steak,' Canada announced soon after they had settled themselves around a table.

'Steak!' said Bob, looking at the menu. 'That's eight hundred kip. It's a rip-off.'

Canada slapped the table lightly.

'This is a rip-off, that's a rip-off, *oh* you're having *steak*, *I* haven't had a steak since I left home.' He addressed the table in general. He was never personal. He went on. 'Why are travellers so god-damned *mean*? Like it's immoral to spend money or something. They haggle over anything to save five lousy cents. Me, if I want steak, I'll *have* steak.'

'All very well if you've got the money,' said Bob, still staring at the menu.

Ruth tried to catch Galen's eye. A taboo had been broken. They had been so conscientious about adopting the right ethos. If you let them rip you off they didn't respect you, and you were spoiling it for those who came after you. The less you spent, the more you roughed it, the better traveller you were. For some it was not just economical, it was spiritual. Working off some of that bad European karma, vaguely evening up the score. 'We lived just like the villagers.' After India, there were some travellers who never used knives and forks, or a handkerchief, or a sit-down toilet again.

Canada was untroubled by the niceties of the sub-culture. He didn't look like the typical traveller either. Western males in Asia seemed to become feminised. Like Galen or Bob, or the travellers at the other tables, their muscles became wasted from dysentery, their bodies were lost within their own over-sized clothes. Their hair grew, they adopted bangles or earrings or headscarves, their gestures were smaller, guarding their own space. Canada's denim shorts were tight around well-built thighs. He wore a heavy leather belt around his hips. He was square-featured and tanned like an old-time football star. The exchange of names didn't interest him. He called everyone 'Hey', they called him Canada.

The cafe-owner's wife stood before them, smiling. Young, very upright and finely attentive though a child was hovering by her thigh. A grandmother held a baby, and an older child played around the kitchen door. They smiled at her as they gave their orders. Except Bob. He was deliberating over the omelette or the fried eggs.

'Excuse me, excuse me,' he called out after her as she had turned towards the kitchen. Again she stood before them.

'Look, do you mind, I'll have the boiled eggs instead, two soft-boiled eggs, two minutes each, understand? Two minutes.' He held up two fingers and tapped his watch. She nodded.

'Thank you so very much,' said Bob. He treated her to one of his weary smiles.

Ruth kept her head turned away as Bob subsided, satisfied, on the bench next to her. When they had first met Bob, in the German Dairy, a week and a country ago, she had not been sure whether in these transactions he wasn't trying to produce a comedy turn. He looked as if he was going to be funny, with all those schoolboy freckles and his hair barbered ruthlessly above his ears. He drank milkshakes for his health, he told them, by way of introduction, and his smile seemed benignly goofy under his milk-speckled moustache. Hepatitis, caught in India. Infinitely travel-worn, like all those emerging from the great sub-continent.

Like her, he couldn't seem to get the hang of foreign currency. 'This . . . can't . . . be . . . right,' he had said to the German Dairy's proprietor. 'I . . . will . . . not . . . pay . . . so . . . much.' He spoke in pained, deliberate tones, shaking his head slowly for emphasis. Galen had stepped in, and sorted it out for him. But he'd still felt aggrieved as he walked back with them to their hotel. Ruth's old hope, half forgotten in the serious business of travelling, of finding a fellow clown, died. He wasn't trying to be funny. It was a form of tantrum they were to see every time he had to part with his money.

'Nice place,' Ruth said to Galen, across the table. Galen didn't answer. He and Canada were picking their way through an abandoned Laotian newspaper, testing out their French.

'I thought you guys were supposed to be bilingual,' Galen was saying, laughing.

Their waitress brought them a pot of tea. Galen and Canada looked up, paused, motors idling over. Her swift fingers setting out the cups, her oval face . . .

'They take their time,' Bob muttered. 'I'm starving.' He reached a white freckled arm across her to pour himself a cup of tea.

Ruth's legs felt heavy as she crossed them. For a moment she thought of saying to Bob, 'Do you ever feel like you're an inferior physical species?' Like her, Bob was noticeably of Anglo-Saxon stock. Fair skin inclined to flush up in the heat. Blue eyes often sweat-stung. Beige teeth. Innocent knobbly white feet sprawling across thongs. But this was way beyond acceptable perimeters. *Too personal.* The sort of comment she used to make over wine at her own table, safe in that acknowledged femininity that she seemed to have left back in the West.

Was that what she meant? She felt she'd lost a whole persona somewhere along the trail. Become a mere trudging mate whom nobody seemed to hear. It wasn't just that mascara streaked down your face in the humidity and long hair was out of the question, you just tucked it back as best you could. She hated to catch sight of herself in shop mirrors. A large girl with a bare earnest face. Sexless as a missionary. And fat. Getting fatter. There were no shadows, no roles, no corners to hide in anywhere. Just the fact of yourself coming to meet you border after border.

'The women in these parts are supposed to be the most beautiful in the world,' Canada said to Galen. His steak had arrived. He was feeling convivial. 'Good grub heh?'

'I wish I knew,' said Bob. His eggs had not appeared.

'It pays to order what they know,' Canada said, 'if you're hungry.' His eyes glittered at Bob above his busy jaw.

Ruth finished first. Galen worked slowly through his rice, his chopsticks moving in a ruminative way like the fingers of women crouched on doorsteps, searching through their children's hair. Galen had applied himself to the art of chopsticks as he did to everything, with the natural expectation of success.

Ruth preferred to use a fork. The way you could scoop and order and round up with your aggressive Western prongs. And the fork gave her more contact with the food somehow. Sometimes she felt that the closest relationship she had these days was with the plate of food in front of her.

'Ah here we are,' Bob was saying, clearing his spot on the table. The eggs had arrived, lolling in a soup bowl. 'Not quite the usual presentation,' he had to add, but cheerfully enough, holding one down and tapping around its crown. He smoothed his moustache back, his spoon dived and was dropped clattering onto the table.

'Bloody concrete,' he said, reddening under his freckles. The eggs were both hard-boiled.

'He's infantile. It's embarrassing. It's so . . . *colonial*.' Ruth nudged Galen aside on the walk back to the hotel to share her anger with him in the dark. Bob had stood up in the cafe, waving his eggs at their waitress, calling out 'Look here.' They had left him personally supervising the timing of two more eggs in the kitchen.

'Well,' said Galen. 'So what?' He kept walking fast to catch up with Canada.

'I'm fed up with him. We've had him hanging round us since Chieng-Mai.'

'Oh God,' said Galen. 'Chaos in Laos.'

'Oh very clever.'

'Honestly,' said Galen, 'when are you just going to shut up and enjoy yourself like everybody else?'

'Don't lecture me,' cried Ruth. She wheeled off and sat on the steps of a building they were passing.

'I'm going on,' said Galen. She saw him meet up with Canada at the next corner and, both hunched over with hands in pockets, disappear into the shadows on the long avenue.

Ruth didn't sit there for long. The flap of a single pair of thongs was fast approaching. Like her, Bob had no sense of direction, and hated walking alone in the dark.

Back at Ted Akhito's, there was an hour left to them before curfew, but it was not inviting. A naked bulb hanging in the middle of the dormitory cast a subdued, yellowish light. Canada and Galen were making rapid male preparations for sleep. There was a flash of Galen's long hopping white legs, before he was magically prone, sheathed and flattened. It would have been indecent to watch Canada as he thrashed and muttered his way into his sleeping-bag and turned his face to the wall.

Galen re-surfaced. He lay half out of his bag, trying to read *Anna Karenin*; he maintained that he could not fall asleep without a dose of the printed word, but in this light he had to run his fingers under the lines like a ritual of prayer. Perhaps it was a gesture of waiting for Ruth. At home she always fell asleep to Galen's lamp and the soft turning of pages. She would have leaned across him, and said, 'Where are you up to?' *Anna Karenin* was her book: she had read it for four whole days in the hold of an Indonesian cargo boat. She had been carried along by the book as much as by the boat, the story had unfolded to the rise and drop of the seas. Nineteenth century Russia would always be associated with the dazed hustle of their arrival in Djakarta.

Bob came panting up the stairs.

'There's not a soul to be seen out there. Do you think it's a sort of pre-battle hush?' He spoke loudly, as if he were rejoining a party.

'The light!' growled Canada from his corner. 'D'ya need that light?'

'All right, all right,' said Bob, 'it isn't curfew yet.' He lingered at the end of Galen's mat, ready to con-spire. But Ruth had turned to unpack, and Galen was closing his book.

'Christ I'm tired,' said Bob. He flapped across the

room to the door. They heard a hiss, 'Where's the ruddy switch?' and the light went out.

Ruth was left crouching by her pack, unresolved. Galen was still. She had intended to unpack, shake out her hair, write in her diary, all without reference to Galen, but within his range of observation: it would have been a wordless interaction that brought them to the conclusion of this day, and the battle between them that each day's travelling seemed to bring. Then one of them might have been ready to make a sign, that across these strange deprivations, their unity survived.

Darkness had pre-empted her. She was now a mere night scuffler. She moved like a thief, each sound was a betrayal. Unlayer her pack. Possessions as familiar as her hands. Book, sarong, diary, toothbrush. The layers descended in relevance. Right at the bottom, occasionally disturbed by the hands of customs officers, was a woollen sweater still smelling of home, and the photos of her family.

On the other side of Galen, Bob was crackling out his sleeping-bag. It was covered in a crisp papery plastic. For lightness. They had heard a lot about that bag. How it had been specially made for walking tours in Wales. Double thickness down, much too hot for Asia, with complicated aerations, all zip-controlled. Rolled up to the size of a giant green salami. A room-mate, French, had tried to rip it off in Calcutta.

Zip, crackle, deep sighs from Bob, more zips, more sighs. A final crackle. Enough to make the back of your skull crawl, Bob's horny feet manipulating plastic.

Galen had yawned, was turning over. Now to inch her way into her sleeping-bag, lay back her head. The big windows let in a grey translucence that had settled over the room. The night outside was silent. *You'd hardly know there was a war on*, she would write to her parents when they were safely out of Laos. She wrote them hasty air-letters of cool-minded reportage, casual feats of endurance. My goodness, they would write back, you have to be young!

Beside her, Galen had started moving, in a series of subtle, strait-jacketed shrugs. Ruth listened, and understood. He was taking off his passport pouch and money belt, and kicking them to his feet. 'Trust nobody,' they had been told. She shut her eyes. For yet another night, they were to lie side by side like brother and sister, burdened with old knowledge of each other. Galen, her husband for nearly half a year, had become a traveller, a different person to her. But he remained after all, like her, a well-warned child of the bourgeoisie. She turned over then, ready to sleep.

'Look after her,' Galen's father had said. Of course he hadn't had a tea-towel over one shoulder, down on the wharf, he was wearing his suit as he did whenever he left the farm, but that was how she saw him. Waving them off with a floury hand.

Every time Galen had taken her home, Norman would make scones. Rubbed butter into flour with trembling old brown hands. Cut the dough with an upturned sherry glass, up and down, swift as a process worker. 'Open the oven door for me darling,' he would say to Galen. Out the kitchen window, just beyond the chook sheds, you could see the bare brick walls of suburban houses. The poultry farm was in an outer suburb now. There had been nothing but bush and market gardens when Norman bought the place, and flatness, a convex landscape after England, Galen said. He'd been twelve. His mother died that year. He always called his home 'the farm'.

It took him an hour by bus to get to uni. He was always late for morning lectures. When she first knew him, he used to disappear mysteriously from pubs or parties. Slipping off to catch the last bus home. He got a lot of work done that way, he said.

Meeting Norman that first time, she'd been a bit breathy and overdone. She used to think she had to keep Galen entertained. She'd admired the scones, admired Norman's history book collection, pranced around the sheds and admired the chooks. Smoked like a chimney, dropping ash in her tea, but you couldn't do anything wrong in Norman's kitchen. As they were leaving (they were going to a party in Ruth's mother's Mini, Galen at the wheel), Norman had said then 'Look after her Galen.' Galen never answered.

In the humidity, Galen's face was very sallow. The acne scars across his jaw seemed to darken, reminders of an old battle. Now that he was so thin, he looked more like his father. Like this, from the side, his head bowed over the letter he was writing on his knee. She watched a tear of sweat escape his headband and linger in the hollow of his cheek. She could never imagine Galen with his mother. He seemed to spring straight from the mother and father both in Norman.

'Looks like rain,' Bob said.

They were sitting in the courtyard of a monastery, halfway up the hill overlooking the town. It didn't look like they would get much further. They were sated, even by the rich smells that hung in the humidity, of dung and damp undergrowth, and rotting overripe fruit. Even Canada, having paced the circumference of the courtyard, was sitting down now, smoking, over by the gate.

That morning, their pace had quickened with the promise and strangeness of a new place. Luang Prabang, after a night's sleep, was a beautiful country town. There were red blossoming trees along roads that still gleamed from last night's rain. High above the town, a golden dome shone from a hilltop, like a fairy-tale turret. Townspeople smiled at them, curiously. They shared cigarettes and sign-language with a group of soft-faced, schoolboy monks. This was how they liked to be received, as a species of scruffy pilgrim.

'Stomach's feeling strange,' said Bob. 'Think I'm in for another attack of the runs.'

Galen wrote on, rapidly. *I am sitting on the steps of a tenth century drinking-fountain,* she read at the top of his page, *in thirty-five degree humidity.* Facts she hadn't been aware of.

A bell had rung and the monks had disappeared.

The sky that hung before them over the town was now a luminous grey. Palm trees in the courtyard started to rustle and wave. Nobody else seemed to be around.

Canada stubbed out his cigarette and started back down the hill.

'Coming?' said Bob to Galen.

The four of them moved towards the town like an awkward beast whose legs wished to go different ways. Canada was off-hand, accompanying them this morning as if there were nothing better to do. He walked ahead, restlessly peering into doorways of the ochre-coloured buildings, disappearing up alleys, looking for action. His presence made Ruth uneasy.

She was used to travelling at Galen's pace. He always had an air of elation about him, discovering new territory. He loved to plan their route, and fit together the puzzle of map and reality. His passport pouch swung out and back to its bay within his hollow ribcage. The tails of the black and white scarf he wore as a headband flew out behind him. Travelling was a feast of the eye, he said. Was there such a state as pure vision?

While she trailed, glimpsing the backdrop through a web of thoughts. Like watching ants as a child, guessing at purpose and connection in a teaming other world. Distanced by the huge eye of the self.

Sometimes she found herself silently in step with Bob. He always seemed to be holding his words in check, until he caught up with Galen. Bumping together, they didn't even bother to say sorry.

'Ouch,' said Galen suddenly. She had walked into him and trodden on one of his thongs. He held it up by one dangling tentacle.

'Sorry,' Ruth said. Galen was very attached to those thongs. His Bangkok thongs. He called them art objects. The crinkled rubber was printed with a series of red and green music notes, gay inconsequential crochets and quavers, worn away now to the hills and valleys of his feet.

'Damn,' he said. His eyes, looking at her, were as dark as the black checks in his scarf. *'Why can't you keep up with me?'*

The rain didn't matter. Running in the rain had been one of her specialities in the old days. Theatrical liberation like moonlight swims and talking for a whole evening in her 'Juliet of the Spirits' voice. Funny, you couldn't see the rain falling. Just the puddles widening, dimpling, somehow connected with the descent of the huge grey sky.

Already the aisles through the market stalls were running miniature rivers, gorges, lakes. She had to hitch up her skirt, pry up each footstep, her shoulder-bag slapping against her hip. Not such a short cut back to the hotel after all. Galen in bare feet would be nearly at the Melody by now. Untrammelled.

Most of the stalls were empty, the mats rolled up where this morning's produce had been laid out. Just a few women under one of the big umbrellas, smoking and laughing. Probably at her, the only person out in the rain. Eyes down, picking her way home as fast as she could. Focus on that emptiness three paces ahead. Do not look at me. Alone, it was always like this.

'Hey,' Canada said, appearing at the top of the stairs and turning back to the others. 'D'ya hear about the two German guys? They hired themselves a boat and went downriver. Haven't been seen since.'

'Pathet Lao got 'em I spose,' called out Bob. 'Anyone know for sure?'

'Ask Ted Akhito,' said Galen, on his way to the dormitory. The others laughed.

Ruth looked up from the mat that defined her territory. It was late afternoon, they had taken what you might call a long lunch. Whenever she was not with them they seemed to come a little closer to the action of the place.

Surprisingly they came and stood around her mat. Galen crouched down beside her. Bob started moving his hands together and apart in a little concertina movement that she had come to recognise. He was shuffling an imaginary pack of cards.

'We've decided to play bridge,' he told her.

'I don't play,' Ruth said.

The three of them were damp and breathless, seemed to be sharing a joke. Boyos returning from the pub. Galen put a hand on her shoulder. He was still barefoot.

'Bob's going to teach you. Bob's going to be your partner.'

'You know I hate playing cards,' Ruth said to him.

Bob and Canada were already settling themselves around a spare mat under the window.

'Come on,' Galen said. 'We'll be nice to you. Promise.'

Bob was dealing.

'You sort them into suits,' he said. 'Descending order of value. Ace, King, Queen, Jack – 4, 3, 2, 1.' He was frowning, busy, spitty-sharp. Bob came into his own when he played cards.

The faces on the cards were stern and mediaeval as they spilled out of her hand. Bob went on, about contracts, tricks, trumps.

'What?' she said to Galen.

'Just listen and play,' Galen said, not looking up from his own cards. 'You'll pick it up.' That's what he had always done.

On the other side of her, Canada lazily pulled cards in and out of the fan in his hand. He lay on his side, one heavy thigh lapping the other. His eyes had never flickered once in her direction. Why had she let herself be drawn into this? Listen. Keep up. Play.

'Nine clubs,' she offered, hopefully.

Bob flung down his cards.

'You haven't been listening, have you? You don't understand.'

Ruth couldn't help the slow smile spreading across her face.

'I can't seem to see the *point* of the game.' She heard Galen begin to laugh.

'Hey,' said Canada to Galen. 'How long have you been travelling with this chick?'

Galen couldn't stop laughing. He rolled onto his back and up again, his headband fell across his eyes.

'Oh boy.' He put a hand on Ruth's knee. 'This is for life,' he said.

'*Mais où est* Ted Akhito?' Ruth asked the clerk in the Air Lao office again.

'*Ça ne fai rien* Madame, *vous pouvez payer ici*,' came the same reply.

Ruth turned back to the others. 'It's no good. We'll just have to give him the hotel money and hope for the best.'

'Ask for a receipt,' said Galen.

'Bloody irresponsible,' said Bob, counting out his notes. 'I think we have every right not to pay.' But they had already decided that it would be too risky just to leave the town without somehow paying the mysterious Ted Akhito, whom they had never seen since that first night. He probably had friends in high places.

'Hurry up,' said Canada. Outside, the Air Lao cattle truck that ferried passengers between the airport and the town had started up its engine. As before, they were to be its only passengers.

Ruth was the first to sling her bag into the back of the truck. The others hoisted themselves up while she climbed over the boards at the side and swung in. The truck lurched off. They held on to the cabin, standing up.

'All right?' Galen asked Ruth. She nodded.

After their long walk to the Golden Dome, Ruth and Galen had told the others that they would be leaving Luang Prabang the next day. Bob said it was funny, but he'd been thinking of leaving too. Canada just seemed to be with them as they were buying their tickets. You could get used to a place very quickly, they said, it was always a relief to be moving on.

From the truck they could see behind their street now, to paddy-fields spreading under water, islanded with palm-trees and bamboo huts, dotted with bending, slow-moving figures. The truck was speeding up. Now, in their final glimpse of the town, they could grasp its strictly civic plan, its streets and squares set out under the Golden Dome, the steaming river that curved around it and disappeared into alien hills. Like the two Germans, who had never been found. A flock of camouflage-splattered helicopters rose like smoke in the distance. In those hills and jungles there would be the sort of scenes you see in newsreels at home.

'Hey!' Canada was pointing across a square. There, surely, hurrying out of a building, was the neat white figure of Ted Akhito.

'Well I like *that*,' Bob said. But they were all smiling. They had rightly been judged not to be security risks. They were too lazy. Too cautious. You'd hardly know there was a war on. If you played by the rules.

The town was behind them now, shadowed by its own hills.

LILIES

When Christine Hollins came home she knew what she wanted to do. Find a place in the bush somewhere and talk, properly, with her mother. Then at the airport, in the flat white light she had forgotten, she saw her parents, shrunken, aged, looking anxiously in the wrong direction, and she paused. She felt it was another person who was approaching them.

Her parents now lived in a flat in the Bishop Byatt Retirement Home. But there in the tiny living-room were the Sydney Town prints that used to hang in the rectory hall. And the Persian scatter rug and the green leather wireless chair and the fluted daisy teacups from a thousand parish afternoons. Like her parents, they seemed to have lost authority.

'Well, nice to have you back, Chris,' her father said as they settled rather formally around the room.

'She looks tired out,' her mother called from the kitchenette.

'You've put on weight,' said Helen.

This too was the same. Her family had never been very good at celebrations: gathered together they could only follow the right forms. For years they had done their living in separate rooms while her mother scuttled up corridors with a summons to meals or the telephone. Even Christmas had been a vague affair over a Mills and Ware's pudding, snatched between services, shared with the odd lonely parishioner.

Now they balanced the daisy cups on their laps, nibbled on biscuits. Her father pursed his lips with concentration as he reached for the sugar, stirred, sipped to taste.

'Where are the kids?' Christine asked Helen.

'Back at school, thank God.' Her sister wasn't any more maternal with the years. Or didn't show it. The light cast an almost metallic gleam on her long blonde hair. The line of her black-rimmed eyes was like a wire.

'Another cup?' their mother asked.

Helen stood up. 'Actually, I must be off. I have to see someone before I pick up the kids.' Helen had always slipped off somewhere.

Her mother's cup clicked in its saucer.

'We're dying to hear all about your trip.' She smiled.

The flesh falls away, the colours fade, only the forms remain. Like this featureless room, with so much left out, left behind. Christine looked at her mother, trying to remember, glints, flashes, a distant grace . . . You've willed it away, she thought, but even the anger was an echo. She was suddenly so tired that her mother jumped in and out of focus before her eyes. Crouched in her chair, bending to sip, she was the figure in the front pew who dipped in prayer . . .

Within a week Christine had found her shack in the hills and was gone.

Violet Hollins came down with flu at the end of summer. Nothing dramatic, but it left her coughing weakly in bed for nearly a month, and by winter had become a way of life in the flat. John Hollins stayed cheerful, cooked their evening chops, and thanked everybody at the Bishop Byatt for their kind invitations which Violet kept on refusing.

Her daughters visited her. She dressed then and shuffled into the living-room in a cardigan buttoned askew. She sat with her head shaking slightly, leaning forward when they spoke as if following the lines of a play.

'I must bring the kids over. That is, when they can fit it in.' Helen rolled her eyes, but added: 'They've been asking to see Gran.'

Christine saw that Helen, in her own way, was as touched and guilty as she was. They made the tea now, moving gently round their mother. They offered her shopping trips, drives, films. She shook her head, smiling. But when they got up to go, she followed them to the door.

'Now what was it?' Her hands smoothed her thighs where an apron used to lie. 'There was something I was going to tell you . . .'

It's too late, Christine thought as she drove home

Then one afternoon she arrived at the flat, knocked, called out, let herself in. She found her mother sitting in the grey light of her bedroom. She did not seem to notice as Christine pulled up a chair in front of her. They were silent while outside, rain trickled from the gutters.

'Hey Mum.' Christine spoke out of the terror of the last few moments, that she no longer existed for her mother, had denied her and lost her for good. 'Listen, why don't you come and spend a few days with me?' Her mother turned to her with unaccusing eyes.

'A change of air would do you good. Come on, I'll help you pack.' She would not allow her mother to refuse. This was suddenly the right time for them both.

Violet nodded slowly and stood up. She looked around her. 'I'd better leave a note for Daddy,' she said.

Christine drove fast through late afternoon traffic. Was she overdoing things again? There was no electricity at the shack, and the nights were freezing. Would her mother even notice where she was? Then, crossing the Causeway, she was suddenly between two realities. She had done this before, or dreamt it, crossed a river into fading light, her mother beside her, taking her home. Where had she seen it? In London, before she had decided to come back? She hummed a little into the silence of the car as they sped up into the hills.

Violet noticed that a change came over Christine as she guided the car down the long rutted driveway to her shack.

'There's Jesse barking! He hears me coming way back on the road.' Her voice was eager.

They pulled up, scattering hens, amongst old sheds and rusting farm machinery.

Violet straightened up beside the car. In the half light two ducks watched her, very white, solid and grave in the long green grass. A foxy dog danced behind a gate. The air against her cheeks was cold.

'Looks like we're in for another frost tonight.' Christine had opened the gate, was hugging the ecstatic dog against her chest. Violet followed her across the yard. They paused on the verandah.

'How do you like my view?'

Beyond the yard, green pasture fell into a valley, disappeared into a line of trees and rose again to meet the sky that arched above them.

'It's so quiet.'

'I might be a hundred miles out, here.'

'Don't you get nervous?'

'Jesse's my protector, aren't you boy? Come on, it's getting dark.' She crossed the creaking verandah and unpadlocked the door.

The last light shone through a four-paned window into a dim kitchen. Christine lit kindling waiting in a wood stove and set a gas lamp on the table.

'Make yourself at home, I'll just shut up the chooks.'

Violet heard her voice calling, young and echoing, out in the darkness. The gas lamp hissed softly. Light swayed up on the ceiling. Beyond its circle were dark shapes and corners. She sat very still at the table.

———

'It reminds me of a time . . . do you remember Casson?' They were sitting over empty plates, the lamp between them.

'The rectory by the river and swimming off a boat and some boys we used to play with all the time . . .?' Christine leaned over and topped up Violet's glass.

'The Spences. So you remember them? You must have been, what, five or six when we came back to the city?'

'Yes, but the country made a big impression on me.' For some reason her memories of that time were speared with sadness, twilight over the river, low rocky hills around the town that threatened her, a sort of Sunday night feeling of being lost and alone.

'Of course we had electricity, but we had a wood stove and it was very quiet like this.'

'What happened to the Spences?'

'They went to Melbourne after Casson and we never saw them again. Just Christmas cards. I haven't thought of them for ages.' Violet looked across Christine to the forgotten life of a fire.

'You know,' Christine said, watching her, 'you and Dad could easily find a little place around here. There are plenty if you look, and they're quite cheap and comfortable.'

'Oh we couldn't possibly. Dad isn't a country person. And he loves the Home.'

'What about you? You haven't looked exactly happy recently.'

'Haven't I dear? Convalescent blues.' Violet put down her glass.

Christine leaned forward, flushed from the fire and wine.

'Come on Mum, don't give me that. Are you going to stay a convalescent for the rest of your life? How can you bear it, living in that place, all ping-pong and sing-song and isn't it nice? Why have you just given up like this?'

'Oh Chris.' Violet waved a hand in front of her eyes. 'No dear, don't, you don't understand. It's all right there really, it's not much different from before. It's me, I'm tired, I have to catch up . . . somewhere . . .' Her head had started shaking again.

Christine stood up and put on the kettle, closed her eyes against the fire. What had she done? What did she know after all? Their lives were so different. She slumped into the chair by the stove, her hands searching out Jesse's back.

Violet was sitting very still, letting her heart beat out its panic. It passed more quickly then. The darkness. The light actually seemed to dim. Lately it had been happening more often, triggered off by the phone ringing, a moment's indecision in the supermarket, a cat calling in the night. As if the darkness was gathering all around her, waiting for her to forget that she had ever been alive at all.

It was quiet again. There was the lamp, the fire. It always left her clearer for a little afterwards, the mind unrolled itself, even and sure. She was almost grateful to it.

Back at the Home, no it had started years before, she

and her mind often seemed to have come apart. Couldn't remember what she'd got up for in the morning, and then what to do after that. Until she just had to trust to her body's long habit of living to do it for her. Always feeling there was something she had to remember, something vital, for which she needed time and quiet. There wasn't much of that at the Home. 'Keeping busy', they all said that when they asked after each other in the courtyard. What had Chris said, that it was a silly place where they played ping-pong? But they knew that, all of them. Keeping busy: it was a sort of motto of the place. Her last parish.

And there was Chris, looking miserable. Poor old Chris, she had meant to help, she had always been like that, running to you bursting over with an idea about this or that, or something she'd made for you, and the next moment in tears, stamping her foot, and you didn't know where you'd gone wrong, where you'd let her down. John understood Chris better, that she had to try things, she had to battle with her own nature all the time. You didn't see it in John, but he was a battler too, hours in his study, praying, reading, coming out quiet and cheerful again, a conclusion reached, food for next week's sermon. You had to respect him for it, but it was lonely in the beginning outside his door, part of the world that had to be forgiven.

Christine had inherited it somehow, this drive to saintliness. Along with his high forehead, his short strong limbs. But it had been hard for her to find her way. Was this it here, alone? In workman's boots and those rings studded up her ears? And what about Helen, always smiling through her hair . . .?

My daughters are strangers to me. She sometimes said that to herself to try and work it out. Because this couldn't be the whole story, the way they looked at her sometimes with hard grown-up faces that made her nervous. If she could get past all those little phrases, 'doing nicely', 'going through a phase', 'happily settled down', now 'got their own lives to lead' – the words you use for other people, like a currency across the years – if she could get back to them, Helen and Christine, two heads, one blonde, one brown, bent over the kitchen table, quarrelling over coloured pencils, there was a knowledge there, there must be, that could show you what they had become.

'Why do you live here, Chris?' She had never asked her before. She had accepted it as part of the world's drawing away.

'I'm nearly thirty.' Christine turned to her, reached for her wine. 'I knew I wanted a place of my own back in England, in the end. I wanted to grow things. I don't know why. I found I like looking after things.' She said this almost defiantly. My dog, my chooks, my ducks. Two goats arriving next week. My goats. Jealous even that the cows her landlord ran on the place were not her own. An orgy of ownership, of care. Even of this shack, that she was saving up to buy, scrubbing the old lino, blacking the stove, oiling the flywire door. She looked after it like a baby.

'And what about those photos over there?' Violet

pointed to a fan-like arrangement pinned to the back
of the kitchen door.

'They were all taken during my time with the Youth
Centre in London.' Christine got up and went over to
them. Violet joined her.

'That's me with Eugene Hoffman outside the Centre,
we ran it together, that's Eugene playing basketball with
some of the boys, that's our Christmas party, what a riot,
that's the group of kids we took to the Lake District.'

Eugene Hoffman featured in every shot, a thin
blond young man dressed like a fisherman in a polo-
neck sweater and beanie. It was his face in the
blown-up photo in the centre, caught turning to a call,
beginning a smile that deepened his long jaw, eyes
searching out the caller, deepening and disappearing
into a maze of printed dots.

'Who was he?'

'An American, from Baltimore, ex-priest, social
worker, teacher, traveller.'

'Did you get to know him well?'

'We lived together, more or less.' In sleeping-bags,
above the Youth Centre, breakfasts by the tea-urn,
wearing coats and gloves, planning the day over a tres-
tle table. Knowing at the time she was serving her
essential apprenticeship.

'What was there between you?'

'He was the man of my life.' It was good to say it to
her mother, even if it gave the wrong impression. She
had always known it was possible for a human being to
be like that. She had found him and he had taken her

along with him. Work, ideas, laughter, work, it had been like suddenly mastering an instrument, or she was the instrument, no straining, no false notes. It had seemed easy then.

'What happened?' Did he treat her well, did he make her happy as I could never do?

'His mother was sick and he had to go back to America.' She thought too that he sensed his time in London was over, his work was done. Too many people depended on him, it was time for them to go on alone. He was telling her then, it was no good, her hand on his arm. He had said: 'If it was to be anyone, it would have been you.' She had tried for a while, had the presumption to try to live like him. But love for her had to be through her hands, in what she touched and held and was given back.

'So that's it?' Her mother would never understand.

'Oh there are letters. He says he'd like to come to Australia one of these days. But yes, that's it. And there'll never be anyone else.'

Violet was silent. She would have liked to offer comfort, denial, you are so young, how can you know . . . but they were easy words against Christine's face, this kitchen. Hadn't she too once held on to such an ending, at Casson, when she was in love, with Jim, Jim Spence?

Christine was clearing their plates off the table. 'Ready for bed?'

It was all here waiting for her to put together, to find under layers of living. It mustn't slip away again, the man in the kitchen, the woman by the fire.

'Coming?' asked Christine, picking up the lamp.
She followed her daughter into the other room.

Morning revealed a foreign country outside the window, mists rolling away from silver fields.

'Did you see the frost we had last night?' Christine asked as she stoked the fire. 'I hope you were warm enough.'

'Oh yes. The best sleep I've had for a long time.' The night had done its work for Violet. She had slept heavily, moving in and out of dreams she had forgotten, but which brought her straight back to the morning, ready.

'I must be off,' said Christine, pulling on her boots. She taught three days a week at the local high school. 'I'll be back about four. You can keep the fire going, I've chopped some more wood.' She had not slept well, aware of her mother's presence across the room. She wished she had not spoken of Eugene last night.

Violet nodded at her. Christine had never been very sociable in the morning. But Christine lingered. 'You'll be all right here, won't you? Why don't you go for a walk? There're some arum lilies growing down by the creek. You've always liked those lilies, haven't you?'

Yes, yes, go! You don't know what it is you are offering me. Violet sat listening as the car engine turned over and died, once, twice and then away, steaming, bumping up the drive.

It had been a larger room than this, a real old rectory kitchen, but the light was the same, the bright innocent sky over the sink, the floor dappled from trees outside the verandah. One bulb above the table. None of the spotlights and stainless steel of modern kitchens, everything concealed. A pile of wood by the stove, a box of oranges wedged into a corner. The heat and cold and blowflies rushing in the door.

Another era. Life at walking pace. Radio serials, Mother's Union meetings, children's voices down at the river all through the long afternoons. No trouble with falling congregations then, everybody came to church on Sunday.

It was their first parish. They were very busy. They tried very hard. John with his painstaking sermons, his visits to all the farms, even the shacks in the hills. And she, with fêtes and socials and afternoon teas, let alone two small children. The kitchen was her scene of battle, her introduction to the mysterious ways of things. Of Things. To this day, a pot burned if she turned her back, backs and fronts joined together if she sewed on a button, her sewing machine would only go if she hummed and looked out the window and pretended she didn't care. But then she had wondered how she would ever keep the household creaking over from day to day. How long would the women of the parish forgive a no longer new bride for her misshapen pikelets, her husband's creased cassock, the curtains that hung unhemmed in the rectory lounge-room? She felt their eyes on her in that kitchen, sweating, prodding, stirring her lumpy gravy over a copy of *Golden Wattle,* pouring her unjelled jam down the drain at the back steps. It was like a revenge, she used to think, by all domestic objects around her, for having ignored them up till then, reading a book in her grandmother's house, being looked after.

And yet it was in the kitchen, making one of her uncertain cups of tea, too strong, more water, too weak, if I give it a stir . . . that she first noticed Jim Spence looking at her, laughing. He'd taken to dropping in at odd hours, always just seemed to miss John, and would sit watching her blunders as if he enjoyed them. One day he took her hands as she wrung them and said: 'You're like a little girl. Don't ever grow up.' Watching her, smiling as she blushed. It hadn't occurred to her that her struggles could be funny, could even be endearing. It was as if she had moved onto a stage. It was irresistible.

Had she thought much about him before this attention, as apart from Dot and Jim Spence, one of those couples on bank postings, who came and went, and remained outsiders? But Jim Spence had been to school with John. 'Wonderful to find you here,' he said, and presuming friendship, took them over for the summer. 'Old Happy Hollins,' Jim called John. He didn't seem to take it seriously, that John was now the rector of the local church.

'What do you do for Saturday lunch? Right, how about a picnic by the river?'

'Dot says she's just baked a cake, what if we walk over after tea?'

'You mean you play bridge, then we've got a four!'

'We're used to moving about in this job,' Dot confided to her over the dishes. 'We settle in quickly wherever we go.'

They sought out the Hollinses daily, as if they needed them. Picnics drifted on to dinner: night after night they put the children to bed, sat on the rectory verandah, drinking beer, swatting mosquitoes. The children formed a foursome of their own. She could see her two little girls slick-haired like seals, squealing as the two Spence boys bombed them from over-hanging branches into the dark green water. Dot quickly saw that Vi needed a hand. She rushed out and brought in her washing if the dust was blowing, took over her kitchen for the dreaded annual cake stall. Twelve blowaway sponges that you practically had to hold down, and the benches clear. ('I wash as I go,' said Dot, elbows up at the sink, setting up a sort of rhythm, like a jazz musician.)

John and she accepted it, this brief take-over: they didn't know what else to do. They were used to accommodating people, fitting their life around others' needs. And it intrigued them a little, a breath from the easy frivolous world that had always passed them by. They muttered protests about sermons and Sunday school, but it was summer, the whole town slowed down to the pace of a ball tossed in an idle game of tennis. They rather enjoyed for a while being Happy and Vi making mistakes over the bridge table.

Dot and Jim were strikingly oddly matched. Jim was short and slim with heavy brown eyes, straight black hair. He made you think of cricketers, Errol Flynn, or an officer on a British cruise ship. He had an eager, interested air about him, liked to yarn in the pub, make irreverent comments over a few beers. He was, by anybody's standards, a heart-throb in his tennis whites. While Dot looked more like a Girl Guide leader, broad in the beam, sporty calved, hair clipped back off her face. That face, she could see it now, clearer than Jim's, the downward slope of the eyes and mouth, the mole with the hair on the upper lip that seemed to say 'Trust me' as she leaned forward over her knitting, talking. A great talker, talked as rapidly as her hands moved, accounts detailed down to the last minute, the last penny, the last second cousin. She listened too, her eyes were alert, she noticed and could stay silent. She was everybody's mother, good old Dot, she remembered the tomato sauce and the towels, gave the signals of departure. 'Well come on Jimmy,' she would say, gathering possessions. 'What, are you tired?' Jim would say, looking round for an unfinished bottle. Until she would touch his arm. 'Please. Home.' And he would get up not looking at her.

You couldn't help wondering what had drawn them together. 'She's a nice girl,' John said. 'A stable influence. Spence was a pretty rowdy type at school.' She sensed that John didn't have much serious time for Jim. He listened to his war stories, his cynical stances about farmers and bankers, and said very little. But John never talked about other people. She was alone with her fascination from the start.

For yes, though she didn't have the words to name her feeling, she had noticed Jim Spence, turned to watch him, as probably many women did. She gave herself up to watching him, in his old army fatigues, brown arms emerging from khaki, coaxing up their barbecue fire, neat as an Arab on his heels, quick, skilful, male. When he smiled at her it was as if she had been chosen. His glamour spread to Dot, his children, all of them, until there was a sort of hectic shimmer over the lamp-lit verandah, the dusty tennis courts, the shaded, sluggish river.

Jim Spence catches her eye across the table, brushes her arm as they walk home, feeding tired children witticisms for one another's ears. Appears at her kitchen at dusk to smile at her by her stove, until she feels she can do no wrong. Until she wills it, he opens the gate of their front garden as if she had sent for him, she is there watering the McCartney rose in the summer night. He comes straight to her as he should, she is waiting like all the heroines in all those novels she read in her grandmother's house. Except meanwhile John is putting the children to bed.

You can remember humiliation too. Here she was, an old woman in a dressing-gown, deciding she must dress, pulling yesterday's clammy clothes over her stiff body; this body that once seemed beautiful to her because he said it was. And she, brought up to distrust beauty, to think of herself as a soul without a body, now swivelled on long-tendoned ankles down the main street, dazzled the baker with her Monday morning smile. And pitied poor Dot her hairy calves as they dabbled their feet in the river together. Even then she had suspected that for this, time, if nothing else, would make her pay.

And she had sometimes wondered if the others noticed! That night, towards the end, when Jim had said he fancied a walk. Any takers? They had left her to say shyly she would go. Exultant children, their quick footsteps passed the bright verandahs of the other houses, to stop in the shadows where the street lights finished and make their declarations. Quick we must go back. Returning too gay and generous to John sunk in a book, while Dot made tea in silence.

And then, sooner than expected, the Spences' new posting comes, they are to leave for Melbourne in a fortnight, they are terribly busy, meet only once or twice more with their friends the Hollinses. Summer is over anyway, cooler evenings seem less festive in the rectory lounge-room. Dot knits on with itemised reports of travel preparations. Jim drinks and smokes and doesn't look at Violet. When John begs work, they all stand up together.

Everything falls away. Parish duties slide past her as if her term of office were running out. John, the children, come and go around her. She is waiting, when can she see him, tell him, I am ready, take me with you, take me where I belong. She never leaves her kitchen, but he never comes.

Then their last evening, Helen's birthday party, balloons lurching in the windy twilight, the children's voices querulous in the long rectory garden. Dot is sprinkling bread with hundreds and thousands, talking, and suddenly her voice is thickening, 'the strain of it, always on the go, always having to make new friends, why couldn't we just be a family together?' Shoulders shaking over the sink, just as the children run in demanding their party, voice choking, 'as if I'm not enough', what is Dot saying? That it has happened before, an intense friendship with another couple, Jim's even more intense friendship with the wife? That it will happen again? Too late, Dot blows her nose and is serving up the sausage rolls, the men come in and take up positions round the clamouring table. She cannot even look at him now, and what is Christine, tear-stained from Pip Spence's teasing, whispering in her ear: 'Anyway, I like Daddy better than Mr Spence.'

Everything spoiled, streamers fallen into half-eaten cakes, a jungle of grabbing and shouting, nasty cream-smeared faces. His eyes follow her as he crouches behind his sons. Next day limp-bodied balloons catch at her as she crosses the verandah. They were making an early start, Dot said. He's gone.

A fork scraped a bowl, fat hissed, an egg spread across a pan. Winter clouds moved outside her window, children sat quietly, mysterious angels. Without his eyes none of this existed. Nobody broke the silence around her. John said nothing. She was grateful for the warmth of his back. While the other lay with her, walked with her, watched her, listened to her endless muttered debate. The drive to her days was to their finishing, to leave the children sleeping, John in his study, and walk those darkened roads. Smug lights within the houses, insolent smoke tossing from the chimneys, now she was an outcast, burying herself in the bushes by the river, rocking thigh against calf over her loss.

She grew angry with him, old brown eyes, moony face, the friendly man without any friends, the scoffer at security working his way up the bank, the lover who never followed through. Guilt grew, until Dot's face went with her too. She knew now that her days were also lived in this suspense, must be a series of watchings, yieldings.

Summer was coming. She was weary. When would this double life be finished, would it last as long as the hope that she couldn't after all let die? When could her life be light, self-forgetful again, with the simple pleasures, simple shames of those around her?

Then their time too was over in Casson, they moved to the city, a new parish, the children were now both at school. Shyly she turned to them again, but they brushed past her: they had learnt to be alone. Perhaps she was never to be in step with them again? Her days were filled briskly, sometimes she could even miss the daydreams. How long had it taken for her cells to shed him, five, ten years to have forgotten even to say, I have forgotten him. Until he was felt only as a vague stirring in the blood from time to time, an excitement about the first summer evenings, a dark-eyed man, a garden gate. Now, years later, this room.

Violet looked around her. She was standing in the middle of Christine's kitchen. The fire had gone out. Would Chris be annoyed? It must be well past midday, the sunshine outside was shadowed. She should go for a walk before it rained. At least be able to tell Chris she had seen the lilies.

Jesse jumped up delighted from the verandah and led her as if scenting a trail, across the yard, through the gate. He raced on down the hill, far ahead of her. She took it slowly, the luscious green was unexpectedly gravelly, she had to watch her way. The air smelt fresh, of clover. She would like to leave the whole affair back in the staleness of the kitchen. It was, after all, nothing by today's standards, didn't they call it a 'bit on the side', just to name it then had been shocking enough. Yet she had been ready to lie in the bushes with him, she would have left with him on the next train out of town. It had affected her terribly. She could see that now. Beyond the guilt, which in time she forgot along with its cause.

No, it had left her terrified at where the dreams might take you, the lack of substance they revealed. She would never dare to look again into a shimmer, to follow her own voice again. She was unformed somewhere, a child. Rightness was a conspiracy that others knew about, better to follow the path marked out by John and Gran. If it was narrow, it was clear, forget about the light and shade on either side. And when reminders came that these might still exist, panic closed her eyes.

Her foot turned on a stone, she skidded, waving wildly, landed on all fours. 'Damn it all,' said Violet, turning herself back and sitting on her bottom in the middle of the hillside. A huge pale sky moved slowly with its clouds above her. Cows in the next paddock shifted bite by bite. She shut her face and felt the sun and wind lightly upon her face.

This was how I was meant to be. That was what it had been about. With Jim she used to shut that thought away as it turned up like a cat at the door. This was how I was meant to be. An answering smile into the sun, yellowed teeth, porous noses, squinted eyes; answering imperfections. Being yourself until you were drunk with the giggly ease of it and could lie back laughing your silly head off. And then afterwards, the peace that descended, the long sweep of the oars bringing them home, the ripples spreading to the banks, the whole boatload of them blessed.

To have gone on like that, would she now be calling 'Come and get it' over a barbecue, waving plump arms in welcome, a cheerful, ripened self? It would have been bridge and beer and camping holidays: would it have lasted, the recognition between them? They were weak, she and Jim, perhaps had needed the solid buffer of Dot and John. Who had aged better. She still played eighteen holes, Dot said in her card a few Christmases ago. Jim had heart trouble, was having to retire early. Is there a moral quality to ageing? Poor old Jim, she hoped life had not found him out too much.

She ought to have been faithful to it, what there was between them, seen its truth however shallow, instead of turning away in fear. It had existed: it was part of her.

John had kept faith with her all these years. Beyond duty, disappointments. From the very first, as she stood in the pew beside her grandmother, he had insisted on seeing her as virtuous as himself. And she had only ever given him a sisterly rubbing-along.

There was her sin, that she had committed once, smiled upon by her grandmother and her friends, as they helped to fix the veil upon her hair. She had carried arum lilies, though her grandmother thought they were more for a funeral than a wedding. But her mother had carried lilies when she married her grandmother's son. A different affair that, a train and a coronet, the bride's hand resting on the shoulder of the man sitting in front of her. To obey until death, five years later.

My mother is ded, she used to write in her room in her grandmother's house. Nothing could be deader than ded. Except Dad, who had gone away and left her too. There were only those photos left for her, which she crept in to look at in her grandmother's lounge-room. Gran wouldn't approve somehow, Gran didn't like her mother, she knew it. Her mother had been Catholic and had died so that Edmund went away. Or perhaps she had been one of those who *kicked up her heels, was not quite . . .* : in those photos her face was not quite serious in spite of the hand on the shoulder. What would life have been with such a mother?

She rose stiffly and set off again. She must find those lilies.

Nothing was becoming any clearer. The Lord had his purpose for each and every one of us, John said. Could you say that a death long past had blighted a life, left it with an emptiness somewhere? Discount the years of living, doing . . . She saw herself, an old woman, and behind her, cold rooms in dusty houses, spoiled food, ill-made beds, wilting gardens, the quiet man lonely in prayer. And what about the children, not born out of passion, who had grown up silent, apart from her, as if she too had not been there?

She glimpsed the lilies like a cluster of white birds among the bush of the creek, and pushed her way through to them. There was a boulder by the water to sit on and watch them. She was scratched and shaking, she felt a familiar drumming, was it growing dark already? *No*, she said, holding her head rigid, her hands rubbing the gritty surface of the rock, not here, not yet, there are many ways to look at a life, look now at the lilies. 'Consider the lilies of the field, how they grow.'

Here amongst the dimness of the trees, the water rushing by, was the sort of foreboding of her grand-mother's lounge-room, the waxen flowers, the heavy frames high on the mantelpiece, taken down by a shy child's hand. The smile of her mother waiting for her.

She was right to come here. Calmer already. The flowers have thick white flesh. Heartshaped around their powdery stamen. They stand so straight on their ridgy stems, some are almost leaning backwards. They grow in theatrical arrangement, like a band of nuns and brides. There are older flowers amongst them, thin brown stalks waving a pod of seeds.

They will all die in the summer, and reappear next year. They come and they go, they toil not . . . perhaps this would do, this acceptance. Stages in a life. Her mother cut down, she grown old, her daughters in some sort of prime. They come and they go. Helen playing out her blessing before her time was over. She knew her, knew that smart swivel, that smile for someone else's eyes. And Christine. Looking for God, her whole house was a shrine to the man in the photograph.

Violet felt a hush, a prickly rustling, then the sudden rush of rain. She had taken too long to get here, it was nearly dark, she was late. Through the bush, the shack was still there against the sky, it was pouring with rain, it looked thundery, but she must get back. Christine would be waiting.

She ran from the shelter of the trees, started to scramble up the hill, slipping, grabbing, gasping to herself, I must get back.

Christine was sitting on the verandah, with a cup of tea and Jesse by her knee. The clouds were still and heavy, covering the light of the sky. It was going to rain, where was her mother? She would go and find her when she finished her tea. She liked to sit here after teaching, between the house and sky, she was at her most private at these moments.

The headmaster at her school was waiting for an invitation to see her place, he'd said again today. One small cloud detached itself from a larger grouping and seemed to skid in the growing wind, straight towards her. It was going to happen. She was prepared.

She wondered again, if you thought hard enough about somebody, if every lover were really only him, could it be his image that was implanted, his spirit that was passed on? She shivered. She was entering dark territory. She thought, there's an awful arrogance in loving, in trying to harness a whole delicate universe to your own. She would almost like to ask her mother how it might be.

It had started to rain, quite heavily, and standing up, she could just make out the tiny figure of her mother slowly advancing. She must help her, bring her back. She set off into the rain.

Ask her, ask your mother, struggling up the hill, see if she can tell you somehow, your children are born in forms you never dreamt of, you go on to see them grow up strangers, and yet one day you find them living out your patterns, the patterns rutted across their souls.

Burning Off

Vic and Angela lived right in the town, down by the river. Wes and I lived out a bit, under the hill. As the summer came we spent a lot of evenings sitting out on Vic and Angela's front verandah.

Up at our place, the first that Wes and I had ever shared alone, the darkness seemed to lap around our ankles. The town sprawled out below us, a far-away marquee of lights. But here with Vic and Angela we were deep within a community of sounds. Frogs croaked in the still air by the river, Angela's little sprinkler whip-whipped by the gate. Half a block away Poddy Stratton's TV droned under its giant antenna. The girls in the schoolteachers' house behind us sent scraps of laughter echoing across the town.

'I thought they were having a night off,' Angela said. 'The big blonde one told me they all wanted to wash their hair.' A few cars went by. Most were turning up to the schoolteachers' house. The teachers were said to be a 'good crowd' this year. They joined in, they were having a ball.

No doubt we were being observed too, sitting there like a flashback in the light of a kerosene lamp hung by the door. There was a campfire smell from the mosquito coils that Angela had lit for each of us. Vic's was too close, he knocked it over reaching for a can. Angela relit it. While Wes kept playing, discreet runs that went nowhere, as if to himself.

Poddy Stratton liked to surprise us. Prowl up the verge so as not to crunch the gravel. 'Hod enough for you?' He'd pause by the gate as if he'd just seen us. Vic raised a can to him, Wes put down his guitar. They worked in Poddy's garage when it was busy. Angela pulled out a spare chair. She'd been in the town almost a year now and no longer asked, 'Where's Maxine?' Everybody knew that by this time of the night Maxine Stratton would be under the weather. Poddy went everywhere alone.

Poddy sat forward, legs apart, and fitted his stubby finger through the ring of a can. His pull was vicious, froth ran onto the floor. 'Cheers,' said Poddy. We all sat forward a little, in his honour, our visitor.

'Ye-es,' said Poddy, as if continuing a conversation, which in a way he was. 'It's gunna be a record summer.' His voice was pitched to reach the end of the verandah. He scanned us with his dark, ringed eyes. Poddy afterhours, shaved jowls and sports shirt sleeves ironed out in right-angles above his biceps, had a headmasterly air about him, a self-appointed distance. 'Useta think about putting in air-conditioning.' He wiped his long upper lip. 'That was before your friend Goof took charge of course.' He had assumed from the start where our sympathies would lie. 'I tell you what, everyone's gunna feel the pinch this Christmas. All your university types, your bra-burners, unionists and what have you. They aren't gunna like it any more than we do.'

He waved his hand at us, our bare feet, the ragged deckchairs, the cockeyed flywire door. Which side did he put us on now? We sagged back. Once I had taken him on, look there's a world recession, think what's been done for the etc, but I'd lost energy in the end, retreated — well anyway, it all boils down to, maybe it's just a temperamental, it's not that I'm really into . . . (Wes, where are you? . . .)

'I hope he doesn't stay long,' Angela said in the kitchen. She was trying to light her little camper stove to make a cup of tea. 'He'll wake up Nat the way he carries on.'

'I hate it when we all just sit and take it,' I said. 'Pod's pet hippies.' I muttered like this sometimes to Angela, when we were alone. Angela never seemed to hear. She was always doing something, providing something. I hovered behind her with the vague reflex feeling that I ought 'to help'. I tried to wash out some cups in the sink but it was full of drowning nappies.

There was a cough from the bedroom, and a long surprised wail.

'There!' said Angela. She paused on her way out. 'It's all Gough's fault of course.'

I was left, free to prowl. Since Poddy had come, you could disappear behind that beaded curtain in the country, 'women's work'. You only had to turn up with the tea. The flame beneath the kettle flickered near to extinction. Angela must be running out of gas.

Angela's kitchen was a lean-to, tacked onto the back wall of the cottage. The city owners asked no rent on the understanding that Vic would build a proper kitchen. He had laid the concrete slab for the floor. The dark end of the room still held the cement-mixer and a jumble of tools. Into the weatherboard wall, between the louvres, Angela had knocked a dartboard of nails. Here hung her pots, her mugs and nappy-pins, her dusty bunches of drying rosemary and everlastings. Postcards from friends in New Zealand and Bali and Nepal were wedged in between the boards.

From the doorway I could see onto the verandah. Vic now held his son, loosely, high up on his chest, his dark face blank as if to say 'this makes no difference to me.' Poddy was still talking. I thought how people in middle-age seemed to occupy their own features, they seemed overdrawn, stamped with use. Like babies, they were a different species.

I remembered how my own parents used to entertain on summer evenings. They called it 'having a few couples over'. For this my mother would sweep the porch and sponge down the leaves of her pot-plants, wearing a snail curl criss-crossed with bobby pins over each cheek. She would put out guest towels and at the last moment, as the bell rang, shed her shorts and tread into a skirt. Fussed. For a handful of heads on a lit porch — sniper-like my sister and I knelt and picked out favourites — the anecdotal growl of the men's

voices, some woman's helpless nervous trill like punc-
tuation, echoing out into the suburb. The vast starry
night was undisturbed.

It was in the kitchen, if you padded out in your
shortie pyjamas, where the women got the supper,
heads bent over the hissing kettle, that the evening's
true exchange seemed to be taking place.

Were we after all so very different?

And, spying like this, would I have picked out Wes
to like, to watch, *mine*, as he yawned, as his bare satiny
shoulders curved guard again over his guitar?

The first thing we had done when we came to the
farmhouse was to set up the stereo on its packing-case
frame in the empty living-room. At last, full volume.
The wet paddocks, the stolid hill received Zappa, Jeff
Beck, the Allman Brothers. This was the environment
we were used to.

'10, 9, 8, 7, 6 . . .,' shouted Pod on our doorstep
one knife-cold night. 'When the hell is blast-off?'

Wes started putting on more and more country
blues. Even if we were talking, after a while Wes's eyes
slid sideways as his head chased up a beat. Those nostalgic voices were stronger than our own. In the
mornings I would know that he had gone by the
absence of music. These days he was leaving earlier and
earlier for the garage.

I could not train myself to become a morning person. I had counted on this just happening in the

country. Change of regime = change of person. Was this part of my work-ethic upbringing or was it really profoundly Zen? Funny how much they all seemed to be linking up; Bad Karma = Reap as Ye Shall Sow etc . . . I lay on the mattress on the floor and tried to think about this. The sun slanted in through the broken venetian blinds.

The Inner Light grows in Silence and Concentration. I had to shut my eyes not to read this on the sun-slashed wall, not to see myself, felt pen in hand, on our first night here. My own uneven letters mocked me like graffiti. Yet still I did not try to remove them, or even cover them up.

In the city, in the big house where I had met Wes, the walls carried signs like a political meeting place. Indian gods behind the kitchen door. Over the stove, a newspaper cutting of Whitlam and Barnard waving after they had announced the conscription amnesty. A big mandala above the fireplace in what had come to be called the meditation room.

I'd thought then it would be easier to meditate in the country, to get up, work in the vegetable garden . . .

The vegetable garden was no more. Such as it was, some lettuce-pale silver beet coiled up like flags and other, unidentified fronds, had disappeared entirely one weekend when we were in Perth. Tours of inspection now included not only the pen where we *could* have chooks, but the vegetable garden's graveyard, its frail wire netting looping among the grass, its scare-crow climbing canes.

Anyway, why were vegetables such an index of virtue? The eating of them, their growing, the disposal of them back to the earth?

. . . *in Silence and Concentration* . . . The 'S' was oversize, it seemed to leer at me . . .

The house was not silent. It was a hollow contained within a sleeve of animal life. In the ceilings and walls, under the floor, rats, cats, possums were they? skittered and thundered on ceaseless missions. The sleeve had holes. At night they gambolled in the passageways with the whispery abandon of out-of-hours children. Now the house itself creaked hospitality as its joints expanded in the heat of the sun. Crows bleated out in the paddocks. The day was cranking open before me.

Some time before we came here, this house had been dispossessed of its land and left to perch as a rental proposition on the crossroads between the town and the hill. A previous owner had tried to turn it into a city house, *à la mode*. You cleaned your teeth over a water-buckled vanity bench. The toilet had just made it inside, wedged in, not quite square, home-tiled next to the shower. (While the old dunny lurked outside among the grasses, its round white pedestal crouching in intimate darkness, its door forever on the point of being closed.)

A breakfast bar butted across the kitchen on spindly legs where a big wooden table should have been. The fireplace had been boarded up. On the sink a single cup trailed the tail of a tea-bag. The guitar sat in the one comfortable chair.

There was only the country women's programme on the radio. It was like being home, sick, in the suburbs at midday, part of a community of grandmothers and invalids waiting behind lowered blinds. The heat here islanded you to the shelter of your own roof.

Outside the kitchen window the long yellow grasses marched up from the paddocks, consumed the fences, halted at the edge of the firebreak beside the straight gravel road. Although the day was still they shimmered and rocked, an imported pastoral ideal. I grabbed my shoulder bag and shut the front door behind me with a bang that sent Wes's Javanese windchimes into brief, oriental applause.

It seemed quieter out on the road. Just the regular swish-swish of my thongs on gravel, throwing up little ankle wings of dust, and a great airy stillness around me. Crows rose and fell in the distance. The sun swamped everything. The drab homespun belly of the hill was exposed, too close behind me. I walked fast towards the haze over the town. I became an engine pumping up heat. I was haloed an inch over with my own heat. I thought about Coca-Cola in thick glass bottles. I thought of shopping centres, as of great humming cathedrals. I thought of pine trees and of wading into the cold oil of the sea on a hot day. Although I had never been to a dinner party, I thought about soft lights and crystal glasses, and the fine picking up of lines of thought. Cheeses and wines, meat in cream, all that refined acid food that made you aggressive and decadent. And interesting. I trod out my own stale band of thoughts, oblivious to the landscape. While my higher mind slumbered, unsummoned for yet another day.

There was always a moment, as Angela and I turned into the main street, that I saw the town as distanced, through a lens, and our approach to it as something slow and heroic, a response to a sudden call for 'Action' . . . The two women trudge on, faces to the sun, their long skirts blowing against their bodies . . . The pusher rattled a pony-cart accompaniment, a flimsy candy-striped city job that jolted poor Nat sideways, his towelling hat across his eyes, his fat fists clenched on either knee.

'Whoa there boy,' sang out Angela, swooping down and straightening him, her long hair still damp from the paddling pool where I had found her, balancing Nat on her naked brown stomach. She and Nat smelled of talcum powder.

The main street narrowed down to vanishing point before us as it sped on into the wheat-belt. The shopfronts rose into turrets and mouldings, the clock in the Town Hall struck midday against the white-blue sky. But as we entered the town, past the dusty Municipal rose garden, the wide street swallowed us, and the shops broke into their familiar sequence, the Co-op, McIntyre's Newsagency, 'Verna' Hair Salon, the Post Office, Kevin Scragg's, The Bright Spot.

Why was shopping so consoling? A relief from the

daily round of giving out, these small smooth purchases bumping against you, a newspaper, stamps, a bucket and spade for Nat, fresh bread, the first watermelon! It was like nourishment . . . especially with Angela who did not worry about confusing wants and needs, who rummaged and fingered passionately while the Co-op girls, school-leavers with engagement rings, clustered around the pusher. 'Isn't he *gor*-geous!' they cried.

The pusher rolled on, Nat unblinking, wedged among the parcels.

'Just a minute,' Angela said, when we had nearly passed the butcher's. 'I've got to get a chop for Vic.' Vic was an unrepentant meat-eater. He added a chop or some polony to Angela's wok vegetables and united them with tomato sauce.

'I'll wait outside with Nat,' I said. I did not even like to catch Kevin Scragg's eye as we walked past, his knowing salute, chopper in hand. He liked to ask you how you were finding life in the country, and to read your T-shirt, eyes lingering, for the benefit of the other customers. You knew, by the little silence as you made your way to the door, that you were going to be talked about as soon as the bell rang your exit.

I pushed the legitimising pusher back and forward under the window. At the kerb a girl in high-heeled sandals was stowing groceries and a baby into the back of her car. She gave me a quick church-porch smile across the pavement. Loretta Wells — one of the Wells. Did she see me as a sort of poor-white, a younger version of Mrs Boon, who shuffled in to town with a shopping trolley from out near the drive-in?

Through the window I saw Angela's bangles shiver down her arm as she took her tiny white parcel from Kevin Scragg's outstretched hand. The hand held, for a moment the parcel was a tug-of-war with Angela laughing and shaking her head.

'Let's go,' she muttered as she joined me, her escape jangling behind her. 'I'm not going in there if he's on his own again.'

Poddy's garage was a block further down the road. Out in the yard Wes's ute and Vic's Kombi were nosed up next to one another.

'Vic!' called Angela. We stood at the top of the driveway leading down to the black mouth of the workshop. A transistor was playing loudly in its depths. We waited. Vic came out slowly, paused at the door, took out his tobacco.

'Want to come to the Bright Spot with us?'

'Na – got a job on.' He squinted up at us over the paper bandaided across his bottom lip. He clicked his tongue at Nat. I cleared my throat.

'Is Wes about?' I hardly ever spoke to Vic. He wore footy shorts and workman's boots; he propped one shapely leg across the other, leaning on the workshop door. You could glimpse an earring through his tangled hair. 'Wes!' he called out over his shoulder.

Poddy's red beanie shadowed Wes at the entrance. Wes was carrying a coil of rope and the transistor. They were moving towards the yard.

'Any chance of a lift home?' I said.

'No way.' Pod answered for him. 'He's gotta follow me in the truck.' Wes lifted his shoulders above his armful and gave an idiot-grin. He called himself a grease-monkey these days. He marched off, Pod right behind him. With his pony-tail and his big boots he looked like the garage mascot.

'Wait at our place.' Vic gave a nod in the direction of the river. 'Have a sewing circle or something.' He breathed out smoke and smiled broadly at us, conscious that he might have gone too far.

'Do you see yourself living here always?'

'Always?' Angela frowned as if it was a word she didn't know.

I knew it was a low-consciousness sort of question. All because I couldn't bring myself to ask: Are you happy? I drew up hard on my strawberry milkshake. There was a lot of it, it tasted of crushed chewing gum, I felt it flooding through every cell of my body. *Daily renewed sense-yearnings sap your inner peace* . . .

We were sitting at one of the laminex tables in the Bright Spot, the traditional end to our shopping trips. There had been times, when Vic and Wes were with us, playing the pinball machines amongst the town's milling adolescents, that we had recognised the Bright Spot's fly-spotted nostalgic charm. Today we were the only customers. Most of the chairs were stacked on the tables up near the kitchen. A whirring fan bowed to us from the counter.

'Actually,' Angela said, 'Vic's talking about moving on. He'd quite like to try opal mining up at Coober Pedy.'

The plastic streamers in the doorway swayed and kicked in a gust of afternoon wind, straight from the desert. A jumpy brightness was suddenly flung across the table.

'Do you want to go?'

'I don't know.' Angela pushed back her fringe and for a moment her small forehead stared out, white, next to her hand. 'I don't mind I guess.' She looked past me towards the door.

We looped our bags over our shoulders and prepared for that moment of darkness through the plastic streamers. There seemed to be a new silence between us as we set off again, into the glare of the long afternoon.

My parents had come to visit Wes and me. This time Evvie, my sister, was with them. It seemed crowded in the kitchen round the breakfast bar. Outside the whole country spread, bland in the late afternoon sun. But for all of us the world had shrunk, temporarily, back to this, wary faces across a shadowed table. Between us was the cake-tin with the Highland Tartans border. We ate the cake from it over our crossed knees. Christmas cake, my mother's year-round speciality. Before she left I would give her back the tin, empty. It would come back full again.

Evvie didn't eat the cake. She filled in time examining the kitchen. She was seventeen now; all at once she had very long legs in very tight jeans. Her blouse, satin with little ragged caps of sleeves, was the sort of thing you find by a dedicated haunting of the op-shops. Her blank survey of my kitchen said *Not for me*.

'You've been making jam!' my mother said, smiling.

'Mm. Fig.' She would never know how I had flung the figs, my only crop, into Angela's big pot, bored, martyred, mad with itching . . . 'You can take some home with you if you like.' With any luck my mother would forget. Though out of desperation for some proof of this lifestyle, fruits at last, she would probably persist in pushing the tarry substance across her morning toast . . .

'Still no job turned up for you?' my mother asked me. 'You'll be getting broody if you hang around too much.' Her laugh turned uncertain. She had to go on. 'I'm too young to be a grandmother!'

My father stirred. His big form was hunched up in one of our frail chairs. I hoped she wouldn't go further. I hoped she wouldn't say: 'Mind you, there's a lot less hypocrisy about the young people of today.' But she turned and looked out the window. 'Oh this poor dry countryside,' she said. She sighed.

I knew how to look out that window, to see, defined against her, the grasses moving for a moment across that other landscape, *the country*, luminous in fading light, waiting for us.

'How's the guitar going, Wes? Do you get enough time to practise?' My mother had turned to Wes.

Wes looked up. 'Oh I get around to it now and . . . haven't had a really good session for a . . .'

'He's been working really hard at the garage,' I said.

My mother smiled at him, nodding. 'It's a wonderful chance to learn a trade.'

Then my father did something surprising. He uncoiled his hand from his elbow where it had seemed to be holding him contained. He stretched it across the table, his red, whorl-jointed hand, part of my former life, and picked up Wes's restless fingers.

'These aren't mechanic's hands,' he said. He put Wes's hand down gently. He didn't look at anybody. He cleared his throat in a business-like way.

I was sitting, crease-eyed from a heavy siesta, on the front steps of the farmhouse. From time to time I ducked in through the open front door to put the needle back onto my favourite sides of Wes's records. This was something that I was too shy to do when he was home. I felt I probably liked them for the wrong, unmusical reasons, for the feelings they gave me, their melancholy landscapes: I waited for certain songs, to retaste that sensation of the right chord struck, again and again . . . Bonnie Raitt singing 'Guilty' and 'I Thought I was a Child', Maria Muldaur's 'Midnight at the Oasis', Randy Newman's 'Louisiana 1927' . . .

'They're tryin' to wash us away
They're tryin' to wash us away',

I droned, private, flat, stamping empty time on the step below me, calling up something to happen.

The step was still warm from the day, but the glare was gone. Lights began to trace the streets of the town. Dogs barked.

A pair of headlights was advancing up the road with the darkness. I heard the home-coming changing of gears. The ute.

'Did you listen to the news tonight?' Wes called as he came towards me up the path. 'Have you heard?'

'What?'

He stood before me on the steps. 'Gough's been sacked. Kerr's sacked Whitlam.' He wore the half-smile of the news-bringer.

'*When?*' I stood up too.

'This morning. It came through about midday. Fraser's forming a government.' He was edging past me up the steps. 'Pod's been at the pub all afternoon,' he called on the way down the hall. 'It's pretty wild down there. You'd think they'd won a war or something.'

He came out again with his guitar.

'Where are you going?'

'They want some live music.'

'You're going back there? Now?'

Wes gave a swift loop of the ute keys over his fingers. His eyes flickered. I felt the wordless authority of his feeling, that chose when he came forward, or kept back.

'I'm going to play,' he said.

———

The fire when it came was swift and stealthy.

On a day when the sun hung venomous, whitening, striking sharp light off leaves, I heard a distant crackling like a friendly winter hearth. I looked out the window and saw a low line of flames snake across the paddock as if it rode along a fuse.

From the verandah, down the hill, a truck was crawling up the road, the fire's keeper. I could just make out the figures of some men by the fence, and then they were lost in billowing smoke.

I thought: Do they know I am here?

The fire took over. The house was darkened. I ran from room to room shutting the windows. A roar seemed to run under the roof. I heard the windchimes' futile alarm.

I stood by the kitchen window and watched the flames pass the house in vast erratic tacks across the grass.

from
LETTER TO CONSTANTINE

LETTER TO CONSTANTINE

Constantine, you asked me to write. Write, you said, as if setting me a task. These are not times for writing, I cried. But you shook your head.

Constantine, it has been nearly two years now. For nearly two years I've been thinking of what I would write. For a long time I never stopped talking to you. You were my companion, we were on the same journey. Your presence was natural to me as a dream is on first waking. In this dream we still breathed the clear desert air.

Two years, they say, or used to say, two years and you can get over anything. 'Get over': like a mountain or a long stretch of road. A particular landscape has at last fallen behind you. Retrace your steps and there will be a different light or season. You have a sense of perspective again.

I do not breathe that desert air any more, but it carries voices, and they reach me.

But I have always been a milky, imperfect mirror of my times. Last night for the first time in years we sat on the balcony of this apartment, Steeg and I and some neighbours who had also found their way back. It was a freak summer night inserted in this watery spring. Everything came closer in the warm salt air, the sounds of gulls and cyclists, the hushed chatter from the other balconies, the vegetable smell of the Botanical Gardens. Light, we kept it light: we drank some young raw wine and did not look too hard at one another in the late light of the balcony. Something had been restored to us, we knew, a past and future, a private life: we have not after all been damned. People are beginning to read again. They contact old friends. They even write letters.

Today as I write, rain lashes the balcony, and once again I can see no further than my own opaque window.

But you Constantine, you lost your country, your family, even your profession long ago. You gave up the anxiety of possession. For you there has been no way back.

Writing to you now, it's as if I'm stepping down into the town where you live, the town of your last address. I have made one last bus ride across the desert. I'm setting off down the streets where everybody knows you. It's a border town, the streets end in barricades of barbed wire. The hills that I see beyond the wire are the hills of your country.

I am directed to the widow's house. The shutters are closed, she takes a long time to answer.

'He's not here,' she says. 'He goes away for weeks at a time.'

She has been sleeping, but yawning, she serves me with a glass of tea. She's a countrywoman of yours, you come from a hospitable tradition.

'He crosses the border, you know.' She laughs, and there's something familiar about her mouth. 'They say he has a girl there.'

It is dim behind the shutters but I see that every surface in this room is covered, with woven hangings and carpets and long-fringed brocade shawls. Before my eyes two gold-embroidered peacocks nest together. There's a market in this town, I've heard, for goods smuggled across the border.

'You can wait if you like.' The widow tucks up a strap, bends to rub her bare, high-arched feet. She looks up and smiles at me suddenly, and I see that her front teeth have a flirt's gap between them, like yours. The gap of a flirt, or a traveller. 'He always turns up.'

'I have to go back. I have my work.'

'Leave a message then.' She shoves a writing pad towards me and a gold-tasselled pencil. She smiles again.

'There,' she says. 'Explain.'

Our times, Constantine. The years between my first meeting with you in the old life, and the second. By the time we met up again I thought I was old. Everyone seemed old, even the children.

It had come late upon us in our prosperous old city. In our quarter everyone I knew grew a little richer

each year. Everything became a little more conven-
ient. It was expected, like a birthright. Everyone's
children were born healthy. Nobody died. The domino
crashes, riots, bankrupt governments happened across
borders. Then the borders closed.

Small things at first. Restaurants closed, country
houses were shut up. Only the children had new
shoes. Then the eviction notices, the fuel cuts. Nothing could be sold. Nothing could be used. A
neighbour, a merchant banker, tried to set fire to his
car. With his family in it. He had to be taken away.

Then everything went. When the first of those winters came, like most other people I had lost my job.
The gallery had closed. Who wants art in such times?
Only music stayed. Didn't they used to call our city
'Little Vienna'? All day long on the radios, in the freezing apartments, there was music. Brass bands tramped
past us on the streets as we stood outside the shops in
queues. Our opera singers and nightclub artistes were
rounded up to give free concerts among the rows of
tents in the Botanical Gardens. All through those winters they fed us music.

We were lucky. All through, we were lucky. Steeg's
job was classified essential. He could live at the laboratory to save money. All the same, by the second
winter – perhaps the worst – my life felt like a starving body, feeding off its own fat and muscle. I spent my
days scavenging and hoarding and standing in queues.
Out on the streets, under those colourless skies, I kept
my face closed. I did not want to look at anyone. I

wanted to be left alone to listen out for rumours, tips, clues. When beggars approached me as I took the boys to school, I shook my head. If I give to one, I said, hurrying on the boys, where will it end?

I took in boarders. A couple with a young child heard that I had a room. The boys slept in my room. We moved the piano in there too. At night, after I had listened to them practise, we went to bed. I heard my boarders through the wall. They had no work. He walked for miles for firewood which he shared. She lay all day on their bed while the child crawled over her. At night she whispered to her husband, her voice breaking, on and on . . . I'm going to scream from the balcony, I'm going to jump . . . I don't care . . . I don't care . . .

He seemed to think he had to earn his way by movement. He ran on errands up and down the stairs. He seemed to smile and smile without seeing anyone. One day his smile fell on me and warmed me. Feverish, for a week or so we raced through the streets together on our quests. At night I lay with open eyes and dreamt of fire, its savage bite and heat, its swift annihilation. But when he turned to me, on the stair landing, pressed me against the wall, I felt no warmth, only the coldness of his lips and hands. Fire burns on air, I thought, and I had no breath to spare.

They left to look for work. Word had started to come through that there was work, work far from the city, in the north, across the desert. There was a hum in the cafes again, under the tattered awnings, by the fountains choked with rubbish. Corporations had regrouped, the government was borrowing, work cards were being issued. Whole towns were on the move, looking for work. There was work to support the workers. Dormitories, canteens, schools for workers' children. Work registers. I was one of the first to queue.

When I registered my former occupation as *Art Historian*, it looked strange to me. I might as well have written *Princess*. What could they do with me? But the winters had brought about their own transformations. I was issued with a work card. I was to become a canteen worker in the desert.

The boys were accepted into one of the new schools, a music school, said to be the best in the city. We were lucky in this too. They would become musicians. They would always have work.

I took them to the harbour before I left. A man with a little dog had set up a brazier by the sea wall. I bought five hot potatoes from him in a cone of newspaper. I was his only customer. The boys chased the little dog through the mist that swirled around the rusted iron tables. Were their voices too shrill as they cornered it and tried to make it beg?

They came as soon as I called. They had become polite: Are you sure? they said as I offered them the last two potatoes. Even the younger, who is chunky and stout, like a sportsman, not a pianist (though in fact he is the more talented), even he held back. The desperation of his hunger had always been a secret understanding between us.

We ate in silence. They kept the end of their potatoes for the dog, and smiled as it licked their hands. No doubt, I thought, they have made their own bargains with the dark streets. No doubt they had their own version of what we saw, the shrouded ships and cranes of their childhood, the tatty beach, the dark fluid shore.

As you know Constantine, all my life I have lived by the sea. In the little town where we first met, my home town with the switchback roads between the dunes, the horizon was a white electric bar that seemed to draw in everything, sky, sea, sun, like the gateway to some distant blazing country. To travel inland was to lose my orientation, lose that mirage of ultimate escape. On that journey into the desert I kept looking for the horizon, as if I couldn't believe in any destination that did not end in water.

I had bribed my way, late, onto a bus. Bus drivers! Already rich from others' desperation, they flourished as fuel bandits, couriers, black marketeers. Ours was tiny, in high-heeled boots and an oversized fur jacket. He watched us load our own miserable luggage in the early morning rain. Then he swung in and started up, his little bitten nicotine-stained hand wedged onto the horn. The money for his bus would have come from under a mattress, I decided, or the bottom of a wardrobe, a mother's hoard. He drove as if fulfilling a childhood dream.

he road out of the city was thick with buses. We ssed dozens, each with its hunched intent driver, its waying topknot of homely possessions. We passed cars, battered out-dated models, loaded to the roof with barracking passengers. We passed packs of cyclists, too wet and grim to look around. By late afternoon we hurtled along the desert road alone, like the front-runner in a race.

First impressions. They hold their own place in your mind. Their image comes to be connected in its own way with your later knowledge. So many others must have first seen the canteen as I did, at nightfall, all its lights on, twinkling like a crystal in its valley of pale sand.

I stood in line by the front desk with the others from my bus and looked into the low, round room, its tables pooled with light. It was vividly unreal, as places are for those who arrive at night. There was something suspenseful about it, the dusty smell of it, the distant clash of dishes, the row of doors in shadow all around: it seemed to exist only for its own life, to be between performances, waiting. I saw it for a moment as already in the past.

Fawzia was at the desk. Not Fawzia to me then of course, but *the one in charge*: I smiled, as I had learnt to smile, at a grey-haired woman with powerful shoulders whose shirt was strained across her chest. She did not smile back. She took my work card and punched it in so fast and hard she could be angry. There was soup and bread, for me as for everybody, she said. She paused. Sweat rose and fell in a mist across her glasses. She pointed to a door. I would find Lucien out there, she would show me a bed.

The door opened directly outside. I was in a walled courtyard, unlit. For the first time I noticed how bright the desert stars were. At the trough by the back wall, Lucien was singing as she washed her hair. Her face loomed, white and young and round beneath her turban as she walked towards me. She wore loose trousers tied at the ankles. She was humming again as she led me inside.

Someone was standing in the doorway, a small balding man in an apron, *like a waiter*, I thought, *in a foreign country*. Something seemed to catch us, haul us to face each other, after more than twenty years. We peered at one another through layers: you, Constantine, your face, marked in a dozen tiny ways. In another moment I would see this new definition as inevitable.

'Constantine? Do you work here too?'

Then you threw your arms out in your old open-handed way and I saw that your right hand was curled up into a black glove that hung limp as a leaf at the end of a bough.

'Magda!' you said. 'How you've changed!'

There was no mirror in the cubbyhole that Lucien led me to, or I would have looked in it straight away. How long ago had I looked in a mirror? Except for two beds the room was bare.

e sleep wherever we can find a bed,' Lucien
lained. She was sitting on the other bed, combing
er wet hair.

I lay back, turned my face to the wall. The blankets
smelt sour with use. I spread my jacket over the dubi-
ous pillow. Voices from the canteen echoed and broke
like a party outside the door. I sighed.

'*Where is my little sister?*' Lucien sang, in a sudden
clear soprano.

'*Who sighed like the pigeons in the summer chimneys.*'

'What song is that?'

'It's called "The Country House".'

'I don't know it.'

'Of course you don't. It's *my* song.'

'Oh. Are you a songwriter?'

'I don't *write* them.' Lucien flicked off the switch
and lay back in the dark. 'Nobody writes any more. I
make them up as I go along.'

'*Now the little birds fly round and round,*' she sang.

'*With no light to direct them at all.*'

I did not sleep for a long time. When I shut my eyes I
saw the country slipping past me, framed by my bus
window. Town after town, all alike, aged, as people
age, without hope of redemption. Roofs had slipped,
balconies sagged, weeds grew up blackened walls.
Abandoned farmhouses had stripped windows like
empty eyes. It seemed to me then that the years
behind me had grown old and wasted too.

I could name causes, give explanations. We had done little else for years. Yet the true disaster I could not name. I had survived, behind glass, but I had not been spared.

I heard one bus arrive, another depart. Their horns echoed across the desert like agonised, plaintive wails.

I had thought that in the morning we would talk, Constantine. Perhaps we would sit across a table over breakfast, I thought, and talk about the town beside the sea. Perhaps I would find a way to reclaim my history.

But we didn't talk that morning, nor any other. There was no time for talk. There was no time for personal histories. That morning I stood, scarcely awake, tearing at the flesh of my regulation orange, and watched the day's first bus load surge across the hall.

They seemed to come in waves. No sooner did the tables empty for a moment than I heard the next clarion horn from the last hill, or the cicada trill of bicycles arriving at the door. Then in they came, out of the desert air, energy released into a void.

They did not talk. Do you remember how they flocked straight to the noticeboard and peered in silence for bulletins of work? But when they pinned up their own notices, marked *Work Required*, the little slips of paper seemed to shout and jostle with each other. At the tables they wedged their bags between their feet, bent their heads low over their soup. Sometimes when their bowls were empty they talked a little, very carefully: they exchanged work rumours.

...mes they slept and if their place wasn't needed
...might sleep a full day or night. Some wanted
...ep first, some food, some a chance to clean up. But
...hey all wanted work more than anything.

Fawzia sent me to the entrance desk. She showed
me the computer. There's nothing to it, she said. You
punch in the numbers on the work card. If they have
work, one free meal will be credited to their company.
If not they will have to pay.

But the computer chewed up the cards I fed it. It rang
like a telephone and flashed *No Credit No Credit*. The
queue broke ranks and crowded round the desk. Fawzia
had to rescue me. She stabbed at the keys without looking at me and ignored three offers to replace me. I'm a
computer operator, one man said. His face was hawklike
in its thinness, his hair grew in odd tufts as if something
had eaten into it. He walked away shaking his head.

Just have a joke with them, Fawzia said as she
rushed on. Cheer them up a bit. *You* have a job. But
when I faced those crowds, no jokes came to me. They
didn't seem to see me: I knew the edgy blankness of
that gaze. The men wore coats too hot for the desert,
big crumpled coats with heavy pockets, as if they carried their families with them. The women stood with
folded arms, eyes creased into a line: sometimes one
hand would drift up as if to knock away something, a
memory, a headache, for which there was no time.

There were no children.

'Do you have children?' I asked Fawzia in the
kitchen late one night.

'Five.'

'Do you miss them?'

'They're all grown up now. That was another life.'

'I miss mine.'

Fawzia joked when she worked. She slapped down soup and winked and stuffed her mouth with bread. Lucien bent low among the tables, her arm across a shoulder, whispering advice. And you Constantine, you carried plates along your arms up to your neck, and then put another for good measure on your head. You were everywhere at once and everybody watched you: your maimed hand made your precise delivery more of a wonder.

In the silence beneath the clatter I stumbled with my tray.

I tried to remember myself as a worker, long ago, in the gallery. For a moment I thought I could smell coffee. Coffee that I made for myself as soon as I reached my office. Coffee that I drank with my colleagues in the courtyard. In spring the smell of coffee mingled with the lilacs, and in autumn the lilac leaves blew around our polished leather shoes. I was researching the work of an artist – who? I made notes of details: larger patterns promised to emerge. I attended meetings. I drank coffee as I planned what I would say.

I did not understand the ceaseless hungry sequence of your tasks. Tell me what to do, I wanted to say, tell me *exactly* what to do. I did not understand work. In my old life I had kept work at bay.

———

A liverish yellow light hung over the desert. The atmosphere crackled, our hair swung out in brittle spokes. A hot wind started up, blowing straight towards us from the factories in the north. The canteen windows rattled night and day.

One morning we woke up with eyelids like little fat translucent worms. Our faces swelled up like baking bread, overflowed into wondrous folds. The skin on our hands and necks broke out in tweedy bubbles. If we looked at one another we had to turn away to hide our laughter and the sudden tears that wet our tiny gritty eyes. Lucien rubbed oil into her face, humming steadily.

People staggered in amongst a spray of sand. They wore strange cloaks and headdresses made of spare clothes, curtains, towels. Some were bent double, coughing. They lay down straight away against the walls of the hall, curled up around their bags. It was said they had drunk contaminated water.

The buses could not get through. The computer flashed *No Credit No Credit*: then all power failed.

We never stopped working. We took water to the sick from the good well in our courtyard. We wiped the sand from their eyes, the bile from their mouths. Sometimes they cried out when we bent over them in the stuffy darkness: ours were the faces of bad dreams.

I came upon you Constantine, binding the blackened feet of an old woman with smooth expert bandages. She lay back, her mouth open, her legs trustingly splayed.

'So you finished your medical studies,' I whispered.

You held up your black glove.

'What use is a surgeon with one hand?'

The wind dropped. Buses arrived and took away our sick. We opened the windows and swept the floors. When we looked at one another we saw ourselves again. Except our eyes seemed wider, our smiles more real. Our tread was lighter, as if after an illness. Once, in passing, you reached across and touched my hands.

Our supplies were very low. Fawzia decided that you and I should go to the Headquarters to reorder provisions. We boarded the bus at dawn, a little battered van going deeper into the desert than I had ever been. I took some water with me in a glass bottle.

You slept, I looked out the window. I saw birds rise with the sun and circle the endless plains. I thought of your country, a desert country, and your old stories of the desert, of ravage and recovery, of duration beneath change.

Your city was famous for its hospitality, its casinos, its sensuous starry nights. You carried photos which you showed me in your room in our town. Your father in a lambskin cap, your flawless sister, your four brothers who each had a fiancée and an air-conditioned car. You in every photo, the eldest, the most handsome, with the wicked gap between your teeth, the lush waves of your barber's-model hair. You with your arms thrown wide around them all.

In your room you cooked for me, the food of your country, though there would be a meal for me at home. You liked to feed me with your hands, with flat bread dipped in oil. Eat, eat, you said, you need to fill out. In the air you traced a sinuous ideal. I had an impulse then, to lie back on your forbidden bed, yawn, loosen my belt, expose my belly, spread out my hair . . .

Our town did not take strangers seriously. In summer we rented our spare rooms to them, put up the prices in our shops. We abandoned our beaches to them: we had our own relationship with the sea. Our eyes had narrowed, our lips tightened, from constantly surveying our horizon.

I never meant to take you seriously. How could I? You and your friends were the laughing-stock of the town. You were not like our usual tourists. You were medical students who could not return home because of trouble in your country. Arm in arm you walked our switchback roads and we winked as you passed. If you met a townsperson, you bowed and paid lavish compliments about the weather. If there was bad news from your country you would cry openly amongst each other, stagger from the post office, your letters pressed against your hearts.

You paid court to all the single women of the town. A chance encounter and you would send flowers, letters, mention marriage. After a week or so you were mainly to be seen with women tourists much older than you, or young girls, like me, who looked in mirrors all the time, greedy impatient girls, waiting to leave for the city they called 'Little Vienna'.

You attended every dance in the hotel by the shore. You wore gardenia buttonholes, your suits shone with gold and silver flecks. At the end of your last evening you asked the band to play your national dance. People began to leave. I looked down as the floor cleared. But you linked arms and lifted up your heads and sang your sorrowful desert song into the empty hall.

The bus set us down at the entrance to a long avenue of pines. Here at the edge of the plains the trees grew tough and thick, so dark they could be black. Do you remember how the light beneath them fell, as soft and flickering as snow? Beside you I was conscious of every step I took.

You carried nothing. It occurred to me then that in the canteen I had never seen you seek sleep, food, or even conversation. Yet once you had licked the salt from my face as if you wanted to possess my whole life. I tasted of the sea, you said.

What had happened to you over the years? You'd told me only that your hand was crushed when you were working as a postman in the north. The slots of the letterboxes there snapped shut like the mouths of turtles! Letters can be dangerous! you said.

The pines rustled like surf. I caught the flare of light between branches. Soon, very soon, I would speak.

Come over here, I would say. *Let's sit down for a little. Look, I have brought water.*

But the avenue turned, and the Headquarters was suddenly before us, an old country house, two-storied, shuttered, standing full in the sunlight. A brand new yellow jeep was parked by the door. High up a faded curtain hung out of an open window.

Our steps quickened.

'Lucien used to live in a house like that,' you said.

Constantine, it has stopped raining. My window has cleared, I see it is late afternoon. Across the balcony the sky is washed out, ready to give up. The world keeps on turning, from light to dark, from dark to light again.

Constantine, there was a time when all the tracks across the desert seemed blown away. Now I realise we were at the apex, at the point of crossover. But then I could not think of beginnings or endings. Like a desert creature I had given up everything. I knew only the outline of the plains around me, knew it like the backbone of some lurking, familiar animal. And I knew the work.

I came into the hall now like an actress, slipping a reminder note into my pocket, tucking back my hair. *Can I help you?* I knew now how to listen to those husky whispering voices. I knew how to look for a faint answer in their gaze. It gave a swirl, a lustre to my work, I could do nothing wrong. I did not know where this finer timing, insight came from: I worked as you all worked, without question. One shift overlapped another. I lost track of nights, days.

And yet already there was a change. There were less and less work bulletins, and then none at all. We heard the boom was over, the factories had closed their doors. Fawzia had scrawled All Positions Filled across the noticeboard.

People were no longer in a hurry. They started to wander in the desert because there was nowhere else to go. They caught buses from canteen to canteen: they might miss a bus or two, and stay. In the right season the desert could be very pleasant, they said. The clear air was good for the chest. One man had found a goat which he tethered at the door. She wasn't allowed on buses so they walked everywhere. He was looking into breeding, he put up a notice for a mate. He made some calculations on the back of his work card. If you kept moving, he said, there was a living to be made.

We stopped using the computer. What use were work cards now? We waved the people through. We sat at tables with them, talked, played cards. You lost a week's pay at poker. A fortune-teller read our palms. A bus driver sold Fawzia some whisky. Lucien slept for hours at a time.

Of course the musicians were Lucien's friends. I see that now. They parked their old truck and set up tents beside it without a moment's hesitation. They were young like Lucien, and mainly female, though in the clothes they had adapted for the desert, loose layers neck to foot, sex didn't seem an issue. They seemed to know us, they called us all by name. They helped us clear the tables: they said ours was the best canteen. Then they asked if they could hold a dance there. Fawzia is all for it, they told me as they unrolled their posters and stuck them on the windows, Fawzia says okay. They put their arms around me and kissed my cheek. I caught a whiff of wood smoke, and something else, like incense.

At sunset they gathered brushwood and made a bonfire in the car park. It blazed for hours into the night, like a ship arrived in harbour. Before the evening shift had finished, Lucien put on her coat, an old debutante's coat with a tattered fur collar, and slipped out to join them. I saw her silhouette against the fire, her head tipped back in laughter. I had never seen her laugh like that before. We heard them practising, odd riffs of a fiddle, more laughter, a spatter of drums, a clarinet's nosy whine.

But they did not laugh when they stood in line across their stage of stacked tables. The kitchen lights behind them outlined their legs and torsos. They loomed above us, faceless. One of them gave a sign.

From the first drumbeat the sureness of their sound shocked us. Music! It took us over, like another landscape. We stood struck. Then I saw people running towards them, as towards an ocean. Then Lucien stepped out on stage and sang.

The sound was high, pure, choral, but with a minaret curl between bars, like a wail. It was at once familiar to me, known and yet lost to me. It was your desert song, sung without sorrow, despatched in a new beat far beyond us, a new echo in the desert. I closed my eyes.

The music never stopped. The canteen was dark and more crowded than it had ever been before. Thin ragged shapes, three deep, swayed in the shadows around the stage. Where had they come from? A gang of bus drivers stood smoking by the door. Around me I saw men loosen their coats, nod to the beat, their faces tranced, benign as uncles. I saw women unfold their arms, smile, rock a little in a shy way. I even thought I saw a baby in the crowd, a tiny dark-thatched head bobbing over the horizon of a shoulder.

'All this of course will have to be cleaned up,' I heard Fawzia say. Later I saw her on the stage, her arms uplifted, without her shoes or glasses. Her arm movements were wild, entreating, I could not tell whether from love or rage.

Lucien had become the evening's favourite. 'Lucia!' The people stamped and whistled. '*Bis* Lucia, more!' Lucien never failed us. She grew pale and heavy-eyed, she had to sit down sometimes for a glass of water, but her voice stayed true all night.

'Look at her!' Fawzia shouted. 'She's clothed but she's a naked soul!' Hair stuck in wet strands around

Fawzia's face. She threw off her shirt. 'Look at her! Isn't she an angel?'

'Yes! Yes! Sing for us Angel, more!'

I came upon you Constantine, dancing in your old way, a nightclub singer's smile upon your face, your good hand tracing its enticements and the other following, though there was no audience in that dark, packed space. We danced together then to Lucien's songs. She sang about the old things, the coldness of the nights, the buses passing one another, the stars that shone. About seas and plains and mountains, journeys, starts and endings. She sang until her eyes closed and she lay down, and all the musicians lay down, next to their instruments, on the stage.

All around the canteen people were sleeping. I turned off the last lights and watched the dawn enter the hall in stages, like a slowly widening pupil. I heard the first flutter of the birds. I saw a yellow jeep drive softly into the car park. In the doorway stood a man with yellow hair.

Constantine, they are putting up a merry-go-round in the Botanical Gardens. I can hear the ring of hammers in the twilight air. It is the spring festival tomorrow. There will be flowers, music in the streets again. It will be just as it used to be, they say, why not? It will go on even if it rains.

Not all of us are sure about this. We have always been a sceptical people. We have adapted to another knowledge now. On these streets we have been known to jostle, mug, steal from one another. We have been known to cry.

There is debate about everything. About the desert for example, the great lake, the ten-year plan. Some say the desert belongs to everyone. Leave it as it is, they say. As a reminder. As an abstention.

Ah, but we know about this, don't we Constantine? *Sold to private interests*, said the man with yellow hair. *In view of circumstances, a complete revision of personnel. Classified work card area only. Last bus leaves at nightfall. Thank you all very much.*

You were the last to leave. Lucien left in the morning, soon after everyone was roused. She left with the musicians, climbing up onto the back of their truck. The wind blew her coat open and I saw her put one hand across her belly as she swung over the rail. The truck circled the car park, somebody blew a reedy pipe. Lucien raised a small fist above her head in its tattered fur collar.

The thin hair blew across your forehead as you stood on the road and waved.

Fawzia took longer. For hours she picked her way around the canteen, muttering, looking for her glasses, her clothes, looking for *something*. She left with the goat man. She strode off to the north under a large knapsack, into which she had stuffed a few favourite kitchen utensils. The goat man trailed her a little: he kept the goat close to him, firmly in hand.

We stood together at the edge of the road. At that

moment, after sunset, before stars, all the plains seemed to hang purely in air. Already the canteen, unlit, was fading behind us. I saw a bus appear at the top of the hill.

'Constantine? Will we meet again . . . in this world . . . ?'

You laughed, made one of your open-handed gestures.

'The world is of our own making,' you said.

The bus wailed, you leaned down close to me.

'Write,' you said.

$\mathcal{A}$NGELS

1.

I slept, I woke, I slept again. In one of my waking times
I thought that yes, I had caught the Russian virus. I
thought that I had never been to Russia and was therefore extremely vulnerable to a Russian virus. When I
woke up again I saw the snow.

I sat up. The roof garden glowed like a Mediter-
ranean beach. Seagulls arrived and scrabbled outside
my window. Although they had been coming for weeks
now – Maida and Faye threw them bread – I saw
them differently. They seemed like a new species come
to a new world. Snowbirds. I fell back on my pillow
and slept.

The flat was small but the women's voices echoed at
me as if they were calling from the end of a long hall.
Back from the cold streets their laughter was vast and
relieved. I could hear in their voices the breath of
snow.

I hoped they wouldn't come in to see me yet. I

thought I couldn't stand the onslaught of such energy. But there was more laughter in the kitchen and the crackle of paper – they'd been shopping. Pop! The plug jumped out of the electric jug. A spoon dropped. Then the living room window scraped open. Silence.

I looked out my window. Sure enough Faye came squeaking across the snow of the roof garden. She sat down on one of the benches and lit a cigarette. I had often watched her scramble over the sill in the living room: now I was witnessing the private end of the ritual. The light fell on her from the flat above, outlined her cap of grey hair. A mug of coffee steamed beside her. She looked like a larger species of snowbird, crouched forward in her puffy silver parka.

Then suddenly she turned towards my window and smiled straight at me. She lifted one hand and wriggled her gloved fingers. I lay still, shocked. How visible was I? Was there enough reflected light for her to see my face against the pillow, watching her? Or was she smiling on trust, that I was there, awake, and likely to be watching, somewhere in the darkness?

Maida was on the phone, talking to our daughters. I knew it was them by the way she projected her voice, as if to help it across ten thousand miles. And because she sounded apologetic.

'Oh, what time is it there then? I'm sorry love, I'd have thought you'd both be up by now.'

I could picture Rachel or Jane, yawning by the

phone, examining her feet, wondering whether she should wash her hair. The truth was, no time was the right time to ring the girls. Our calls, like those of out-grown lovers, could only be a disappointment, our concern a bore.

'Did you get our photos?' I asked Rachel the last time I phoned.

'Yes,' she said. 'You both look so *white*. And kind of tense. What are you worried about? I hope you're not worrying about Michael. He's *fine*.'

This time none of the children had wanted to come with us. Michael wanted to stay with his teacher, Mrs Everett. He was very decided about this. Mrs Everett's son, Chris, is eighteen, four years older than Michael. He is white-blond, with freckled lips, endlessly good-natured, a Christian. He plays cricket with Michael every day. He's a credit to Mrs Everett, who is also a Christian. They stood together on Mrs Everett's front steps as we got back into our taxi. They waved, Mrs Everett and Chris, and Michael watched them waving, his suitcase and cricket bat at his feet. Maida and I turned to the rear window as we drove off, but he was still watching them.

'How's Michael?' I heard Maida saying now. 'Have you seen him?'

Maida had tiptoed in to see me. I felt rather than heard her, as an interruption in the teeming molecules of the air around me. The engine in my head wouldn't allow me to open so much as one eye. This jealous Russian virus!

The night she hit me we had eaten in a restaurant near Trafalgar Square. It was no more than a tizzied-up hamburger joint, but it was raining, and the process of getting ourselves back to the flat, on one of those ship-like red buses that swished past us, seemed too much to tackle straight away.

But it was not a place to linger. There was a queue. The light, in mock lantern clusters, seemed to shrink back from us, made us feel the hour was late, our table needed. Before we were disposed of, Faye picked up her coffee and waving her little golden box at us, threaded her way to the lower part of the restaurant. This was fenced off with a tasselled rail and a gate marked SMOKING PERMITTED. Maida and I sipped our tea with that seeping of energy we allowed each other. This was when I started to feel it, the tingling all through my limbs as if I was being reminded of something. All my edges started to draw in, and the rhythm of everything beyond me fell slowly out of time.

My eye travelled the room. I saw on the stand by the door our three coats hanging one on top of the other, Faye's parka which kept its human shape, arms sticking out stiffly like a child's drawing, on top of Maida's Burberry, my tweed. Faye had struck up con-versation with a fellow smoker, a young man with a shaven head and a shawl around his shoulders. They nodded and laughed, brandishing their forked fingers at one another, and butted out in a shared ashtray.

I studied Maida's gloves lying by her cup, small soft brown leather gloves like paws, bearing the creases of her knuckles, the teardrop of each fingertip. Again and again I measured the distance between the two tables. It seemed to me that behind the tasselled rail, Faye had returned to her own unknowable element: when she joined us at the door she smiled in the kindly, absent way our daughters might when returning home from somebody's bed.

Out on the street again it had stopped raining and the city's wet glitter made everything tremble with clarity. A middle-aged woman in a raincoat came walking towards us at the bus-stop. Swinging her bag, shaking her head, her walk was purposeful as if she was rehearsing something she was going to say. I stepped back for her as she passed.

Thwack! Her handbag struck me square in the stomach.

'That was for *you!*' she shouted, thrusting her face at me, and for a moment I accepted the pure, insistent logic of that glare. Then I clutched my stomach, and it did not seem strange that the street tilted and swung its length of lights above me.

'So sudden,' I heard Maida say to the taxi driver. The city tacked with wild accuracy in and out of the window beside her.

'That's how she goes,' the taxi driver called out

over his shoulder. 'Laid up thousands – just knocks them down out of the blue.'

I didn't try to tell them. It wasn't a sudden arrival, more a recognition, of a presence that had been there all the time. For weeks now, or was it years, I had felt it coursing through my blood, like a drug, something fretful and chill, and now it had started to speak.

London stayed quiet outside my window. There were reports – Maida gave me details from the bedroom door – of burst pipes, derailed trains, roads buried under drifts that were *the deepest, the furthest south* . . . statistics thrived. The snow had taken the country's breath away. And the Russian flu now claimed twelve lives.

Maida and Faye were not daunted. Each morning Maida tiptoed into our bedroom – since my fever she had slept in Faye's room – and dressed in the milky light. I woke to a thief-like rustle, the tiny whirr of a zip. Whispering, they let themselves out the hall door.

Once or twice I got up and walked around the flat. I didn't recognise it. Maps and guides were piled up by the unmade beds in Faye's room. Newspapers were spread around the living room floor. On the table was a mound of air letters, friendly blue Australian air letters, opened greedily, in the middle, in the wrong way. I stood shivering by the window and watched the birds fight over crusts left for them in the snow.

This was not the first holiday we had spent with Faye. Once when the girls were very small, before Michael, Faye invited us to share a rented beach house with her and Henry Schmitt and their four children. It wasn't a real beach house, it was an abandoned suburban bungalow, with venetian blinds that no longer opened and an autumn leaf carpet that smelt sour and dusty like the coat of an old dog. Its front porch faced scrubby sandhills that blocked off the view of the sea. Here Henry sat all day, smoking and reading, sometimes absently pushing the baby's pram back and forward with his big toe. Here, I said, light-hearted, just unpacked, a daughter on my shoulders, we will drink gin and tonic at sunset. This was the first time I had met Henry and Faye.

I came to think of the Schmitt children as a tribe. Their fringes hung in their eyes, they had all inherited Henry's pinched nostrils. They never slept. They rode their battered bikes through the house on long hot afternoons when everyone was supposed to rest. When I held up my hand to stop Luther, the eldest, he stared at me and rode across my foot. Our own little girls became alarming telltales.

Even the sea seemed given over to the children. It stretched for miles, warm, knee-deep: no hint of a wave entered that flat bay. I did not know what to do with myself. Each morning I shared the newspaper with Henry across the gritty table. He was a slow reader. While he muttered over the headlines, I started to look through Positions Vacant and Office Space To

Let. Later he puddled dishes in grey water in the sink. I dried. There was no question of conversation with Henry unless you felt strong enough for political debate. I paced the house and plotted my future. I stood on the porch and watched Faye and Maida and the children.

All day long they stood by a swing under tuart trees, supervising turns. Faye wore a shirt of Henry's over sagging bathers and a peaked cap pulled low, like a camp leader. Her short legs were snaked with veins. They slapped sunburn cream on backs, and talked. They talked as they piggybacked children in convoy across hot sand and prickles. In the kitchen they talked and laughed and waved their knives around while the lino beneath them crunched with sand and spilt cordial.

'What do you two find to talk about?' I knew I sounded disagreeable. I had lain all afternoon in this airless bedroom with a transistor on my stomach, listening to the cricket. Maida was sitting on the end of the bed, quiet again, rubbing cream into her sunburnt arms. I thought of how I saw her with Faye, hooting, bent double, as if something had been released in her.

'As a matter of fact, we made a pact today. We promised to take each other's children if anything happened to us.'

'Christ! . . . Don't Henry and I have a say in this?'

'The trouble is, Roy, you never think that anything could happen to us.'

Someone was wailing in the hall. Maida turned on her way to the door. 'I feel relieved,' she said.

'A test run,' Maida said. She wedged my cap onto my head and wrapped my neck in a red scarf. I had forgotten about the cold in the streets. I had forgotten how to look after myself. I looked in the hall mirror. I saw that my hair, pushed down by the cap, now covered my ears. My square face had become rectangular, my stubbled cheeks now fell into my scarf. I saw a man in an outsize coat, stooping to look at himself with dark, diffident eyes.

'Ready?' Maida said. She and Faye kept saying how glad they were that I was better. Yesterday I had sat in the living room and drunk chicken noodle soup and read the paper. Now the fever's gone you won't look back, they said.

It was true that the pounding had gone quiet. But I couldn't believe that this was for long. All the time I was listening out for its return. But we were booked into a guesthouse in Scotland, a famous guesthouse in the North, with open fires and grouse and deer. We had only got the booking through a cancellation. A little walk in the Square, they said. Try your legs. See the snow. I followed them out of the flat, down the stairs.

The roof garden had not prepared me for it, the vast even-handed whiteness laid across the grubby street, the meticulous quiet. A square black taxi cruised gently by. The whole city had been brought to order.

'Gorgeous, isn't it?' they said. We crossed the road into the Square. Here they stooped and plastered snowballs together in their gloved hands, grinning at each other. They ran, ducking and squealing, and their breath held its shape as it rose towards the great black trees.

I walked a little. The crunch of my footsteps made me shiver: I could scarcely bear the clarity of the air.

It was back. I was not surprised. It seemed natural that it would start up again here, in the snow, as if the same witch had set us sparkling . . . The glare enclosed me. All around the Square the houses reared up with grinning windows. I heard the women hailing me from a long way off. My eyes sought out the darkness in the bare thickets by the fence, but I could not see the gate.

2.

I put myself in their hands. Our departure was swift, in a freezing dawn: they helped me down the stairs of the flat whispering, as if they were spiriting me away. They stowed me with pillows and blankets into the back seat of the car they had hired. I sat stiffly, like a packed-up corpse in my cap and red scarf, while they ran back to get our bags.

Faye drove, Maida read the map. They seemed very pleased with the car. 'If you want to stretch out we can let down the back seat,' they said. They said how I would be tucked into my bed in Scotland that night. With feather pillows most likely. And a hot toddy. They laughed.

They found their way to the M1. An uneasy silver light was rising over the rooftops of the suburbs. 'Oh isn't that nice,' Maida said. They found the nice in everything, the courteous drivers, the clear signposting, some horses galloping behind a low stone wall . . . I sank lower and lower into my pillows. My head rolled and jolted on my chest. The car was a capsule of throbbing warmth. I thought suddenly of Henry Schmitt, the last time I had seen him, after years. A glimpse, under a banner, passing me in the lunchtime crowd. I saw his round-shouldered lope, his tight fanatic jaw, as he marched, alone, towards the other banners.

I wondered if I would ever return to the world of men again.

We stopped once, at a roadside cafe, somewhere far to the North. There were already stars in the afternoon sky. Snow lay piled like surf against the steaming windows. It was a place of clatter and scraping chairs, lone men in suits bent over newspapers, families chewing together in numbed, stricken silence. We might have dreamt it as we entered, out of the arctic air.

We were served by a waitress with skin as fine as powder and an accent we could hardly understand. We sat amongst the hiss of fat and steam, under the neon glare. I watched Faye pace like a sentry with her cigarette outside the door. I could have laid my swirling head down on the plastic cloth, and stayed.

Then I saw a boy at the pinball game in the corner. One pointy shoe rocked over the other as his wrists shook it to life. I must note down the game, I thought, and its highest recorded score, and send a postcard to Michael. Michael likes facts. Before the snow came I had sent him a postcard nearly every day. No answer of course, no knowing their effect: I sent them off the way I played these games with Michael, without much skill or hope. Then there is room for something else, that sudden lift or flare. He always recognises it. I look around for him and see it, on his face.

When Michael was nearly three, Maida could take no more. She took the girls out of school and they went for a holiday together. Although there was more work than we could handle in the agency by then, I took a month off to look after Michael. Maida wouldn't leave him with a stranger: she was afraid that would break whatever fragile links he had with us, he would never trust us again.

I told myself it was a holding operation. We had our routines. We steered a careful course around the house, the suburb. There is a playground near us where in summer the slide winks, red hot, and the swing hangs empty in an acre of dead grass. Even now I choose not to drive home that way. Once, in an endless afternoon, I took him to the beach, and while he howled, I gave myself for five minutes to the sea. Sometimes at night, when even the reruns of The Twilight Zone had finished, I carried him around the dripping garden, both of us in pyjamas. Twisting away from me in his big nappy, he looked over my shoulder at the shadows, his eyes as dark and ringed as a possum's.

I had to leave him, once a week, to go to the office for a couple of hours. Maida said that Faye would mind him for me. He was used to Faye, she said, he would stay with her. He did. She clasped him to her hip and as I drove away I saw that she was picking something off a leaf and he was stretching over her to look.

The same old Faye, I thought. Her own house was like a beach house, a real one, weatherboard with a verandah, lost among peppermint trees. It was no good going to the front door, Maida warned me, it was blocked off, one of the children slept in the hall. I found Faye each time in the backyard, reading. They had made a whole room out there. At the bottom of the back steps, straight onto the grass, they had set chairs and a table and an old velour couch. And all around in the trees, slung over branches, were bathers and towels, a school shirt, pyjama pants, a bath mat, flapping peacefully among the leaves.

The last time, just before Maida came back, I was late picking him up. I had a drink with a client and then another with my partner and staff. I found I couldn't always follow what they were saying. My laughter seemed a beat behind the rest. Another drink might help me to catch up, I thought. Faye won't mind. I was careful not to think of Michael. Then I realised I was three hours late. That drive, too fast, to make amends, it was like all the past weeks, years swerving along the edge, *something is wrong*, Maida said, and then everything was out of line, everything had to be negotiated. To think of Michael was like sending off a silent prayer.

He was asleep on the leaf-shadowed couch. He slept like that, suddenly, deeply, after one of his fits of rage.

'About half an hour after you usually come he started to wail to the skies.'

'I'm sorry. I was held up.'

'It doesn't matter. He survived. It doesn't matter at all.'

She must have smelt the alcohol, and the sweat that slashed my shirt. She must have seen it all. I closed my eyes.

She put her arms around me.

It was so quiet there, the way a noisy place is quiet when it has been deserted by its usual voices. I saw above her head the strange cloths nesting in the trees. And higher still a fierce whiteness blazed around the edges of the leaves. Everything was strange and yet piercingly familiar, and the stillness held us as we waited there. Michael stirred. I gathered him up, and kissed her like a wife, and went away.

3.

The North. It was a moving darkness as if the sky kept pace with us. Lights swung in strings and disappeared and sometimes a denser darkness, a huge curved flank, travelled alongside us and then dropped behind. Sometimes trees were revealed, black bare fists held up to us in the headlights. The car warbled and sighed and the rhythm played through my blood until it seemed the whole journey was fired by the energy of fever.

And then silence.

The car was tent-like in weak orange light.

'Where are we?'

'Three or four miles from the guesthouse, we think. But it's snowing so hard Faye can't see the road.'

Then later: 'It isn't going to stop. We'll have to stay here for the night.'

Their voices were calm and soft.

'Lie between us, Roy, for the warmth.'

Feeble and clumsy in my thick coat, I eased myself into the bed they had made in the back for the three of us. Side by side we stared at the ceiling.

'Abraham and his Two Wives,' Faye said into the darkness.

'If I remember rightly,' I said, 'wasn't one of Abraham's wives *young*?'

They thought this was very funny.

They seemed cheerful and matter-of-fact. The guesthouse was expecting us. Tomorrow there would be a search-party. Or in the light we would see how ridiculously close we were, and would set off walking, lugging our bags across the snowy fields. Thank goodness there are no children with us, they said, hooting a little in the darkness. They would never let us forget this . . . They yawned and snuggled down. It was almost as if this was part of the plan. And all at once I thought of their maps and whispers, their haste, their insistence, dragging me and my Russian flu on and on, right into the arms of the snow . . . they had all conspired against me . . . they had got me where they wanted me . . .

A sound broke out of me that I didn't recognise, the deep rasp of a stranger, talking through me. I felt it scrape against my ribs and throat. My limbs trailed and twitched behind it. Tears ran from my eyes.

They went quiet then. Maida found my cap and settled it on my head. From time to time one of them would wriggle free of our cocoon and switch on the car engine. The heater roared and snow slithered from the gently vibrating roof. Mist ran in rivulets down the windows, like curtains parting, and we could see the dim broken whiteness flocking past.

Something gripped my chest and tightened. I had to reach further for every breath. And as my eyes closed and my fists clenched, I saw it. I saw her face.

Out of this whiteness crawls the Humber, with my mother and father peering out on their separate sides for street numbers, and the boy in the back, bent over something, something new, a pocket-knife. It's a Christmas present. It is Christmas Day, circa 1950.

This is a new suburb, War Service, and we have never been here before. The scrubby grey bush is being pushed back block by block into a valley. The houses are all the same, grey-white asbestos, on stilts at the back for the slope. Nothing is growing here yet, and there are drifts of grey-white sand.

'We need your eyes, Roy,' my mother says. She is rather anxious about finding the house, rather annoyed. Christmas Day is a family day, she says. There is something about Harry Crewe and Natasha – never 'the Crewes' – whose house we are looking for, that has singled them out, left them adrift, free for drinks on Christmas Day.

Then my father spots Harry on his porch, the Humber wheels down a steep driveway and lurches to a stop with the handbrake. My father, responsible for this outing, gets out first. Squinting, clearing our throats, tucking and patting, my family descends on the porch.

There is a lot of handshaking. Harry Crewe is the same as ever, when he comes to pick up my father for golf on Saturday afternoons, except he isn't wearing his tartan cap. He's a solid man with a broad forehead and gold-rimmed glasses. His porch is cool, a slab of glossy red concrete. Natasha is handing round a bowl

of cherries. Not just a little damp bagful, a token quarter pound to be scattered in amongst the Christmas
nuts and raisins, but a great wooden bowl filled to the
top. She shakes it and smiles in front of each one of us.
'Take, take,' she says.

And when I take a little dangling bunch, it is forked
over another, so that a whole linked branchful falls
into my lap. My mother looks alarmed, but Natasha
laughs and leaves the whole bowl beside me. Then she
sits down, not next to my mother, but back next to
Harry.

And though my knife is beautifully heavy in my
pocket, and I am free to wander off now, I opt for the
cherries, which, I can see, are going to be unrationed.
And for Natasha. One after another I put the cherries
in my mouth, and every word that I have heard, but
never listened to, about Natasha, comes flying back to
me. She is a White Russian. She has had what they call
a Terrible War. Harry Crewe met her in Singapore. She
is a woman with no children, but there are other husbands, other wives somewhere. Harry Crewe has
given up everything. There are two sides to a story. He
doesn't come in for a drink any more because Natasha
gets lonely. When my father says the name 'Natasha',
there's a smile in his voice. He says it quickly and easily to include it in his vocabulary, like the brand name
of a new, promising car. He is smiling now, receiving a
drink from Natasha, and Harry Crewe is smiling, and
my mother, they're all smiling because of Natasha.

Natasha isn't young, she isn't as young as her name

sounds. She's as old, maybe even older than my mother. She isn't pretty but in another way she is like the source of everything pretty in the world. She seems uncluttered, as if, wherever she came from, she could not bring much with her, not even a surname. There are no folds or drapes to her outline. Her hair is coarse and dark, parted, close to her head. She has a long olive-skinned face and her long eyes have a bruised darkness about them. When she smiles, looking into your face, her eyes have a secret life to them, close to something extreme, which might be tears.

My mother talks to her slowly and clearly like she does to our ironing lady, who is a New Australian. But Natasha talks back quickly and laughs, and her laugh breaks ragged and violent across the porch.

Like the men I sit there with my hands on my knees and I look out across the sand to the Humber, held back, mid-turn, down the driveway, and far away down the street I hear kids' voices, rising thin as smoke, arguing over their new toys.

They had turned off the car engine. With every cough I sank back further. I saw our car, a tiny speck amongst the whiteness, and the whiteness spread and became a map of a tiny country, and the map spread and became the globe in Michael's room, set to spin so all the countries blurred together, and the tiny speck, of course, had disappeared.

'I'd give anything for a smoke,' Faye said.

I couldn't speak. But in between my gasps, I listened for their steadfast breathing. I am glad you are with me, I wanted to say. But as if they had heard me, they pressed closer to me, their heads beside my shoulders, their hands in mine. An arm pillowed my heavy neck, and I felt a wing of precious breath catch across my cheek.

'Isn't this what you've always wanted?' someone whispered. 'To die in a woman's arms?'

The Woman Who Only Answered Yes or No

Everybody is so nervous. So very nervous. And everybody is in love . . . This magic lake. But how can I help you, my poor child, how?

The Seagull, Anton Chekhov

You ask me how I came to make the film of the woman. Who she is, how I met her, why she interested me . . . Do you know, this is the first time in a long career that I've ever been interviewed. My career? Scriptwriter – once, other people's scripts. That was how I met Steiner. That was a long time ago.

This is your first interview too? How did I know? Believe me, I know about *asking* questions. It's just a case of one question really, the one that might call up a whole life to explain . . . Let me tell you first how I was working on Steiner's *Seagull*. How I was stranded on location in the hotel by the lake, with Bernadette – who plays Nina – and Jacob, Steiner's nephew, the assistant cameraman. It was spring, the ice had melted into the rivers, all the bridges were swept away. The telephone lines were down, the ground was too marshy for landings. Steiner was coming in the summer. Summer did not come. For weeks we waited, while it rained.

And the woman? She worked in the hotel. In the bar. Would you like a drink? Just a little one? I'm going to pour myself another.

Yes, they reached us eventually. Steiner hired a *barge*. Have you seen *The Seagull*? Good. Because you see, *The Woman* is a film within a film.

Why did I make it? Ah, well there you have it. The one question. The one I ask myself.

I might find out by telling you.

Because I like your face! Because there's a long night ahead. Because I want to entertain you. *Because I've decided to trust you.*

The idea to make a film of *The Seagull* came to Steiner in a dream. You won't find this mentioned in any interview: producers are not known for backing dreams. But he told me about it a few nights later. In this dream, he said, he was flying, across a mighty stretch of water that gleamed silver against distant plains. Closer, and he made out mountains and fields and rivers branching into marshland and patchy beaches amongst banks of reeds. On the shore was a lone building, a wooden inn or country house, its windows shining silver like the water. This seemed to be his destination. Tiny figures on a balcony were running up and down, pointing past him, to the clouds. He looked up. Out of the clouds huge black curving shapes were hurtling straight towards him. He swerved and saw they were not birds or stars but letters. He recognised the Cyrillic alphabet. These are the titles, Steiner thought, and I am reading them. He woke with the words *The Seagull* in his head.

Straight away he'd stumbled out of bed and found Chekhov's play and opened it at random, and read: *We should show life neither as it is nor as it ought to be but as we see it in our dreams.* Treplev's speech.

Right from the start, he put his faith in Treplev.

First of all, he told me, he had to find that wooden inn beside the water. He had a memory of a childhood holiday in an old hotel beside a lake. He would ask his mother about it. He was going to look for it as soon as possible.

Then he got out of my bed and smoked some very old, very good Nepalese hashish that he kept on the mantelpiece at my place so his children wouldn't find it. He would like me to work with him on the script, he said.

The opening sequence of his film, he called out from the kitchen, lit up, large, white and naked as he rummaged in my refrigerator, would be much as he had dreamed. By the time the titles finish a young woman's voice is heard chanting, above the wind and the cry of birds. You can make out a figure on the beach, the lights of the country house behind her. It is Nina, rehearsing the speech that Treplev has written for her, the one beginning: *Men, lions, eagles and partridges . . .* Treplev is watching her, his glasses glinting amongst the reeds. This is the speech that caused an uproar at its first performance in St Petersburg, when the audience booed and shouted: 'Intellectual rot!'

The success or failure of his film, said Steiner, would depend on how convinced we are of Treplev's talent. He would show the speech in context, as a response to the landscape, to the childhood knowledge of the lake that Nina and Treplev shared.

'Treplev is starting with poetry,' he said. 'Doesn't any serious young writer start with poetry? And the speech does have a sort of cosmic pull to it.'

'In a youthful way.'

'Youthful talent, youthful aspiration and intensity, attract me more and more as subjects,' Steiner mused.

I must explain that all this occurred at a low point in Steiner's career. His last film had not been a success. He had not fulfilled his youthful promise, the critics said, he had become irrelevant, obscure. Steiner knew *The Seagull* might be his last chance. They want relevance! he said. Let them have the workings of the nineteenth-century Russian soul.

The play itself, it seemed to him, was a meditation on success and failure. Trigorin, the older successful writer, and Treplev who fails. The pragmatist and the idealist. Of course, he said, the idealist has to die.

'What about Nina? She survives.'

'Nina does not have talent. She's a lonely, deprived child. She doesn't talk of acting but of who will watch her act. She doesn't want art but the artistic life.'

'Not in the end. After Trigorin has seduced her. Not after she's lived a little. After she's died.'

'Do you really believe as her carriage drives off — oh that carriage! — disappearing off those plains like the last word off a page — do you really believe she is off to reach the heights?'

'I wouldn't mind betting there'd be a performance in a provincial theatre that at least three people would never forget one night.'

'Three pairs of hands clapping . . . Is that what you call the heights? Her career is a substitute for love. Even Treplev knows this. *She screams superbly and she dies superbly*, Treplev says.' Steiner paused. 'You can't bear failure, can you? You want every story to have a happy ending.'

'And your film's a tragedy all round.'

'Aren't all our dreams potential tragedies? Happy endings are something we invent when we wake up.'

The Seagull of course had enormous, unexpected popular success. It's the film which made Steiner an international name. It set off a fashion in certain circles for doomed young men in wire-rimmed glasses: 'a version of the hero', the weekend papers said, 'for our pragmatic times'. Steiner woke up one morning to find himself a Trigorin, not a Treplev. With Trigorin's dilemma: *What success? I've never satisfied myself. I dislike my own work.*

The script was not a true collaboration. I became

less and less involved. We did not speak of this. Steiner
hates post-mortems, and I, perhaps, still hoped for a
happy ending. In the credits I am named as script edi-
tor. But a true collaboration must share a vision, like a
love affair.

Steiner found the hotel of his childhood, still alone
beside the lake, just as he had dreamt it. You know it.
That weathered silvery facade, those high-ceilinged
rooms dominate his film like a monument to the
unconscious, nostalgic yet oppressive, as Treplev
would have found it.

You will have seen the balcony with its carved
wooden balustrade that fronts onto the shore. Do you
remember the scene where Irina, all in white, is playing
cards with Trigorin at a little table? Those whites! The
tablecloth, the seagull which Trigorin watches drifting
past, the long white lace curtain that billows out from
Irina's room . . . A solitary candle burns late at night
in the farthest bedroom: Treplev writing, Treplev who
cannot sleep, his ideas too big for the page.

In the weeks before Steiner's arrival there were
only three pairs of shutters open on that balcony,
Jacob's and Bernadette's and mine. There were no
other guests at the hotel. Outside each room was a
deckchair but we never combined them. Soon after we
arrived we all found ourselves sitting out there, in a
row, staring at the rain like patients in a sanatorium.
Within five minutes we all went inside again.

From the moment I arrived I felt that I had stepped into Steiner's location, that the hotel was built to the dimensions of his memory. We stood, dripping wet, in the hall and rang the bell at the empty entrance desk. Nobody came. We did not know then that there was no one to answer except for Anastasia. A yellow-brown light seemed to swirl down the stairs, and hang around the potted palms, the dusty mirrors and cracked vinyl couches, as if an army of 1950s tourists had once smoked there.

I could see Steiner in that hall, Steiner as a child. I could see him look at me over his shoulder as he followed his mother up the stairs. A large, fattish twelve-year-old, already pubescent, in a school suit a little tight across the chest, and a new haircut that made him look priggish and vulnerable. I saw him everywhere. Running round balconies and slowing down when he saw an adult coming. Making friends with the cook and having two lunches. Rounding up the other children and organising them. Kissing the prettiest, that is, the most subtly pretty, of the girls. Having a cigarette with the youngest and most dashing of the adult guests. Getting up to no good and lying about it. Being forgiven. Being believed.

Steiner when he came, auctioned off the deckchairs and the vinyl couches, the mirrors and the pleated lampshades and potted palms to the villagers. He made a bonfire of the wall-to-wall carpets. On his barge he brought a team of painters and carpenters. He'd had time, fuming, far across the water, to scour the antique shops and the homes of the old and wealthy who had an interest in the arts. He brought rugs and chairs, a piano, an entire dining suite, paintings, lace curtains and velvet hangings, a brass bedstead, an old copper samovar. He restored the hotel to how it was meant to be. Even when he was a child, he said, this was what he had planned.

As the weeks passed, Jacob's dark blue fisherman's cap was often to be seen hanging off a corner of his deckchair, a dog-eared book spreadeagled on the seat. Jacob was generally inside his room, asleep.

Bernadette too slept most of the day. There was no phone to disturb us, no letters from our agents. No telegrams with the big chance. Bernadette, after sleeping, would shower and come out onto the balcony. She would stand at the balustrade and turn her head from side to side to dry her hair. Her hair grew lighter while I watched, flew out in white-blonde strands around her. I could smell her wonderful freshness in the air.

I envied them the heavy sleep of youth. Sometimes in the long afternoons I sat in my deckchair, a sheaf of paper on my knee and stared slack-jawed at the horizon, as if a ship might suddenly appear and sail straight towards me. Once Jacob stumbled out, his red curls all lopsided, took up his book from his chair.

'Got to . . . wake up . . . somehow,' he muttered. His book was called *Illuminations*. He squinted towards me. 'What are you writing?'

'I am just . . .' I began, but a gust of wind lifted up my top page and blew it across the balcony. Jacob and I watched it dip and swoop above the balustrade, our heads swivelling together, before it disappeared.

One night I thought that I heard footsteps on the balcony, whispers, Jacob's door clicking shut and then Bernadette's. But in the morning Bernadette was as indifferent to both of us as ever, Jacob as vague and dishevelled. *It is all a dream*, Nina says. We all seemed like dreamers on that balcony, waiting for Steiner to make the dream real.

The hotel appears completely isolated in Steiner's film. But just across the hill was the village, its white-spattered roofs running down to a fishing bay. We arrived in the rain, on the last bus to cross the bridge. Ferenc met us in the square. He ran the local taxi, but he told us no car could now reach the hotel. It was a ten-minute walk, but in this rain it would take half an hour. Yes, Jacob could leave the camera equipment at his house. 'I will tell the woman to look after it,' he said. This was the first time we heard her called that.

Ferenc is in *The Seagull*. How could Steiner resist that face? He plays one of the workmen on the estate. He helps build Treplev's stage. When Irina makes her grand farewell, Steiner focuses on Ferenc in the servants' line-up. Ferenc was not born in the village: his eyes never lost the watchfulness of a stranger. Something – a blow, a missing tooth – had made one side of his mouth droop, so that the other twisted upwards. As he bows for Irina's mean little rouble, a strand of thin grey hair falls like an ironic forelock across his face.

Steiner also uses Anastasia, little Anastasia, whose legs, always flying in service, were as short as a child's, but whose cheeks were brown and shiny, patterned in wrinkles. When Steiner's barge arrived, Anastasia rushed over to the village to beg her relatives to bring food, help her with this horde. But on the barge Steiner brought a chef with his knife already in his belt, barrels of red wine and virgin olive oil, sacks of wild rice and pasta, fresh oranges, chickens in a cage, even a huge cheese lashed to the deck.

When Steiner wanted extras for the harvest scene, the whole village came walking down the road over the hill. 'Oh those faces, those faces,' Steiner murmured, as if they were the harvest. But he didn't use the woman. He tried to, but even as an extra, her presence was too powerful. He had to edit her out.

The dining-room was Steiner's favourite room. He loved the wide French doors that opened onto the lake. When the sun shone at a certain angle, you could see the pattern of waves moving across the ceiling. In the film this is Treplev's study, where his old uncle has a bed made up, because he is dying and can't bear to be alone. How Steiner loved creating a writer's desk!

He modelled it on Chekhov's own. A glass ink bottle, a handful of pens in a brass tray, four tall candles in a row. A little bronze statue of a peasant family clustered together. But the frenzy of the desk, the uneven stacks of books sprouting strips of paper, the piles of ruined pages, is Treplev's.

This is the room where Nina comes in secret, to say goodbye to Treplev. She has had Trigorin's baby in Moscow, he has left her, the baby has died. She is off to a theatre in the provinces. This is where she tells Treplev: *You know Kostya, I've come to realise that for an actor or writer the great thing isn't fame or money, it's knowing how to endure, how to bear your cross and have faith.*

Every day at mealtimes, Jacob said that without a doubt the film would have been scrapped by now. Steiner would have lost too much money to go on. He had heard on the family grapevine that Steiner's backers had been reluctant from the start, had regarded the project as too literary. He personally thought that Steiner had sold out, that he was trying to make both an art movie and a costume glossy, trying to please everyone. He had lost touch with his own material, Jacob said.

'I think the material is fairly close to him, actually,' said Bernadette.

'Like a dream?' I asked her.

'Yes.'

Jacob said that right from the start he had never really believed that the film would come off.

'Why did you accept the job then?' Bernadette asked.

'Because it's the only work I've been offered for two years.'

'The film will happen,' said Bernadette. 'My mother said she'd pray.'

Through the swing doors burst Anastasia with our plates of mutton and dumplings and the bottle of wine that Jacob had requested. She always forgot the corkscrew. Jacob had to hail her and make turning motions in the air.

Bernadette could no longer face mutton and dumplings. She followed Anastasia through the swing doors and came out with rye bread and honey and some little pears, brown and wrinkled like Anastasia's face.

'You will get hollow-cheeked,' I told her, 'before the film has even started. Nina is only hollow-cheeked at the end.'

Bernadette said she'd thought of sending her mother a message by morse code, for a parcel to be dropped by helicopter, like Red Cross food relief. 'The trouble is,' she said, 'my mother would have herself dropped by parachute as well.'

I did not know when Steiner had become aware of Bernadette. She was not then well known. She lived in an old apartment with her mother, who had a nervous complaint. She had worked in fringe theatre and in short features by some of the younger film makers. I had just begun to recognise her white-blonde hair and the spare, almost bitter planes of her face.

'Nina must project an unusual emotionality,' Steiner said.

I said I thought that Bernadette's face was intelligent and self-possessed.

'We all know intelligence is no protection from the emotions,' he said.

Bernadette cut her finger to the bone one night as she sliced her bread. At once she turned white, dark rings appeared beneath her eyes. Jacob rushed for Anastasia, I wrapped her finger in a napkin. Bernadette sat very still and watched the blood soak the cloth.

I began to wonder about the Nina Steiner would get.

The final version of Steiner's *Seagull* ends not with Treplev's suicide, but with Nina's carriage racing into the darkness. In the carriage window you can see Nina's profile, staring straight ahead. Bernadette's Nina has gone beyond dying and screaming. In the end this is Steiner's final image, a moving window, Nina's face.

One night Jacob, echoing the first line of *The Seagull*, said to me: *Why do you wear black all the time?*

Without thinking I gave back Masha's line: *Because I am in mourning for my former life.*

'Really?' This was the first question Bernadette had ever asked me.

Then I remembered that Masha was hopelessly in love with Treplev, who couldn't bear the sight of her. That she drank in secret and regarded herself as a tragic figure.

'I started wearing black when I was very young,' I said. 'I don't know why. Nobody else did then. Perhaps I wanted to look pale and mysterious, like a movie star.'

'Of course!' said Jacob. 'The movies then were all in black and white.'

In the blackness of the French windows I could see our three heads reflected, tiny in that empty room. I thought then that we only talked because of loneliness, and that what I thought was not what I said.

There are angles and views of the hotel in Steiner's film that I can no longer be certain that *I* saw. That worn bench against the kitchen wall, for instance, with gnarled branches for its legs like old knees – did I see that? And did I ever look up when we were at our table in the dining-room and see the reflection of the lake swaying on the ceiling? Yet when, in a cinema a thousand miles away, I saw that reflection, I remembered a sensation of being underwater and for a moment I could almost smell mutton and dumplings and hear Jacob call 'Anastasia – corkscrew?'

I must not have lingered, as Steiner does, by the three aspen trees on the path to the lake. I never saw their thin white trunks like that, twisted by the wind, nor the rooks nesting in their pale leaves. Of course, it was not warm enough for the rooks to have returned by then. The rooks came when Steiner came.

There is one view of the hotel which remains untouched by Steiner's vision. My room. That room, with its big sagging bed, its rickety escritoire, its three-sided mirror in walnut veneer, was like a parody of all the hotel rooms on previous locations. Whenever we walked in, Steiner would say, 'You have the desk.' Already he was on the phone, checking that he could dial international. At once the bed was covered with memos, notes, scripts. Steiner could work anywhere. The room filled with people talking, Sophie and Raoul and George. In the mirror I adjusted my little black hat before we went to dinner. True to Steiner's word, the desk stayed clear.

When Steiner arrived, he took Jacob's room. Jacob moved out with the rest of the crew to billets in the village. Bernadette's room was converted to Irina's: that long white curtain billows out through Bernadette's door. The interior of my room was not used for the film, I was able to stay there. At first Bernadette slept with her mother in a small back room: after a week or so she moved in with Steiner.

One day the rain stopped. The sun shone, the lake receded, the little stony beach was revealed. In celebration, the three of us went swimming. Jacob and I stood on the beach in the thin yellow sunshine and looked out across the lake. Bernadette was swimming up and down, parallel to the shore. We were looking for signs of the city across the water, the old resort town where palm trees grew along the boulevards and seagulls rose above the square. Was Steiner waiting there? I thought I spotted the glint of something, a tower perhaps or a descending plane. Jacob had lost his cap and squinted beneath his hand.

'I hate the summer light,' he said. 'All those hard edges, all that white. It's depressed me all my life. When I was a kid I used to think, this is what they call "reality". I used to spend all my time at the movies in the summer. Those movies, those *art* movies Steiner sent me to, they became my "real life".'

He rushed suddenly into the water, grabbing at his shorts, and struck out furiously to catch up with Bernadette.

Why do I dream of Jacob? Last night I dreamt he came to visit me, whistling, in a narrow-shouldered suit, with a broken briefcase tucked under his arm. But I was busy, I had no time to talk.

In the new stillness and clarity of the air we could sometimes hear the distant shout of voices. Anastasia told us that work had started on the telephone lines. But the bridge – here she shook her head several times – the bridge had not even begun to be repaired.

Now that the road was drying out, Ferenc arrived in his taxi from the village each afternoon. He had opened the bar again. This was a wooden room added on to the back of the hotel. By day chickens scratched around its porch, but at night, when Ferenc turned on the porch's coloured bulbs, it shone out onto the road, the only light for miles on those dark plains.

Now that the bar was open, Ferenc said, it would stay open every night of the year. Ferenc was a professional. By the time we came in after dinner, he was polishing glasses, the floor was swept, the candles flickering on the tables. As soon as he saw us, he slung his towel over his arm, slid three tumblers towards us, and paused, looking at us through his forelock, the bottle of plum brandy tilted in his hand.

The regulars were already seated, their caps and jackets slung over their chairs. They were men from the village or from even further out, come to work on the telephone lines. The room warmed, smoke rose, the men played cards, had drinking competitions, sang. It was comforting to be amongst other people again. They called us 'The Movies', Ferenc said. Sometimes at the end of the evening it seemed that all the faces in the room were turned towards our table. They called for plum brandy for us, and as we raised our glasses to them they laughed as if we were children, and raised their glasses back.

When Steiner called the bar 'inauthentic' and had it pulled down, Ferenc walked off to the lake. Steiner followed him, put his arm around him, promised to rebuild it, but Ferenc shook his head. He had other plans, he said.

The first night the woman came she was late. We were all settled at our tables, the air was warming and thickening, when a tall dark woman in boots entered, a shawl thrown over her shoulders, her hair blown back off her face. She crossed the room and tossed her shawl down behind the bar. She eased her boots off, clop! clop! onto the wooden floor. Then she stood up, folded her arms, and looked straight ahead.

'That was an entrance,' Bernadette said.

Although nobody had stopped talking or even turned in her direction, it now seemed that the laughter was louder, the pools of light deeper over the tables.

She had come to help Ferenc. She washed up, served drinks, collected glasses from the tables. She moved around the room straight-backed, noiseless in little leather slippers. She did not smile or frown or look at anybody, but did everything in a calm, unhurried way. She never forgot an order. Nobody hailed her, joked with her, jostled her. She wore each night the same black v-necked blouse. She was broadcheekboned, hawk-nosed, and the dark glossy hair caught loosely behind her head was streaked with grey.

We speculated about her. What was she doing in this village? Was she married to Ferenc? They did not seem to need to speak or even look at one another. Sometimes Ferenc watched her across the room as she leant over a table, but if she looked up, he turned away.

As for Bernadette and Jacob and I, we watched nobody else.

How can I explain her effect on us? It is not enough to say that she was striking, that she was the only woman, apart from Anastasia, we had seen for several weeks. It was her indifference that intrigued us: a woman who had renounced the desire to please.

'I bet she used to be a dancer,' Jacob said.

One night as she cleared away our glasses, Jacob cleared his throat. 'Do you come from around here?'

'Yes.'

'From the village?'

'Yes.'

'Lived there all your life?'

'No.'

The woman moved off with her tray.

'Did you hear that *voice*?' Jacob said. 'Maybe she was a singer . . .'

That night, at the door as we were leaving, Jacob asked Ferenc: 'What is your wife's name?'

'Wife?' Ferenc gave a burst of laughter. 'She is a widow. And I, I think' – here he thumped his chest – 'I am a living man.'

Across Ferenc's shoulder Jacob called out to the woman: 'Goodnight!'

'She is my sister,' Ferenc said and closed the door behind us.

We asked Anastasia about her.

'Ferenc's sister?' She looked puzzled.

'The woman with the deep voice.'

'The one who only answers yes' – we nodded brightly – 'or no' – we shook our heads.

'Ah! Berthe!' So Berthe was her name. But even Anastasia did not call her that. It seemed the woman Berthe helped Anastasia in the hotel sometimes. That she had worked in many hotels in many countries. That she had no children. Ferenc's sister? Well . . . Anastasia cackled a little.

After that I became aware that what I had thought was silence in the hotel was composed of many sounds. When I heard a broom sweeping, a rug being beaten, the clatter of dishes far down the stairs, I imagined the woman's austere rhythmic movements. I grew restless in my room, set off for walks around the lake. One evening as I climbed the hill towards the village I met the woman coming the other way.

'Beautiful evening!'

'Yes.' She wore her boots and shawl, she must be on her way to work.

'No more rain!'

'No.'

From the top of the hill I turned and saw that the first stars hung over the lake, and the coloured lights were twinkling around the bar. The woman had nearly reached the porch. Jacob was sitting on the porch steps.

The next evening I joined him there.

'How light it is now,' I said, as the tiny figure of the woman appeared at the top of the hill, for in that moment, everything, the lake, the plains, the distant mountains seemed to lie in a great circle around us, their separate shapes and colours forging a horizon, a world in all its strangeness.

'Jacob,' I said, 'how much film did you bring?'

From the start, the woman and Ferenc showed no reluctance to have us come into their life with a camera. The film was to be based on what she, Berthe, did as she went about her day, I explained. There would be no questions, no interviews. She could always choose to close her door. It was not a documentary, but an interpretation, hers as much as mine. The woman shrugged as if such distinctions didn't matter. Hadn't she said *yes*?

Each morning we set off early from the hotel. The lake breeze blew into our faces as we reached the top of the hill. Our step was light, Jacob had found his cap, Bernadette's hand had healed. Is it worth recording here that throughout this time the hours went faster, people seemed glad to meet us, and the days of this late spring had a deepening warmth?

As we came into the village, children raced past us, satchels flying, up the alleyways to school. Dogs barked, chickens squawked, bead curtains rattled in shop doors. Ferenc and Berthe's house was on the square, a wooden house like all the others. We knocked. A silence seemed to fall around the square.

'This is the part I hate,' Jacob muttered. Below us the masts of fishing boats jostled in the harbour. Behind us rows of three-paned windows winked the lake's reflection up the hill.

But the door always opened. 'Ah, The Movies!' Ferenc bowed and tipped the peak of Jacob's cap. In the hall our equipment was waiting where we'd left it the night before. In her bedroom the woman was tying up her hair. In the kitchen a pot of coffee was stewing on the stove. 'Please,' we said each morning, as we filed through their house, 'please, just carry on.'

In that dark little house I became aware that I was filming exile, that every shot was composed towards that end. The silence of exile. The print of Ferenc's newspapers in the kitchen that no one else could read. The faces in the frames beside the woman's bed that no one else would know. The quick strange words they sometimes exchanged, as startling as a bird's flight across the room. We filmed the woman as she watched the postman ride into the village, the first time after that long winter. We filmed her as she read the letter that he gave her, silent in her bedroom, a shaft of sunlight on her head.

Did I hope to uncover a mystery? We worked by suggestion, hunches, clues. One image led to another, seemed to find an answering echo within me. The time we came upon her standing in Ferenc's room, for instance, where the radio was playing. A certain melody had drawn her in. Played on the accordion, its carnival brightness drifted into melancholy echoes above the crackle of the radio. She was looking through Ferenc's window to the pear tree in blossom in her yard. When

the music ended she went outside and stood beneath
that old tree so that the petals swirled round her like a
great white tent. Suddenly she stretched up, raised herself upon her toes, her fingertips against its trunk.

'See, a dancer,' Jacob whispered.

That tune on the accordion became the music of the
film.

How much did we affect her? How conscious of the
camera was she as she moved from room to room?

'She has decided to trust us,' said Jacob.

'She's a performer,' Bernadette said. 'Do you notice
how she never shuts a door? She's a natural. She's been
waiting for this chance all her life.'

Her face became familiar to me, like a lover's or a
child's. At night in my hotel room as I planned the next
day's shooting, I could see her face all the time in my
mind's eye. Sometimes I did not sleep but worked all
night, glad now that only the wind knocked at my
door. Sometimes I lifted up my head from my desk and
felt my lips pressed firmly together, my eyes blank
with indifference to my surroundings. If I looked into
the mirror, I thought, I would see her face.

Sometimes at breakfast Jacob said that he too had not
slept. He could hardly wait to air his worries. 'This
piecemeal way we do things,' he said, 'where will it end?'

'This is not Steiner's way,' he said.

I had no answer. All that I had were some images of
a woman's life, on unprinted reels, images I had not

even seen. The archival footage of the civil war in her country, the sequence of the young woman in the fur coat hurrying down a bombed-out street, the troupe of travelling players fleeing with their tent, all this came later, existed then only as ideas in my head. I did not yet know what the film's truth was, the images' linking thread. Each image that we filmed seemed to end in silence. I only knew my destination was my vision of the woman on the hill. In the end, I told myself, silence will speak.

'We are running out of film,' Jacob said.

On our last afternoon in her house, the woman moved a table out beneath the pear tree and on a cloth laid out wine and preserves, a slab of coarse yellow cake, a bowl of hard-boiled eggs. Ferenc invited us to join them. Jacob set the camera on the kitchen step and ran to take his place at the table. There we have it, five minutes' cinema-vérité, the film crew at tea with their subjects.

It is all there. The ragged pickets of the yard, the gauzy light beneath the tree, the old woman next door dozing in her chair. The wasps hovering over the pre-serves, Bernadette's silvery hair. Jacob sits on an upturned box. He has a mock fight with Ferenc over a plate. There are not enough plates or chairs. 'A brother and sister travel light,' Ferenc says with a wink. Later I saw that the camera caught a certain quickness as the woman turned her head.

We drank a toast to the film's precarious future. Bernadette raised her glass to the woman. 'May it make you famous,' she said. The woman stood up, handed a piece of cake, a glass of wine through the pickets to her old neighbour. Her smile was gentle, her nod patient: soon, I thought, she too will be an old woman. Like me.

Jacob reached up and shook down the last petals from the branch above him. For a moment the light shone full on to his long white face.

'Jacob, you look older,' I said.

'Summer is here,' said Bernadette.

Ferenc offered us a ride in his taxi as he left for the hotel, but we preferred to walk. Slowly we made our way up out of the village, carrying our equipment. There was just enough film left for the last shot, of the woman coming down the hill.

We never took that last shot.

'Look,' Jacob said.

Far below, like a giant blot upon the silver water, a great flat boat, square-sided, was moving slowly towards the hotel.

'Steiner,' said Bernadette.

We turned off from the road and stumbled down the hill's steep flank towards the water. As we ran we saw Ferenc and Anastasia in her apron running to the beach from the hotel. We could see people on the giant deck now, dozens of people, perched on crates,

hanging from cranes and ladders. A white shirt, tied by
its sleeves, billowed from a mast, like a flag of truce,
or rescue, or victory, castaway-style. We could hear
snatches of music through speakers, blaring into our
quiet world.

We reached the beach just as the music and the
engine cut out, and the barge, its huge anchor poised,
rocked in silence on the swell. We could see their faces
now, staring across at us, Steiner and all the old crew,
Sophie and Raoul and George. Sunlight caught on the
water between us, the air was still and warm. They were
just in time for the summer. Their faces looked fresh and
mildly curious, as if they were coming to a picnic.
Steiner, taller than everyone, his nose red from the sun,
looked severe, as he did when he was very pleased.

'*Men, lions, eagles and partridges . . .*' Bernadette
muttered beside me. All at once, as the waves lapped
my feet, my longing to be on that bright deck was so
great that for a moment I thought I could see myself
there, in my little black hat, leaning over the rail
between Steiner and George.

Steiner took up his megaphone.

'Bernadette!' His voice boomed god-like over the
water. 'Have you taken up fishing?'

Bernadette was still carrying the tape recorder with
the microphone on its improvised fishpole.

'We've taken up lots of things,' Bernadette shouted
back, 'without you, Steiner.'

But Steiner was turning away from the rail to let a
small figure in. A grey-haired woman swathed in a

scarf, stepped into his place and blew a little kiss to Bernadette. Bernadette went very still.

Suddenly Jacob rushed into the water, his camera rolling, his long legs splashing like a crane's. He waded out right into the shadow of the barge, shooting off our last few feet of film. 'Jacob, look out!' everybody cried. The anchor crashed into the water beside him, the barge lurched forward. Jacob lifted up his camera, stepped back, stumbled, fell. But at the last moment the anchor rope tautened, and the barge scraped to a halt, aground.

In the end I use the footage that Jacob risked his life for. Jerky, swerving, water-splashed, it has a quality of panic and urgency. The faces on the deck peer down frowning at the camera. The shadow looms, darkens the lens, takes over. My film ends with the arrival of the barge.

Why does it end that way?

Towards the end of the filming of *The Seagull*, I met the woman on that hill again. I did not have Jacob or the camera with me: the woman was going to meet Jacob, and the rest of the crew. She spent most of her time at the hotel now. It was evening, late summer. I often slipped away at that hour, to escape those post-mortem drinks on the balcony and to think about my film again.

The woman waved and picked her way towards me across the ruts of the road, which were now baked clay. Below us the lake was dark, the sky silver, as if everything was in reversal. Far away a single seagull flew, black, into the horizon.

The woman seemed out of breath as she reached me. She put her hand on my arm. '*My film,*' she said. Her voice was hoarse, her lips cracked from the sun. She peered into my face. '*When will you finish it? Will you show it in your city? Can I come? Will Steiner see it? Will everybody know then who I am?*'

THE INLET

Nights at the inlet were long and black and filled with strenuous dreams. Between the dreams, large animals crashed through the bush and stood outside windows, breathing. Meanwhile the inlet was rising. That slap-slap at the door was the edge of the waves.

As soon as I woke up in the morning I left our cabin and headed across the clearing. All along the tracks people in dressing-gowns were walking to the showers in a stiff-legged intent way. Small kids in pyjamas sat on doorsteps. Two big boys started to throw a ball over the nets without speaking. The Frost girls sat in identical pullovers, eating bowls of cereal outside their cabin. In the lightness of the air all the faces seemed dazed.

I met Wendy Shepherd on the track to the water. She was walking fast, head down. Her parents owned the cabins and the bush down to the inlet. Wendy played in short fierce bursts between chores with anyone she could find.

We went straight through the reeds to the big pink rocks where the foam was trapped. We crouched on the rocks and scooped up the foam and tossed it in armfuls through the air. *If mine lasts the longest, that will be a sign*. I didn't know what I was bargaining with, or why I did this all the time.

I stood among the flaring plastic streamers in our cabin doorway. Les Shepherd, with his jerry can, was sitting at the kitchen table. My parents were standing at their bedroom door. All night I'd heard them, sighing and muttering. They had to screw their eyes up to look at me against the light.

'Heather!' my father said softly. He went to pick up the kettle, his sarong crooked on his hips.

'When are you coming fishing with me then?' Les Shepherd said. His jerry can was his visiting card to all the cabins in the clearing. He made his rounds to fill the lamps and fridges just in time for morning tea. He loved to wake my parents.

'I tell you what though Frank, you'll have to tuck your skirt up!' Les winked at my mother. My father lit the camper stove with a little patient smile.

'Sunset's the best time.' Les went on. 'Reckon you'll be awake by then?'

My mother, Lenore, closed her eyes for a moment. Each year we came to the inlet I saw a little more. This time I saw that my parents didn't want to be here at all.

Like me, the Frost girls went to the little beach below the cabins every day. After the cars loaded with fishing tackle and surfboards had bumped their way out towards the big white ocean beaches, and the last outboard had died away to a toy putter far across the inlet, we lay on the pink-brown sand in silence.

Here in the south the blue of the sky had an ashen tinge to it, as if the summer had already passed. The Frost girls turned deep golden in this light. Every half hour they waded through the powdery sand of the shallows, squealing at jellyfish, and raced each other to Les Shepherd's boat moored out in the inlet. Their yellow racing bathers were like second skins.

We took good care to park our towels away from one another. They were about my age, but we never spoke. Each year it was the same. If we met coming through the reeds, or at the showers, we turned our heads. That was our acknowledgement. I knew all about them. The older one was Pauline, the younger one Annette. When their brother was a baby they used to push him on the swings. Their father was young and brown: Les Shepherd called him 'Frostie'. Sometimes Wendy Shepherd sat outside the Frost girls' cabin, kicking her legs while they read magazines.

The Frost girls. Each morning I watched them through narrowed eyes. I listened to them splash and cry out in the deep green water. I watched them race back in to shore, their arms propped out like wings.

On my way back through the reeds I passed the little boy. It was always like that. I never saw him coming, he appeared.

He was humming, head down. He had large feet and wore giant thongs that flapped against his heels. The rest of him was minimal. His shoulders sloped, his calves were barely outlined. I never felt he saw me though once his head brushed my shoulder. He might have been about six, but in another way he didn't have an age.

My parents never did things when other people did. In the long afternoons when the clearing was deserted with only lines of beach towels flapping in the wind, they emerged and set themselves up at a table outside our cabin. Lenore leaned back with headphones, Frank bent over his books. That winter, when Lenore was on tour in America, Frank had started studying Japanese.

Perhaps they slept behind their sunglasses. They had the air of convalescents under the restless trees. The day Lenore came back from America a heatwave struck the city. My parents lay on their bed like bodies washed up beside the fan. I brought them cold drinks and they were grateful. The telephone never rang, they never spoke. They said the heat was unspeakable.

One morning late they threw some clothes into the car, as if a decision had been made. We drove all day until the car darkened from the shadows of the forest and the soft inlet chill blew in the windows. I craned my head up like a lookout. *If I see the water first, that will be a sign . . .*

'Heather, come and join us,' my father would call if he looked up from his books and saw me. But I kept walking. I didn't want to sit at that table. I didn't want to hear what they might say.

Sometimes just as the shadows began to creep across the clearing, we drove to do some shopping in the town. At that hour the town was empty. The main road swept on past the solitary petrol pump towards the forest. Ours was the only car in the gravel playground beside the river. Paddleboats bobbed in a flock beneath the bridge. We ate ice-creams in the dusty golden light.

Once a car pulled up beside us in a spray of gravel. The horn tooted accidentally as a group of Indian tourists burst out from all four doors, laughing. Three men in elegant white pyjamas strode to the paddleboat mooring. The women drifted after them, like children, trying out the swings. The sun caught their oiled hair, the golden borders of their tunics, their gauzy scarves of fuchsia, turquoise, topaz. We heard the tiny dry tinkle of their bangles as they passed.

I could not help looking at Lenore to see if she was watching. This was something that I knew we shared.

Twigs snapped, leaves poured smoke, the little tepee of branches suddenly crumpled and flared. I crouched beside my fire, my face flushed and scientific. My fire shot shadows into the trees, the first each evening.

Darkness came early to the clearing. It seeped in from the bush, up from the ground. The clearing echoed with old-fashioned noises, an axe chopping, mothers calling, kids talking as they trailed to the showers. Their voices seemed to rise with the darkness.

My father strolled out of the cabin with his cask of wine. Lenore followed, arms folded inside her shawl. I loved to cook for them over my fire. I splashed my smoky eyes with rainwater. 'Eat, don't wait for me!' I cried.

My parents balanced their plates on their laps and praised everything as they ate. I stoked my fire, placed the kettle on to·boil. Then I stood at the edge of the bush and threw scraps to the creatures hiding in the dark.

Les Shepherd was a guest at every campfire. He said this glass of wine should be his last. He pulled a chair up next to Lenore.

'You oughta be careful when you go walking round the inlet. You never know what you'll find.'

'Oh no more grisly stories, Les,' Lenore said. 'I have enough bad dreams down here.' The firelight seemed to eat her profile.

'Yep. Police rang me last winter. Keep an eye out for a bloke gone missing from the blowholes. I found him. Just down there. Found *half* of him.'

We knew all his stories. Beyond the inlet was the Southern Ocean, stretching straight to the Antarctic. Les had known this coastline all his life. Freak waves, waterspouts, racing tides swept the cliffs and beaches, took the unlucky, the ignorant, the brave. The nurses with their cameras around their necks, the Scottish rock climber, the local bloke whose wife had left him . . .

'Yep,' Les said, draining his glass. 'Currents. They all end up back here.'

Sometimes a bunch of lights came straggling down the track. Thin beams broke off and chased each other across the shadows. Without a word I took my father's torch and ran towards them.

Spotlight. Any kid could join in. Were those the little boy's thongs I heard, flapping fast among them? No sign of the Frosts, but Wendy Shepherd was at the front, her hair blown back from her forehead, her voice hoarse. She led us to the old farmhouse outside the clearing, where the Shepherds used to live. Spotlight! We ran along the sagging verandahs, our torches flashing into the dark rooms, but found only a pile of beer cans glinting in a fireplace.

What were we looking for? Our torches wavered over leaves that were too still, like curtains dropped. We crouched outside Wendy's new bungalow and watched Kath Shepherd pop chocolates in her mouth in front of television. I flashed my torch through the louvres of our cabin, saw the sarong left tumbled on the bed.

It always ended at the beach. The moon had risen over the water. Our torches lost their power. We milled a little over the bright chill sand, then one by one we slipped back to the fires.

You need three weeks, Les Shepherd used to say, at the showers, at the woodpile, to anyone he got talking to. *For a complete break. One week to just unwind, one to forget everything and the third to remember it again.*

In the third week, as if the seasons had shifted on a notch, there was a change. The sky lost colour and the wind blew most of the day. The inlet splashed the beach in imitation surf. In still moments the sun broke out and lit the clearing with a candle-like intensity.

We drove along coast roads to tourist lookouts, to watch the ocean throw itself against the cliffs. I opened my mouth to shout to the Antarctic but the wind pushed the sound back in my throat. I spread my arms and screamed and screamed with no sound. My father turned to watch me. The wind ripped my shirt open until it flapped like wings along my arms. For a moment cold spray licked my ribs, my armpits, the swollen nipples that were the beginning of my breasts, and my father turned away.

We drove to Albany. I looked for Wendy Shepherd in the streets. She had been sent to Albany to stay with her married sister for a week. She had been running wild, Kath said.

In Albany we ate in a cafe run by old friends of my

parents, David and Paul. They kissed me and Lenore. In that courtyard suddenly everyone was happy. There were vines and pots of geraniums in a dazed light: there was no wind. It was like our terrace in the city where long ago my parents used to entertain people like David, and everyone had kissed me and praised my big words and independence. I took deep sips of my father's wine. I saw that we were wild-haired and smelt of wood smoke: the cutlery and tablecloth seemed tame. David put his arm around me. His shirt was very white and he wore a little red scarf around his neck.

'How big Heather is now,' he said, 'and how wonderfully stern! Bet it's not easy having a famous mother.'

'I'm not *famous*,' Lenore said, reaching over for one of his cigarettes. 'It's my work, for heaven's sake.'

My father ranged pink inlet stones across his papers to hold them from the wind. He sat all day now under the trees. Lenore no longer sat there. She was never round the cabin. I saw her disappear down tracks into the bush, wrapped in her shawl.

One afternoon I followed her as I used to follow her when I was small. 'What do you think I'm going to do?' she used to say. 'Disappear into thin air?'

She went to the old farmhouse. I crossed the creaking verandah, opened the door. She was standing with her back to me, fiddling with her tape-recorder on the mantelpiece above the fireplace filled with beer cans. I had not seen her like this for a long time.

'I thought you never danced when we came here.'

She spun around.

'*Heather*.' Her shoulders dropped. I knew what she was thinking. When I was small, whenever she started to practise I would rush up the hall and bash on her closed door.

'I thought this was a *complete break*.'

I heard the old quick rustle of her skirt as she crossed the room. 'It is,' she said. She brushed the hair back from my face. She could see herself doing that, I knew. It was as if she was showing us to someone.

She would stop now. She would collect her tape-recorder, put on her shawl and shoes. She might start humming to herself. Since she came back from America she was always patient with me. But suddenly I turned and ran out of the room. Even if she came running after me, across the verandah, down the track, back to the cabin, I knew that all the time she would be thinking: *later, when we get home, soon*.

One night I dreamed that I was lying in Les Shepherd's boat, rocked in a gentle current. There were two of us, the boat was rocking us together in the warm sun towards the sea. I woke and lay still in that rhythm, while the wind blew around the cabin. Who was the other? I shut my eyes, but the sun blinded me.

Across from me Lenore sighed. She slept in my

room now. Les Shepherd's second-hand springs were ruining my spine, she said. I left my bed, my dream still warm with me across the cold floor of the cabin, and climbed in next to my father.

The bed tipped me right onto his back. He never touched me any more, but in this trough we were thrown together. I could not move or breathe. I struggled my way out.

The gentle warmth still lingered in my bed, but though I shut my eyes again, the rhythm had gone away.

The little boy rocked back and forward, sucking in his breath. I crouched beside him in the sand. His shin was scraped and bleeding.

'Come with me,' I said.

I made myself walk slowly across the clearing to our cabin. I could hear the little boy panting behind me.

'Hello!' my father said. He was washing up by the rainwater tank. I walked straight into the kitchen and lifted down the tin with the red cross painted on it. The little boy came limping in. I pulled a chair out for him. He sat down, the injured leg held stiff in front of him. I took a bowl and raced outside to fill it from the tank.

'Would your friend like a biscuit?' my father called as I raced back in again.

I knelt before the little boy and carefully wiped his shin. He bent his head to watch. I could smell the faint sourness of his hair. His knee was crossed with scars like badly cobbled knitting. I could just hear him breathing. I laid a plaster exactly across the broken skin and sealed the edges with my fingers. I sat back. *There.* I could have swooned with satisfaction.

It was the last afternoon. There was a hum around the clearing, as if everyone had come alive. Boats were loaded onto trailers, tents dismantled, blankets hung out to air. This batch of families would leave before eight the next morning. Already the cabins looked blank and ricketty, a ring of frail playhouses again.

We would be the last to leave of course. My father was still sitting at his table. Our house would be black and airless as we entered and everything would be just as we had left it.

'Where is Lenore?' I called out. 'We should be packing.'

My father looked up, his finger on the page, his lips moving. *Daijou wa yo*, he said. He often said this to me. It meant: it will be okay.

Just then an old blue utility came veering past our cabin, very fast, heading straight for the water. It had no driver. Behind it came Wendy Shepherd, her feet pounding, her arms waving like windmills. Right on the edge of the reeds the ute swerved, rocked over on two wheels, lurched around again. This time it knocked my father's table, so he stumbled back with open arms. As it swept past I saw a half moon of brown hair just above the steering wheel. It was the little boy. I glimpsed his neck stretched up, his eyes huge with concentration. I ran in behind Wendy Shepherd.

All around us people were shouting and running, snatching up children, as the ute careered between cabins. Les Shepherd stood beside his jerry can in the middle of the track, his mouth open. The Frost girls, coming back from the showers in towel turbans, screamed, clutching their dressing-gowns. But then their father, Frostie, outpaced the rest of us, jumped on the running board, reached through the window and turned off the engine. Silence.

'Move over mate,' he said. He got in. The ute started up again and slowly gathered speed, past the Shepherds' bungalow, past the old farmhouse, faster and faster down the track, until in a cloud of dust it disappeared.

After the fuss about the little boy had died down in the clearing, after my father had picked up his books and packed them away, he said suddenly that he would like one last look at the ocean. I ran along the tracks but couldn't find Lenore. It didn't matter, my father said.

We drove in silence through the town, past the forest's edge, towards the great white dunes. As we parked in their shadow I shivered.

'Cold?' my father said. 'Put on my jacket.'

At the top we knew at once that something was wrong. We joined a small crowd of people looking down on the beach. There was a truck, an ambulance, a police car parked by the waves. Some Indian tourists had gone paddling in a channel, a man told us, without taking his eyes from the scene. They didn't know about this beach, about the terrible blind tides that can take you over the moment you set foot in the water. Four of them had been swept out to sea. Surfers – and he pointed to some black figures sitting way out beyond a line of breakers – had brought in two bodies and were looking for the others. As he spoke, the truck started up and moved slowly along the beach beneath us. On its tray were two bodies, wrapped in grey blankets.

And then down the beach, following the truck, came a man and a woman. He was wearing crumpled white pyjamas. Her long turquoise scarf blew across her face. As they came closer I saw that they were carrying sandals, two pairs each. Brown leather sandals, like those on their own feet. Their faces were without expression.

I stood next to my father, silent like the others on that hill. We watched them stumble, and keep walking, against the wind, looking straight ahead. Walking and walking as you do in a dream, as if part of you wasn't there any more, as if part of you too had drowned.

THE SECOND STAGE

In 1910, the Russian painter Marc Chagall came to Paris for the first time. Two paintings guaranteed him an income from the St Petersburg parliamentarian, Vinaver, which would allow him to survive. He left behind his beloved native town, Witebsk. He left behind Bella, the Jewish girl whom he had met on a bridge in Witebsk: even before they exchanged one word, Chagall felt that this girl had always known him, known his innermost thoughts, that 'this was she – my wife.'

He was twenty-three. He had pink cheeks, red lips, curly hair and a long, wide-nostrilled nose. He stammered, and was not strongly built.

'I feel sorry for you,' his mother said, 'with your shoulders.' She said: 'Perhaps you ought to be a clerk. Where did you get that talent?'

The eldest of nine children, six surviving, he was his mother's favourite.

His teacher Bakst had warned him that he was likely to die of hunger in Paris, and that he must not count on him.

Bakst's school, Bakst's friends in the St Petersburg

avant-garde, Bakst himself with his shining pink and gold teeth, had always upset Chagall, he didn't know why.

When by chance he met his teacher at the Ballets Russes in Paris, Bakst said, 'So you came, after all.' But why should he have stayed? Bakst was a Jew, he should have known. Was it because Chagall was a Jewish boy from a provincial ghetto that his paintings were ignored in St Petersburg, hung in the darkest corners, or, as in the case of the avant-garde exhibition, forgotten in someone's apartment, not hung at all? In Russia he was a Jew, with no country of his own.

He called the light of Paris *la lumière-liberté*.

La lumière-liberté. He moved into a studio at La Ruche – The Hive – an artist's colony close to the Vaugirard slaughter-houses, where painters came from all over the world. He saw Rembrandt in the Louvre, Van Gogh and Cézanne at the galleries on the Rue Laffitte, Picasso and Matisse at the Salon des Indépendants. A miracle started to happen. He painted night and day.

He painted the cows and roosters, the fiddlers and the rabbis, the little wooden houses beside the muddy streets of Witebsk. He painted the births and deaths and lovers, the fires and festivals of his native town as if he were its recording angel: he took the angel's point of view, or the child's, crouched on the rooftop, between the immensity of the dark sky and his mother's warm kitchen.

'What is an artist?' he had asked his mother when he was a child.

He painted himself with a bull's head, grasping the thigh of a woman twined about his shoulders. She is spitting in his face. He called this painting *To My Betrothed*.

He painted nude, by oil lamp, on canvases made from torn sheets and nightshirts. He did not starve, but he was always hungry. At his first lunch with Apollinaire, he was astounded by the poet's colossal appetite. 'Maybe talent consists in eating,' he thought. 'Simply eat and drink and the rest will come of its own accord.'

He took Apollinaire to inspect his paintings. 'I know,' he told him, 'you are the one who inspired Cubism. But I want something else.'

What else?

'Art seems to me to be a state of soul more than anything else.'

The great Apollinaire inspects, sits down, smiles and murmurs: *Supernaturel!*

In 1914 Chagall was invited to exhibit in Berlin. From there he decided to return to Russia, for his sister's wedding, and to see Bella again. He had a three-month visa. No presentiment disturbed him. *The world is a wedding*, as the Talmud says.

The world broke out in war: 'Europe closed before my very eyes.' He married Bella in Witebsk. A daughter,

Ida, was born. Then came the October Revolution. Chagall became Commissar for Revolutionary Art in Witebsk, and founded Witebsk's first Art College. He flew his revolutionary banners all over the town. But they asked him what green cows and flying horses had to do with Marx and Lenin.

He painted murals for the new Jewish Theatre in Moscow. He taught art to the war orphans at Malachowka. He, Bella and Ida were often freezing and half starving. There was very little time for his own work. He began his autobiography as if something had finished.

A poet friend wrote from Berlin: 'Are you alive? They say you were killed in the war. Do you know you are famous here?'

Chagall was given permission to return to Berlin. Bella and Ida joined him and together they went on to Paris. He was thirty-five. He was never to live in Russia again. His autobiography, *My Life*, stops here.

You could say what follows takes the form of a painting. A small canvas, a small moment: in a biography it would not earn even one line. At first sight it could almost be an original for one of those *Scenes of Paris* that tourists buy in Montmartre. It has that light-hearted, consciously naive, nostalgic style that has been around so long it has lost its origins, which might include Chagall's own later style. Your eye skims, ready for disappointment, for signs of the desire to please.

It's a painting of the back view of a house, of its courtyard and the streetlamp beside it and beyond, a horizon of a thousand mansard roofs. It's night-time. The sky above the house is blue-black. The roofline in the background is lit by a carnavalesque red. The long thin house, three storeys high, the shutters and the iron-grille railings at each pair of windows, the art nouveau streetlamp, the little leafy-shouldered statue in the courtyard, are recognisably *Paris*. In the far distance there's even a tiny, high-waisted, emblematic tower. There are no TV aerials: this is Paris, 1923. And there are no lovers loitering beneath the streetlamp. They are in the house, asleep.

You can see inside the windows of this house, just make out the figures sleeping in their beds. The light comes from a lamp that has been left burning on the stairs. That's for the child, on the second storey. In the third storey the light source is a skylight. In the blue-black sky above are splashy comets, impossibly bright stars.

The figures on the bed beneath the skylight are quite clearly defined. A man and woman lie on their backs, classic tomb pose, side by side. A cloth, like a red and gold oriental fan is draped across them. The woman is asleep. Her hands rest neat upon the cloth. She is pale and beautiful with dark, bobbed hair. How do you paint 'beautiful'? The darkness of the eyelashes perhaps, the careful brushstroke of the mouth that suggests fineness, poise. The paleness of her face is like a radiance. Beautiful. Belle. Bella.

The man beside her is awake. His pupils each reflect a pinprick of light. His arms, in clownish nightshirt stripes, are tucked behind his head. He is looking up at the skylight. You can see his long sharp profile, the woolly tendrils of his hair upon the pillow.

And because he is the only one awake in this sleeping house, it's as if he is the point of consciousness in the painting. As if the whole house, floor by floor, exists through his eyes.

The ground floor for instance, the shuttered glimpse of the *salon*. Is it he who sees its heavy cloths and curtains gathered round the ankles of its furniture like old-fashioned petticoats? Does he hear the click of the pendulum of the hall clock in its carved wooden case? It is as reliable as an old man's habits. Work-work-work-work. Only death can stop it.

If he thinks of the hall he will think of the dog, curled up asleep at the bottom of the stairs. This dog! It is a huge long-haired sheepdog, a *Briard*. Its face and eyes, its idiotic paws, are completely covered over with hair. A giant dish mop: Ida cried out with joy when she saw it. 'Take care!' he cried as Ida crouched beside it. He had been bitten by a mad dog when he was a child. And Monsieur says the dog is bad tempered with strangers. Its name is Poppy.

In the mornings he, Bella and Ida come downstairs very carefully so as not to startle Poppy. But here is the miracle. Poppy wags her tail as they creep by, and stamps her paws, her red tongue hanging through her hair.

'Poppy likes *les Russes!*' Monsieur says. They are flattered, reassured. Ida slips to the floor and parts Poppy's hair, and cries out that she can see her eyes and they are lovely and kind.

'Perhaps,' Bella says, caressing the crown of Poppy's head very lightly, 'dogs hold the spirit of a family.'

But he holds his distance. Attack, he knows, can be sudden, unearned, and unaccountable, beyond your wildest fears. Who knows what mad beast lurks there?

They are the first to come downstairs because in this house they are guests. Every day they set off early into the streets of Paris, to make contacts, leave their card, find a place of their own. Bella insists on this. In this, as in all things, Bella knows best. Guests, she says, are most welcome as they are leaving, and so must be on the point of leaving all the time. Their pleasure is largely in retrospect. Their influence is an aftertaste. Their only hope can be to leave a lasting good impression. In this house they are *les Russes*.

So it is they who open the shutters in the blue-and-white tiled kitchen every morning, stoke the fire, make tea, the Russian way. They sit around the wooden table and eat yesterday's baguette, which is kept in a big cane basket hanging on the wall. Perhaps they eat a little too much: today they must make sure they buy some more. Ida slips scraps to the dog, which is against house rules. But when they are alone she likes to pretend that this is her house, her dog.

Before he eats he must always go outside. If he hasn't seen what the day is like, the wind, the light, he feels uneasy, he doesn't know why. In Witebsk the privy was across the courtyard. In the morning he would unbolt the kitchen door into the sudden stillness of outside. Then all at once he heard hens cackling, footsteps, a pail's clink, an old man coughing. It was like standing on the rim of the world.

In this courtyard he stands every morning for a little while beside the statue. This courtyard is very narrow, its walls are high, its tree has lost its leaves. The sky, the tree, the walls, are grey. The statue is lovely, of worn marble, a goddess, with small high breasts and narrow, rounded shoulders. Who is she? Monsieur is vague. A lesser deity, he thinks. Calliope, the mother of Orphée? They call her, jokingly, 'the Muse'. The little oval of her face is blank, unjudging. She remains youthful though the marble is pitted and mossy and her hands have crumbled away. What had her hands been holding? Were they empty? Spread in blessing? Pointing a direction?

After breakfast they prepare for the day's expedition. They fret softly at one another up and down the stairs. They have very little money. They have to count it out and make sure that they are not taking too much, but enough. He hates this, this nervous whispering in the attic. The attic, like all attics, is crowded with old furniture, old hats, failed projects, Sunday paintings. Guests too must not get in the way.

Sometimes Ida will not come. She says she's tired, she wants to be inside a house today. Sometimes they let her stay. They walk faster, just the two of them, down those autumn boulevards, as they have planned for so long. Paris starts to look a little more familiar. Paris starts to hint, drop clues, lay a trail towards its former self.

Ida looks different after a day away from them. When they come home her cheeks are flushed and very round, as if she has not stopped eating all day. She has had cake, and jam, and Madame won't let her drink tea! Madame speaks a little Russian, her father was Russian. She speaks it in a deep voice, laughing, as if she's imitating an old peasant.

Ida speaks some French, Bella has taught her. Bella speaks excellent French, if a little formal and bookish. Her parents were rich, she went to university in Moscow. It is Bella who deals with all the clerks and concierges: he hates doing this. But with Madame and Monsieur, for some reason, Bella stammers and pauses so long she seems to be holding her breath. Last night she woke him.

'*Vous faîtes*,' she hissed.

'What's that?'

'I said *vous faisez* to Madame! It's *vous faîtes*.'

Languages aren't important to him. He can't even remember what language he speaks with Edouard, who is asleep on the first floor of this house. Edouard, the poet, his friend.

Not that they have the long conversations they used to: Edouard has just got married. Right now he is sleeping next to his new wife, Helena. These days there is something preoccupied about Edouard, as if when he talks he always has one arm around Helena, even if she is not there.

Edouard has taken getting married very seriously. On reflection you can see that he has always been interested in marriage. In Montmartre he was the only one of his friends who had ever asked about Bella. Edouard was a very young poet then, who visited Montmartre from his lycée. He was looking for philosophical conversation, preferably in Russian. He had a Russian grandfather, and had heard of the Symbolist poets in St Petersburg. The Ideal Woman was one of his themes. Could a beautiful woman be faithful? Could a good mother, by definition, remain interesting? He used to say that love, real love, could only last three days. But Helena told them that when she met Edouard, he proposed straight away.

He made a drawing of Edouard on the night before his wedding. He, Edouard and Bella sat up late around the kitchen table, drinking Armagnac. Bella talked, he drew, Edouard sat silent with his empty arms stretched across two chairs. In the drawing Edouard's head hangs on his chest like a crucified man. But beneath his black brows he is smiling: whenever Bella speaks, or Helena, or even Ida, Edouard cannot help smiling.

'Is Bella your Muse?' he used to ask.

Edouard has not written poetry for a long time. He is trying to build up a career in journalism. He is the last of his brothers to marry: it is time that he left the family home. All that he has in his head at the moment, he says, are the first lines of critical articles.

In the four years since the Armistice . . . or

Sir: Cubism died with the influenza that killed Apollinaire . . .

He says that he is always writing in his dreams, a beautiful flowing script that is getting harder and harder to read. He wakes to perfect sonnets that he cannot see but only sense, like a landscape he has lost, or not yet found. Or to epigrams of brilliant promise that have eaten their own tails. Or to his final salutation on a letter to a famous poet in which the only line he can remember is: *What, in your opinion, is the connection between Life and Art?*

He and Bella were pleased that Edouard wanted to sit up with them that night, in the kitchen, like a family sitting at a wake. The light over the table caught on their hair, their hands, on all the homely surfaces. It was the first time in this house that he had made a drawing. *Come to my wedding!* Edouard had written. Of all the old friends left in Paris, Edouard was the only one to ask them to stay.

Edouard has the rare gift of loyalty.

Edouard has not written poems for a long time, but he is not tragic. He will never be tragic, he is too sensible.

He called his sketch of Edouard 'The Bridegroom'. Helena loved it.

———

Of course, for the wedding, the Russians had no clothes. He and Bella spent an unspeakable afternoon at the Galleries Lafayettes and bought her some cheap suede shoes. On the day, all day, Bella was white-faced and formal, because of her old black dress. Black is bad luck for a wedding, everyone knows that. Will Madame think that she doesn't know any better? One day, he tells her, he will buy her the most beautiful dress in Paris, a silver dress, a rose dress, spend his last rouble, but meanwhile Bella keeps on looking for something in their battered luggage. All her jewellery has gone to the pawnshops of Moscow. In the end she snatches up her grandmother's red and gold shawl from their bed, wraps herself in it and descends.

Madame surveyed *les Russes* waiting in the salon for the wedding party and suavely said nothing. But Helena gave Bella a rose.

As for him, he hates clothes, any clothes, and hates formal occasions. He is the son of workers, he would rather sit in the kitchen. Conversation in a salon upsets him, he doesn't know why. There is a danger that he might sing, yes sing the old songs that he learnt from the cantor. Like his grandfather he would like to retire to the roof and eat carrots.

All the way to the Mairie, in the Métro, Edouard and Helena remained standing, so as not to crush their elegant clothes. They stood, swinging from handles, and their faces were translucent, as if they had been drained of blood and filled instead with some other pearly substance. He has seen women look like that after childbirth. Or dancers about to go on stage. Their eyes were large and shining, cow's eyes as they wait in the slaughterhouse yard.

Later Edouard introduced him to his brothers as 'the famous Russian surrealist'. Edouard, in his white suit, drinking champagne amongst his brothers in the gentle French afternoon light, said: 'Poetry? My wife is my poetry now.'

He has promised to give Edouard and Helena a painting for their wedding gift. But which? Most of his pre-war canvases are lost, scattered around Berlin and Paris. His next painting, the first painting of this new stage, will be for them.

Bella will tell him if it is right.

In the evenings Monsieur and Madame retire early. He, Bella and Ida, who never goes to bed early, sit with Edouard and Helena in the salon. Sometimes Helena plays the gramophone. She has some records which she says are Latin American. Once she took off her shoes and danced the tango on a table, back and forward, very lightly, as if she were balancing on a tightrope. They should all learn the tango, she said, as they do in America. The tango is a way of life.

'In the tango the shoulders never move,' she called out as she danced. 'The tango is very cool. The touch is ritualised. The faces never change expression. The passion comes by repetition, by accumulation.' Her face was stony, her movements precise. Her breasts and hips were hidden in a long white silk sweater which reached almost to her knees. With her shingled hair she looked like a child who has had fever. She danced up and down above Edouard with a strange, furious glitter in her eyes.

Sometimes Helena comes with them on their daily expeditions. Like them, she is always hungry. With Helena they openly declare their hunger, munch on crepes and chestnuts as they walk, or make *canards* with their sugar in cafes. How glad she is that they are here! she tells them, in her open American way. She has no real friends in Paris. She does not speak French well yet. She writes articles in Polish for a Polish-American newspaper and intends to keep doing so. But sometimes it seems to her that her audience is fading, her writing becoming less fluent. She is afraid that like her Polish mother, she will live between languages and have nothing further to say.

When Madame lies in bed and makes phone calls, her voice floats up the stairs. They catch words, *les noces, les Russes*. Also *l'Américaine*, or even, *la Polonaise*.

When Bella and Helena walk ahead of him, men pause and stare. They do not appear to notice, they are always pointing things out to one another. Their slender necks, their little hats sway side to side, as nonchalant as fans. From time to time Helena waves her gloved hands above her, as if she is trying to define something in the air.

Helena, Bella says, is the New Woman.

One night the four of them went out to an old Chinese restaurant in Pigalle. Helena said that she felt like a change from rich French food. She spooned up her thin sour soup in ecstasy.

'Calm down,' Edouard said. 'Take your time.'

'Did you hear that?' Helena asked them. 'Now he's telling me how to eat.' She leaned across the table to Edouard and pulled the brim of her soft hat over her eyebrows and said in English: 'Do you want sex tonight?'

She said the reason that she ate so much was that she felt at home here, in a Chinese restaurant. An outcast amongst outcasts. French society was impenetrable, she said, smug, structured, tight. Haw-rible, she said, in the American way. Edouard kept on watching her with his small steady smile. And do not be deceived, she went on, Edouard at heart was a traditional Frenchman, for all his bohemian ways. All Frenchmen were, at heart. She caught Edouard's eye and suddenly took his hand.

'Hey Edouard?' she said softly. 'Isn't that so?' In the red light of the Chinese paper lantern above the table, their white-skinned, tightly clasped hands seemed to glow.

He was reminded that he was in the presence of lovers. This was your first thought if you stood at their bedroom door. You saw at once the drying bouquet of violets, the two glasses beside the champagne bottle, the familiar clothes mingled across a chair. Their voices greeted you hoarse and jokey, one voice from the shadows of the bed, but you did not enter. You called out your message from the door.

It worries him that Edouard's parents do not join them in the evening. He would like them all to sit together in the kitchen. Edouard shrugs his shoulders when he suggests this.

'*S'il vous plaît Madame*,' he said one evening, with a flourish towards the salon. But Madame continued up the stairs. She was old, she said, she was tired. Four sons survived the War, and now the last of them had married. She was entitled to go to bed! She reached down and patted his head as if he were a boy. Russians are so emotional! she said.

'Take my chair, Madame!' he wanted to call out. 'Take my chair and sleep!' He would like her to fall asleep while listening to him, as his mother did, her head lurching lower and lower, one eye half open as if to say 'I'm still with you.' His father fell asleep too, every evening at the table, worn out from carrying barrels of herring fish.

'Take my chair!' he would like to call out to Monsieur, as each evening the dapper little man bowed goodnight with his book under his arm.

Monsieur is a retired surgeon. As a young man he had wanted to be an actor, but his mother would not allow it. Now he sits all day reading poetry and history, or takes the dog for a walk. If he speaks it is of the geography of France, its variety, its beauty, especially in the South where they have their summer house. Their *dacha*. It is he who has painted all these uncertain canvases stacked up here in the attic. His is that hesitant hand!

'Take my chair, Monsieur,' he would like to say, 'and let us speak a little about art.'

Monsieur reminds him of Vinaver, his St Petersburg patron. Vinaver, who stood in front of his young protégé's paintings and rubbed his long gentle fingers together and said: 'I'm afraid I am an outsider to art.' Vinaver in turn had reminded him of his father in Witebsk. All his life he has been helped by good, sad men. If you talked to them, a little light kindled in their eyes, as if they were on the point of waking up. Something a long time ago made them decide to go to sleep.

On the night of the Passover his father would hold up his glass and tell him to open the door. Open the door and let in the prophet Elijah! But Elijah never came in, only the cold and the streaming stars.

No wonder their sons attempt poetry.

His father is dead now, run over by one of the trucks he had loaded with his barrels.

'*What is an artist?*' he has asked his mother, knowing that he must at all costs escape the herring fish warehouse. His mother tapped her fingers on the oilcloth of the table.

'My son, do what you have to do. Survive.'

In this house Madame lies in bed, and plans her sons' lives on the telephone. His own mother tapped on her sisters' windows up and down the *shtetl*, consulted the rabbi, bribed the teacher, plotted his way out into the world.

Madame lies asleep now on the second floor of this house. His mother lies in her grave.

He has a longing to stretch out, face down, on the ground somewhere, like a dead man, or a dead man's weeping mourner, but where in Paris can he lie? In the courtyard, next to the little statue? If he lay there long enough would he hear then, very faintly, across the earth, the shuffling of old women in their slippers, the sighs through their broken teeth, the mutter of their prayers?

Ida too sleeps on the second floor, in the little room next to Madame and Monsieur. The children's room: there is a high bed encased in railings, and an old scratched bureau on which are clustered the moth-eaten bears and lop-eared rabbits of Edouard and his brothers long ago. Ida says there is a ghost in this room, which shakes her bed, and rattles the shutters. Monsieur says it may be the Métro which runs beneath the house. Each night Ida begs to sleep in the attic. Each night he lights the special lamp on the landing and tells her of the miles of tunnel deep beneath the city, and of the night workers, the bakers and the dancers and the watchmen who ride the trains. Only she, Idotchka, like the princess in the story, can hear those trains. Ida listens gravely, nods her head: she is a princess, her mother's daughter. Each night he makes her stay.

He is surprised at his hardness of heart as a father sometimes. Didn't he know about the nights of childhood? When he had cried out, didn't his mother call him to her bed? But his mother's body was so huge and loosened, broken with child-bearing, that he was afraid of being lost in another sort of darkness.

In this attic there is no room for a child. The more he grew the more he was afraid.

Bella sleeps on her back, so as not to crease her face, in the valley of this sagging bed. He lies halfway up a mountain. If he joins her in the valley they have no choice but to clasp each other as they had done in the boarding house in Moscow, clasped each other like the old couple on top of the stove, for warmth, and to keep each other from falling.

Bella sleeps. The red and gold shawl, like everything she touches, lies smooth beneath her hardened slender fingers. The next bed she sets this shawl upon, she says, will be their own.

Where was our last home? they sometimes ask each other with Ida, on train rides, to make a game. In Witebsk? In Moscow? Malachowka? They tell Ida about the *dacha* in the forest, with the window where they held her as a baby, to show her the white trunks of birch trees, the broken fence, the cow grazing in the nettles of the wilderness.

On trains Bella and Ida can never sit with their backs to the engine, or they become sick. From Witebsk to Moscow, to Berlin, to Paris, they have sat facing their destination. He sat opposite them. He never minded. It was a better view really, watching something after you'd passed through it. Keeping your back to all that lay ahead.

Bella has been waiting all her life to come to Paris. The girl Bella feasted on cake at her parents' home but was always hungry. *What is an artist?* they asked her. *Look, he puts rouge on his cheeks! You will starve with him*, they said. Bella licked the poppy seeds and honey from her delicate fingers and wrote another letter to Paris.

But now she is in Paris she is still hungry: he watches her walk heavy with a hunger that she will not admit, that she cannot even explain. It is a hunger for the centre which is always elsewhere: a longing for a homeland, not Russia, not even France, but a country just beyond you.

In Paris, the first time, after four years he had almost stopped writing to Bella.

Bella breathes in steam from her coffee and doesn't say she's hungry, doesn't ask the age-old questions wives ask of husbands: 'Am I too thin? Do I look older?' Bella would never ask that. It is his role to tell her, paint her, recast her, as if she is one of his creations. They reconstruct each other every day.

Sometimes Bella looks at him and says: 'Today you

have the face of a woman.' Or: 'You are a child today.'
What incarnation does he have here, in this house?
Without his work, he has no face. 'What do I care
where I live?' he says to Bella every morning as they
prepare to go apartment hunting. 'I could paint in this
attic. I could work in a hole in the ground.' As a student in St Petersburg he had shared a bed with a
workman, and seen an angel coming through the ceiling! But Bella knows all his stories. She keeps on
counting up their money, murmuring behind her little
veil.

He had left out the angel.

At the time the angel's visit through the ceiling
seemed hardly surprising, seemed to have its own
logic. Seemed earned, in some mysterious way.
Earned by innocence.

Angels do not come for the asking. You can't depend
on angels for your daily bread.

Will the angel visit him again?

Last night he dreamt he was alone, spotlit, on the
stage of the Ballets Russes. He'd been given as a costume
a crumpled peasant smock. Disdainful faces – Bakst?
Diaghilev? – were watching from the wings. He could
hear the audience's murmur, waiting for him to begin.
And was that a pair of black Spanish eyes glittering at
him from the opera box?

Art is a state of the soul more than anything else. Or is
he just repeating himself? Is that what they will say?

He will begin again, very soon. He hears the clock
chime down in the hall. At the bottom of the stairs the

wild beast lifts its head for a moment and then flops back to the floor. A long sigh seems to run through the sleepers of the house, the child and the lovers, the old parents, the woman beside him. Perhaps it is the tremor of those underground tunnels. The pendulum resumes its track, work-work-work-work. Only work can save him. He stares into the darkness of the skylight above him as if it is his frame.

The Angry Girl

You understand, on these excursions we do not often see faces from the old life. Faces from the mainstream, moving swiftly, flashed towards us; they catch our eye like mirrors, faces we used to know.

We saw Agnes on a street we didn't know existed. It's as though we live in another city now. Now we go where the others go.

It was an old street not far from the centre of the city, but complete, with its own post office and factories and cafes. Late afternoon, it opened out to us along the footpath like a little foreign town that only appears in this hazy, nonchalant light. At that hour, just as the paperboys set off, just as the home-time buses banked up at the stop lights, Agnes, as if appointed, stepped out of a laundromat and turned our way.

I swear she saw us.

Did I look down? For in that moment I saw my weathered wrists on the handles of the wheelchair and Amy's hands loose upon her lap.

A group of high school girls spilled out from the back

door of a bus. They dumped their heavy bags across the footpath and lit up cigarettes and tossed their hair.

Excuse me girls, if we could just . . .

By the time they parted for us, calling out to one another as if across great distance, the street had darkened, it was evening, and Agnes was not there.

Perhaps it's true that we've become a shadow. People move round us, past us, but they do not look at us. Perhaps they see us only as an outline that has lost its human shape. As carriers of darkness.

After all, don't we come out only with the light? And aren't these excursions our only true existence?

I thought this, late that night, after we'd seen Agnes.

I went to pick up Amy at the nursing home next day. Morning tea. If you time it right there's just the echo of the trolleys down the empty corridors. I try to slip my entries and departures into these pauses in routine.

Amy's grey head was turned away on her pillow.

'She's had a bad night,' Verna McIntosh said. 'She needs to sleep.'

Amy lay so still her eyelids quivered with the effort.

'Looks like you've got the day off!' Verna said.

Verna's from the country – fifty years on the same farm. Even here her face is splashed vivid with freckles. Her freckled hands shook as she reached for the teapot on her tray.

'Go on, have a cup.'

'No thanks, Verna.'

Far away, as in a school, a piano started up.

One of Verna's virtues as a room-mate is that she doesn't mind silence. Sometimes I've come into the silence in that room and felt I've interrupted something.

'See you tomorrow,' Verna said.

I think she knows that in that place I can neither eat nor drink.

The creepers have grown so long they reach out tentacles across our yard and pick out what they want. They have made the studio their nest.

Meanwhile, someone in the neighbourhood has broken the heart of a dog. If you listen long enough the cries lose meaning. They become the peals of a sea mammal recorded underwater. Long echoes from the depths, beyond melancholy, beyond understanding.

A day off.

In the end, if your house is not your home, where do you go? In the end I took the old route across the lawn. I went to visit Rose.

Rose cried, but Rose always cried, a little every day. Tears seep and swirl around her large brown irises, but stay contained.

'I knew you'd come. Eventually.'

All tears are for oneself, I used to tell her. You are a hard man, she used to say.

She is all in black, with her hair pulled back. Her lips are as pale as her face. Without a word she leads me to the couch, brings me cake and liqueur, sinks, straight-backed, at my feet.

'*What* are you doing with your life?' she says at last. 'Have you seen yourself recently?'

She has caught me off my guard. Is there cake smeared on my face? Did I shave this morning? Am I slouching on her couch now like some old tramp who finds himself in clover?

'You've become a shadow of yourself.'

I wipe my mouth, take a sip of liqueur. I recognise it of course. Smell the berries, smell the honey! Rose would cry. Smell my country in the summer . . . Boris gave it to her. Boris gave her a new bottle each year.

'I know – I *know* – what you've been through . . .'

It's all history now, the rituals and the celebrations. The nostalgia.

'But you can't just throw your life away.'

I look around the room. The sheen has worn off the panelling, I notice, and the chandeliers are coated with candle grease. The lace curtains have started to fray. The room of my nostalgia, Rose called it. The room that Tony built for her. Well, it needed to crumble a little to be more authentic. It suits a little seediness.

'I must be on my way.'

'Forgive me,' Rose says through tears at the door.

'There's no one else to tell you now.' I see the skin drawn back from her face like soft white paper. She takes my hand. 'We have to look after ourselves,' she says, 'now we are old.'

All tears are for oneself. I'm still hard on her, I'm leaving again. *We saw Agnes yesterday*. Is that what I'd come to tell her? Ah Rose, guilt flutters around you but I'm not going to make you to blame.

Perhaps I wouldn't recognise myself. It changes you, this life. We've taken to wearing hats, soft cloth hats that I can pull out of my bag. I've found an airline bag is best for these excursions: for the coats and drinks, the rug, the knife. I like to wear loose clothing now, to feel the air upon my limbs. When I first put my gardening trousers on they fell straight down again. I simply took my knife and cut my belt in half. I'm always walking now. This life has made me thin.

Sometimes as I get dressed I think of Tony, in the soft grey work shirt made for him by Agnes. I see the collar buttoned at his slender throat. His deftly rolled-up sleeves.

Once I thought I was old. Tony and Agnes were living with us then. I couldn't sleep. I lay all night in this room where I am lying now, where the creeper taps against the window. For the first time I saw how late the light burned in their studio.

A twig blazed, I woke. Some children shouted on the road. A whole day had passed without me in it and I did not care. I felt my old teeth raw-edged and heavy in my mouth. I did not want to get up. I did not want anything. I thought: this is how it is to be old.

Agnes came into the kitchen. I saw her crouch in the light of the open fridge and peck at something, fingers to mouth.

I struggled to sit up. 'Yes that's right, Agnes,' I called out. My voice creaked, strangely urgent. 'I know you're hungry.' She left at once, as though she had not heard.

After that I got up. I put on the kettle and the light. I cleaned my teeth. They did not look too bad. I am the same as I have ever been, I told myself into the mirror. It is not true that we grow old. It is all in the mind. It is not true that we grow wise and repent of our sins! It is not true that we die.

Rose's brother Boris knew that we died. Boris believed in the body, not the mind.

'All belief is just a neurological state,' he said, soon after we first met him.

'Oh, don't listen to him,' Rose said. 'I have argued with him all my life. The man of science. Can you imagine? My little brother was always going to be a doctor. And I was going to be an artist.' She waved her hand around her newly finished room. This was the first of the dinners, the first of Rose's celebrations.

But Agnes, sitting next to him, seemed shocked.

'Don't you believe in moral choice?'

'A theological invention.'

'Or love?'

'Culturally programmed. A name. Different oxygen levels feeding the brain. Different chemicals in the blood.'

'Then you are saying we are prisoners of our bodies.' Beneath the glittery wings she had painted on her cheekbones she appeared quite distressed.

'There are plenty of other opinions on the matter, Agnes,' Amy said.

But Boris put his hand on Agnes's arm.

'Convince me otherwise!' he said. 'Every day the evidence grows more overwhelming. Prescribe a different chemical and you have a different emotional state. Watch me Agnes! Watch me change my chemical state. In ten minutes or so I will believe in all sorts of possibilities.'

We watched him pour himself a glass of wine and fill up Agnes's glass.

'I am waiting to be convinced.'

We watched his pale deliberate hands, dust-dry across the knuckles. Rose had told us that the theatre sisters said he had the most wonderful hands. She believed it was because their mother was a seamstress in the old country.

It's true that we are prisoners of our bodies. Who would know that better now than Amy? Am I a prisoner too, as I walk behind her? Yet now that I know our course is inevitable, why do I walk with such purpose?

'Here's to Tony,' Rose said. 'A craftsman of genius. An interpreter of dreams.'

Tony, at the head of the table, smiled but kept on watching the shadows of the candles as they flickered across the panelling and the high-domed ceiling. Rose turned to me.

'I hope you realise your son is a genius.'

'You've been a great encouragement to him, Rose.'

'It is very important to be encouraged. I was not. When we came to this country I had to go to work. I escaped into marriage. I'd lost faith in myself.'

'What did you want to do?'

'Paint. But I had lost my subject. My father was a jeweller. He used to work in a room like this, with the snow falling outside the window. You'd think a jeweller might have known that we were leaving behind our greatest treasure.'

'Didn't you find new ones?'

'Nostalgia is my art form now. And people.' She smiled around the table. 'I find the people to give shape to my memory.'

When Rose first walked in the streets of this city, the buildings seemed to tower above her, she once told me, although our city is not considered high. But as she found her bearings, the streets pulled back and the buildings flattened out.

I think about this now when I walk with Amy down the streets that we didn't know existed. Do we have more time now to speculate on spires, attics, upper balconies? The buildings rise up beside us, their windows glittering. We are always looking up. We are always checking out the sky.

Rose put on music, horns and pipes, heraldic, like shepherds calling across hillsides. She held her hand out to Agnes. They stood together in the middle of the room. The music quickened into a polka. They faced each other, businesslike, and bowed. They passed shoulders and came together again with tiny trotting steps. They cocked their heads and gave each other long combative glances. With the tips of their fingers touching they turned and turned beneath their arms. Agnes's strange little satin dress moved round her like a pair of crumpled hips. Suddenly they broke away and sat down again, laughing. Rose leaned across to Tony.

'I like your wife.' She turned to Agnes. Tears filled her eyes.

'You are my younger self,' she said.

Once, a long time later, towards the end, Rose left her house and came to our door, asking to see Agnes. Agnes was in the studio, sewing. Rose made her way across the yard, towards the distant whirr of the sewing machine. A few minutes later Agnes came flying into the house, crying out to Amy that she thought she had swallowed a needle.

Rose had seated Amy at the end of the table, facing Tony. 'The artist's mother,' Rose said, helping her into her chair like an old lady. Amy hardly spoke. She could not speak in someone's house if she did not want to be there.

In the hall as we arrived, Rose had suddenly cried out: 'Amy! There's something on your skirt! A spot! I think it's grease.'

'Must be from my bike,' Amy muttered.

But Rose knelt at Amy's feet, vigorously scrubbing at her hemline. Beneath the hall light Amy hunched her shoulders. It was everything she hated, fuss, attention, being trapped. A stranger's touch.

What Amy does must be of her own choosing. The door is closed: you are on one side of it or the other. Inside, the curtains are drawn but softly moving. There are no words, only this sure breathing. The curtains blow apart for a moment. The light briefly flares.

I can't help thinking that Agnes is going to come to find us soon. That she thinks about us too, now that she has seen us. I imagine how it runs across her mind, our shadow on the street, and is dismissed. And comes back. I imagine how she'll wake up one morning and know what she must do. It's as if I know it's going to happen. Agnes is going to find her way back to Amy.

Boris questioned Agnes.

'Rose tells me you make films.'

'I've made one film.'

'Tell me about it.'

'Oh well, it's about a man getting up in the morning. Going to work. That's all. It isn't very long. It's called *Spirits of the Day*.'

'Where can I see it? Is it showing at the moment?'

'No. It isn't a commercial film.'

'Could I hire it?'

'I have a copy you can borrow if you like.'

'If I borrowed it and showed it to some friends of mine, would you come? I have some friends who are very interested in film. We could have a party afterwards!'

Later he said: 'You're very modest, Agnes. You don't try to promote your work. You don't drink much. You don't sit back and relax into your chair. You don't go in for pleasure, do you?'

'Yes I do.' Agnes lifted up her head. 'Pleasure of a particular kind.'

Her face caught the light and I saw her as she lifted up her head on the way to work in the studio every morning. I saw that as if for the last time.

———

I felt the light on my face too as I leapt up, waving my knife. The light seemed to come from the yellow liqueur that Rose had poured into my glass, that spread around your throat, sweet enough to make you choke. We discussed choking.

'There is only one thing to do!' I cried, leaping up, the rescuer, the man with the knife. I stationed myself behind Amy. I took her chin in my hand, pushed back her head, placed the knife edge against her gullet.

'Just here,' I said, 'so as to avoid the jugular.'

'Could you really do that?' Rose asked.

Amy, released, took a sip of water without looking at me.

'What do you think?' Agnes said to Boris. 'Would he kill her, or save her life?'

What did Tony see as he looked around that room? A collection of angles, joins, materials, problems posed and solved? Or was he aware of being in a space quite separate from himself now, a new space, every moment further from the cast of his hands, Rose's memory?

All the same, he must have been a romantic, to create a room like that.

The moon is up, shining at a sixty-degree angle through the creepers at my window, full onto my face as I lie there in the darkness. On such a night . . . I could go there now, make my way up the silent corridors. It's me, I would whisper over her bed, I have something to show you.

You might say I set up the scenes, choose the light, appropriate the movies. Bestow my moments . . . Oh don't think this doesn't cross my mind. Don't think I differentiate myself. That all along I haven't known about the workings of desire.

I want to take her to a place where we can watch the moon roll its own huge course. Turn with it, watching, until something on the edge of the horizon is about to cross its path. Wait for it, that moment, see it getting closer, see the tip of that waving branch, waiting. Wait for it, wait . . . *There.*

The moon hung low over our roof as we walked home that night. We walked in a procession across the lawn, Amy, Tony, Agnes, I. Like workers returning to our quarters. Like tired performers.

'Boris is very like his sister,' I called out to Agnes. 'A patron of the arts.'

Agnes muttered something.

'What's that Agnes?'

'He's a *layman*,' Agnes said.

I should have made some gesture. I should have tried to catch her, hold her, so she didn't slip away. Shown her somehow that I knew that she was there. Perhaps she only ever saw us as shadows closing in on her. I should have thought more quickly, seen more clearly . . . But a schoolgirl kept getting in the way.

For a long time I did not think Agnes's film was very good. It seemed amateurish to me: all those shots of the same subject from different angles, like a home movie! It seemed disjointed, it did not tell a story. Just the things a man – Tony – does in the morning. So what? I thought, secretly. It did not come to a conclusive ending. I felt sorry for her after all that effort. I did not speak of this to anyone amongst the general acclaim. To my surprise she won a grant to make a second film.

In the end I asked Rose why she thought it was so good.

'Because something seems to grow in it,' she said. 'Because it stays.'

It's true that sometimes now in the morning, I see the lines and shapes and shadows in the courtyard, that she filmed Tony watching from the studio. A whole architecture seems to be streaming upwards. For a moment it's as if I see what Tony saw.

Or how Agnes saw him. He is never less than elegant. I see him buckling on his belt, with his hammer and his ruler and his leather pouch. I see him taking out his pencil, bending to write something, a note or list. Printing rather than writing: he never was at home with writing. He chews his cheek a little, wistful, as he bends.

I see him looking in the mirror before he shaves, rubbing his hand over his cheek with something like anguish. There is a sense of a secret held within each scene, which she lets stay secret. When I see Tony now I see him in the film. Perhaps that's why I didn't like it. She knew more about him than I did.

How did she look? *Small*, a small figure on the scale of the street. Small as a celebrity looks small when seen in real life. She stepped out of a laundromat carrying a suitcase. There was something in her other hand. A box? Soap powder? In the suitcase would be her clothes, freshly washed and dried, still warm. Her sheets, her towel.

Her hands were full, it was not possible to wave.

She did not seem small when we first met her. She was seventeen, a year older than Tony. He brought her home from a bus after he had lent her a fare. They were sitting at the kitchen table: they always sat at the kitchen table. Everything about her then seemed in danger of spilling over, her ash, her can of Coke which she kept sliding round the table, the T-shirt bulging over her school skirt, even the blood rising to a flush in her cheeks. She kept wrapping and unwrapping her large pale legs around the legs of her chair. We sipped our tea on the edge of our own chairs. The room seemed full of smoke and school bags and a hectic intimacy.

Good tea deserves the very best treatment, she read out from our packet of Darjeeling. 'Oh haha. Oh very true.' Her hands trembled on the packet. She looked us in the eye. 'Don't mind me.'

I was pleased that Tony had a caller, I did not remind him of his homework. I hoped that he might make a friend. There was a distance between us then, and in that space I could see only emptiness. Anyone might move in.

'Friendship takes effort,' I had told him. I did not consider that he made enough effort with anything. He wore his hair long and spread his long legs out on the couch, hour after hour, watching T.V. Other people, other people's children, seemed pulled in their lives by invisible strings. But for Tony, I thought, I have to pull the strings.

I bent down over him, gathered his hair in my hands. 'It is not even fashionable!' I said. *But it is beautiful*, a voice crossed my mind. I saw my hand pressing down and down on the nape of his neck. *Life, real life!* I shouted at him, at this child who had never once raised his voice to us. God knows what I thought I was sacrificing him to.

I was waiting for an angel to stop me.

I think of Tony now, if he were here. How deftly, how naturally he would care for Amy. How he would whistle, take his time. How I would prize it now, his unconcern for time, or time's irony.

Above all, I think of the pleasure she would have, just in looking at him.

I liked to look at Tony when he sat with Agnes. He sat away from her, with his chair turned just a fraction towards her, his back to the window. You were always aware of the space he made around him. When he looked at Agnes his eyes went still with concentration. As a child, I knew, he could fall in love with something he saw, the way the ears sat on a dog, the ring on his mother's hands, an unshaved stretch of cheek that he would stroke with an almost unbearable affection.

Agnes came often. It seemed she was always in trouble. She lived with her father and was supposed to look after him. And to go to church on Sundays, her national church. She climbed out her bedroom window to go to clubs at night. Once her father beat her.

I listened and shook my head, like a good parent, like a parent who believes you must never do violence to your child.

What is her house like? we asked Tony. He said it smelt of pickles and cement. Her father was always renovating: he had filled in his entire yard with concrete. There was horror in his voice when he said this.

We gave her a chocolate egg at Easter. She ate it straight away at the table, very quickly, as if she were by herself. She did not thank us. Afterwards she kept sneaking up a finger to check out the corners of her mouth. Any little kindness seemed to disconcert her. But we learnt later that she always took account of what had been given to her.

We asked her what she was going to do when she left school.

'Would you believe – acting? – *this* week. But first I have to go away.'

We missed her when she went.

Perhaps they should never have lived with us. Perhaps the family track, played too long, wears too deep, wears out. Perhaps it was an indulgence for us all.

Tony was seduced by the chance to build his own space. He made the studio a box of many tiny parts to contain his life with Agnes. He built her a darkroom hardly bigger than a cupboard, disguised by sliding wooden panels. In the morning we could see their two heads propped up in their deep bed beneath the window.

Agnes filmed him building the studio. Later she would use some of this in *Spirits of the Day*. Agnes was thin now and held her shoulders high as she crossed the courtyard. She was careful with herself, after all those years away, as if she knew herself to be delicate. She did not smoke. She used our bathroom to take long hot baths.

She did not like to be away from Tony for too long. If he watched T.V. with us she would come and stand for a moment by the door. He always went. I don't know what pacts they had made.

I see us now as we walked back in the procession from Rose's house that night. The moon hung low, the spires and towers of the distant city were bright as if the night were day. As if the daytime world had been a dream and we had woken up and were returning now. Returning to our dream of home.

I became aware that Agnes was not sleeping. I saw the light burning in the studio like a lamp ceaselessly tended. Even if the light was off, I felt I saw her wakefulness rising like a shadow in the window. I realised that I too was not sleeping, or how would I know this?

She said that she was worried about the new film. The film was to be about her father, about coming to a new country. About coming to a point of acceptance. It was to be called *Regions of the World*. She knew the ending, the final scene. Her father is repairing the roof of his house. Suddenly he straightens up and looks out all around him. Like an old king he makes his survey of the world.

But she didn't know how to get to that point. She found herself unable to approach him, even to visit him. The images she had worked out so far were all of absence. His absence, from her. She was wondering if this was really of importance. If she was not just inventing a false epiphany. If she was not just being indulgent.

'Why aren't you working, Agnes?'
   'Because I hate myself.'
   'Why do you hate yourself?'
   'Because I'm not working.'

'Nothing else is real to me.'
   'Agnes, this is also real.'
   'Nothing else can make me happy any more.'
   'What about a hot bath?'
   'It's too late for me!' She flapped her hands about her head as if to frighten off a circling bird. 'It's got me. It's too late for me now.'

In the afternoons she went out. The day loosened, waved its boughs around, grew tawdry. Rose's laugh was brittle, her eyes tearful if I visited.
   'I must ask Tony and Agnes for drinks again, very soon, all of you.' She did not mention Boris.
   I believe Agnes met him nearly every day.

I sat up all night with Agnes's father, Andrzej, waiting for news of her. By dawn he had grown familiar to me, not by talking, but by my sense of his movements across the room. His sighs, his momentary snores, the heavy shifts of his body resembled my own. At dawn we drank a glass of whisky each to the intermittent song of birds.

'She was always angry,' he said. His face was grey, like mine. Its lines did not look like those of a tyrant or a bully to me, but of ordinary failure. 'Such an angry girl.' He blinked back tears.

Verna shook her head at me again this morning. Amy did not stir. 'Too tired,' Verna said. 'Not today.'

She's always shy with me at first. She does not look at me as I pull the ramp down and then lock the chair in next to my seat in the van. I've learnt to check myself from saying *there we go! that's it!* I've learnt I mustn't look at her as we set off. Her eyes gaze steadily to her left, away from me. *Grant me this much*, it's as if she says.

First thing, we might go to the park. The grass is white-capped with papers, boxes, cans, tiny bleached chicken bones. A brisk wind lifts a thousand seagull feathers towards us. There is a sense of aftermath. It's as good a place as any from which to start.

A day has its own rhythm. *Left or right?* I ask Amy, *north or south? Stay here or move on?* Her nod is always very sure. There seems to be a path to follow if we can only find it. On good days we move as if we're getting closer to something.

We like the backlands. We like quarries, railway sidings, beaches tucked in between factories. Washing dancing on solitary lines. We like old streets on the outskirts of the city. Old buildings worn and darkened and the gaps between them. Wind blowing down streets like little foreign towns.

We never speak with the others that we meet. Other travellers making their excursions. Drunks and loiterers, lovers, runaways: those with secret eyes, those with time. Those who carry everything they need with them. Who have left everything behind.

We've never spoken much. I watch her, gauge, assess, offer an adjustment. I want to get it right, but I'm often clumsy. I didn't know about this, about caring for someone. It's not a case of handling, it's a case of becoming one body. I didn't know about this.

Some days we fall asleep. A warm rhythmic sleep that continues the movement of the van. Afternoon sleep, like rooms with open doors, where voices echo as they pass. I wake up hoarse with sentences: *Her damp hair clung to her like feathers:* or once, *They found a black sword buried in her heart.*

Aren't these the best sleeps, Amy? Side by side?

Some days I never get it right. Some days grit flies in our faces, rain falls in large deliberate drops, the end-less streets are more than we can bear. Every minute becomes more hopeless. Amy does not pretend. She turns her head and shuts her eyes. We can't wait to be apart. No consolation, anywhere.

We're late, it's five o'clock, the corridors are restless. Room after room, they mutter, sigh, wring their hands at the onset of the night. Verna jolts awake as we enter. 'I haven't got the tea yet,' she cries, 'and the men are coming in.'

The van seems faster, lighter when I've left her. I drive more recklessly, put on the radio. I catch the last bars of a piece of music.

The night! We haven't tried the nights yet. We haven't made our way yet through the city streets night-lit, through the crowds, the cries and music in the dense electric air. And on, into the shadows between street-lamps, into the tracts that have no lights, the plains that end in blackness . . .

I have such plans!

I lie here and I'm driving again across my sleepless landscape.

Is it too early to go yet? My legs move as if already they are pushing something. My hands shake as I pack our bag. Oh my darling, where are you? I feel an end is closing in. Is this what Agnes would have said?

When Agnes went missing, Amy rode her bike around the neighbourhood. I stayed by the telephone. We felt she wasn't far away. Tony had left the week before, without explanation. He left a message for us with Agnes in the studio. He said to look after her, for him. He said he would be back one day. He never writes of course.

Amy rode and rode. She had to move, she had to be outside, alone. Her face grew very red, she reeled in, dizzy, panting. All the same she went straight to the phone. 'I'm ringing Boris,' she said.

Boris had a cold. He blew his nose, sniffed, put his handkerchief back in his pocket. 'How would I know?' Boris said, sniffing, hunched in a home-knitted jumper. 'How would I know where she goes?'

Amy gave a cry and fell down clutching her head.

I found her. It was when I'd given up that I heard it, a tiny scratching behind the darkroom door.

'I found Agnes,' I whispered over Amy's bed. 'She's going to be all right.'

'Like you,' I whispered. I listened to her breathing.

'She's not here,' Verna McIntosh said. 'She's at the singalong.'

'The what?'

'The singalong. Down the corridor. Hear the piano?'

'I'll go and find her.'

'Why d'you take her out all the time?'

'Because I want her to be happy.'

'But we don't think about being happy any more. We've given up being happy.'

Later she said: 'I used to wait all the time for him to come and get me. I used to think he'd be worried, they'd all be worried, wondering how I was. I used to worry for them. But I've given all that up now. You're on your own here. You're always on your own. That's what that girl said.'

'What girl?'

'The one with the suitcase. The one who came to visit Amy yesterday.'

For a long time after we were married we did not have children. We did not talk about this. We bought ourselves a little white dog called Pup. How well we trained Pup! He walked to heel and sat and came when he was called. Each evening we took him to the park. We thought that it was good for him to run free and mix with other dogs. He took off in all directions, barking, feigning aimlessness. 'Here Pup!' we called. Our voices mingled in the twilight, not young, not old.

Once Pup, when called, trotted a victor's lap around us. He was carrying a little parcel in his mouth. He laid it at our feet and sat back, at our service. It was a little brown bird with its eyes closed and its wings folded to its sides. Was it dead or only terrified?

I have to calm down, take a breather, get myself ready now. Focus, and yet take everything into account. An end is coming, if not a resolution. I want to get it right.

I think of Tony, if he were here now, how he would set to work, his cheek chewed in concentration. I think of what he'd build for Amy, the witty skylights, the ramps and balconies, taking her outside, bringing the outside in. If he were here she would have stayed.

Once I knocked with a message on the studio window. I thought that I'd seen Agnes sitting up in bed, but it was Tony, wearing Agnes's nightgown. I went away at once and forgot it, like a dream. Perhaps it was a dream, it doesn't matter. That was what I saw when I looked in that window.

I think of Rose, with her skin drawn back like soft white paper, her hair drawn back in penance, as she bends over the dishes she has prepared. In the house she never leaves, tears fall into the dishes she thinks are my favourites. Tears fall as she keeps my dishes warm.

I think of Agnes, when I turned the darkroom light on. How her outline rushed to take shape in the dim light like a body rising out of water. How her body lay before me, private, sleeping, eyes closed, arms at her side.

I think of Amy, with her head cocked towards the piano and the half circle of singers pulled up in their chairs. She sits to one side, so she can watch. *On the Wings of a Snow White Dove*, they sing, patiently, dreamily, as if reading the lines in their heads.

She doesn't sing, of course. She is chewing on her cheek, as Tony does, in concentration. Her cocked head seems alert, but patient, not ironic. She doesn't know that I am at the doorway, watching her, waiting for her, at her service. Her eyes are dreamy too. Who knows what she is seeing, what pilgrimage she's making, what landscape she is visiting, what region of the world?

Maisie Goes to India

In memory of my parents.

If there is Paradise on earth, it is here, it is here, it is here.
Inscription in Shah Jahan's Audience Hall, Delhi.

Fremantle Harbour. A ship is leaving. Its horn echoes along the quay. All at once you realise it's moving, it is silently pulling away. You might have been waiting hours, weeks, years for this departure, yet for a moment you think: *too late*.

You are suddenly exposed. There is nobody else on the quay. The ocean wind, unbuffered now, blows in through the Heads, across barren tarmacs, stilled cranes, rows of empty weatherboard sheds. There are not many farewells on the quay these days. When a ship leaves it's as if the last ship has sailed.

The ship sounds its horn again. It is like a voice, an animal voice, from the deep mists around coastlines, warning of perils ahead. It makes you nostalgic for journeys, journeys you've never made. Departures and arrivals you've been told about, all your life, until you have made them your own.

A horn echoes, a ship is leaving. I don't want to be nostalgic about this. I only want to be present, at this time, at this place, as the small white passenger liner, the SS *Naloja* steams out towards the Heads. The quay is crowded, the harbour is bustling again. On the deck a young woman has just stopped waving. On the quay a young man lets his crumpled streamer fall to his feet. At this moment they are both looking out through the Heads to where the sky meets the ocean. The Indian Ocean.

Maisie is going to India. It is November, 1932.

George has come to see Maisie off. In the bouquet that, he hopes, has been delivered to her cabin, is a letter in which he has written: *Do not forget your dearest at heart.*

Maisie is going to stay with her friend Mona on a tea plantation in the Punjab. She is going to be godmother to Mona's newly-born son. The large figure next to Maisie on the deck is her chaperone, Mona's mother, Mrs Black. Mrs Black, an experienced traveller, is sitting on her shooting stick, but even so her head comes up to Maisie's shoulder. She seems larger than usual because she is wearing all her furs.

———

George is standing next to Maisie's grandmother and aunt. He would rather be with Maisie's friends a little further down the wharf. But when he arrived and lifted up his hat to the old ladies, it seemed rude to move away. To Maisie though, to see him there, in his hat, next to her grandmother, it's as if he's staking a special claim. She doesn't want to focus on this now. She moves her gaze along the quay.

George met Maisie at a Tennis Club dance five years ago. Someone's brother was responsible for filling her programme: George scribbled in his name before the fellow rushed off to play Night Doubles. Maisie turned out to be one of the two girls who spent most of the evening by the door, laughing. When he claimed her for the dance, she and her friend Mona bent double with laughter. It was just, they said, their hands light as feathers on his shoulder, they thought that '*George*' would be somebody else.

Mona met the tea-planter on a cruise ship two years later. Mona set off like this from Fremantle with Mrs Black and now she'll never come back. Maisie says, pulling one of her faces, that she, Maisie, is really an awfully sensible person, things don't happen to her, things like that. But there's a chap in a white uniform and gold braid just beyond her on the deck. There's a swimming pool and a three-piece band on the *Naloja*. Who knows what will happen on a journey?

For Maisie the seasickness will start almost straight away. Throughout her journey she will suffer from headaches, backaches, dizziness, vague womanly feelings of being out of sorts. All her life her grandmother has warned her of the dangers waiting for her body. Maisie feels charged with responsibility for something delicate and treacherous. Like Mona, like all the Englishwomen in the Punjab, there will be days when she lies for hours in a darkened room, when she doesn't get up at all.

George thinks that Maisie is looking in his direction and he lifts his hand to wave. But whatever she's looking at, it isn't him. He lets his hand drop to his head as if he is securing his hat in the wind that has rushed in now the ship is moving out. He hopes her grandmother hasn't noticed: she never has taken much notice of him. George feels as if he is standing in the wind at the bottom of a canyon.

Maisie is looking at the seagulls which have swooped in between the ship and quay. Sea birds. She no longer belongs to the shore now but to the sea. How far from land do you go before birds too drop away?

For some reason she is thinking of her mother. Is

this because her grandmother and aunt, her friends, George, all the people that she knows, have gathered to farewell her on the quay? For the first time in her life she is the centre of attention. This usually only happens once in a woman's life, when she marries. At her age, twenty-two, her mother was already married.

Before she married, her mother also made a journey. In 1908 she sailed into Fremantle from Melbourne, and then took another boat north to Broome. She had a position waiting for her there, in Rodriguez's Private Hotel. Mrs Rodriguez wanted respectable, if hard-up, convent-educated Irish girls for light duties, sewing, menu writing, serving tea. Mrs Rodriguez promised to be personally responsible for her girls.

Maisie's father went to Broome the same year. He'd been recommended to go north for his chest. He was an asthmatic, who up till then had been, if not an invalid, a young man who had spent a great deal of time at home, resting, close to his mother. He found a job as an accountant and pearl classer for a pearling firm. He must have met the new Irish girl at Rodriguez's almost straight away.

Did her family send her to Broome, or did she decide to go herself? Did they try to stop her? *It is such a long way*, they said. *Come back! Come back!* But she said that she had always wanted to travel. Did she too glide away like this, beyond warnings and advice, while seagulls tossed up behind her? There are no stories about this journey. Like Maisie's childhood in Broome there is only a great silence out of which she makes up stories. This is because, when Maisie was five, her mother died.

Whenever she sees birds, for some reason she thinks of her mother.

What did she die of?
  Blood-poisoning.
  How did it happen?
  I don't know.
  You must know, she was your mother.
  You don't know everything about your mother.

Maisie's grandmother has tapped George on the shoulder. They motored down, she says, and now she thinks they might have a puncture. Does he know anything about cars? George doesn't. By his calculations he's about five years from owning one. They'll think he doesn't have two beans to rub together. But he promises to help.

He caught the train down, and nearly missed it, because his sisters were in the bathroom getting ready for tennis. He had to rush his shave. Then his eldest sister said 'Not that shirt, George,' and he decided to change. As his sisters tell him, he's low in the pecking order in that house. He sleeps on the back verandah: all his life he's only ever slept on back verandahs.

There's not enough room in that house, but nobody complains. When their father died there was nothing. But all the children found jobs, even George, who was only fourteen. They've survived. They're surviving the Depression, they're even saving for a telephone! But there isn't any money for cars. Or trips to India.

He wasn't a bad dancer: Maisie asked him where he'd learnt, and he said 'North Perth', which was true in a way. His sisters had taught him in the lounge. Maisie said she thought he might be from England or the Eastern States, he looked so superior. She had a teasing manner, which made him smile. His sisters said he was too serious. Close-up her eyes were so blue they gave off a sort of haze.

He thought she said she'd have the last dance with him, but then she mouthed 'sorry' at him across some other fellow's shoulder. It was 'The More We Are Together', the slow waltz. The lights were dimmed, balloons floated free over the dance floor. This is something that even now he's not sure about. That she might have the last dance with someone else.

Is this ship ever going to leave? Mrs Black is leaning over to her, whispering, so her fur brushes Maisie's ear. The ship seems to be stationary in the middle of the harbour. It's rather embarrassing making everybody wait like this. Are they bored down there on the wharf? Cold? Maisie is wearing a coat, her grandmother insisted, so she won't catch a chill in the sea winds. Like Mrs Black she fears she gives off an aura of mothballs.

But she is sailing to India. She has always wanted to travel. In India she intends to forget all about coats. In India she wants – she isn't sure exactly what she means by this – she wants to please herself.

When Maisie arrived in India she was garlanded with tuber roses, maidenhair fern and jasmine bound in silver thread. It was dawn, the sky was black-tinged, but the mountains around Bombay Harbour were outlined in the sun's first rays. Before them the city rose up in wild steps, like a ragged fortress. Hawks glided up and down in invisible currents, above the tossing fronds of a boulevard of palm trees.

Men in pyjamas, sprung up straight from sleep, jostled five deep round the gangway, waving and shouting as if their arrival was long-awaited. A Mr Baksh from Cooks, in a tweed suit and turban, led the way to Customs backwards, too polite to turn his face. Mrs Black strode out with her shooting stick, calling 'Dekko! Dekko!' which she said meant 'Porter'. (They found out later it meant 'Look here'.) She put a handkerchief, for smells, over her nose and mouth.

The air felt soft and warm and resonating. Black hands stretched out a welcome. Women in bright saris were coming down a hillside. Maisie could only smell the jasmine around her neck.

———

I used to think that 'India' was somewhere in your bedroom. It was still and distant, like your little Kodak snaps. It had a brownish dusty light. It smelt of sandalwood and powder and the clothes you kept for best. I heard it in the sighs of your sleep and the rustle of your dress if you were going out. It was there even in your absence. It was your past, before children, it was your secret life.

It's funny what children pick up. I didn't really think about it much.

What was it like there?

Just like living, anywhere.

Breakfast was 'hasri', lunch was 'tiffin'. 'Tea' meant the English sort, with cake. At sunset they had drinks on the verandah overlooking Mona's garden. Each day they watched the sun cross the red dust of the compound, climb the red-stained arches of its walls. Time passed as slowly as the bullock drays plodding by the gate. As slowly as childhood.

On the edge of the verandah, Mona's baby, Gordon, lay in the folds of his ayah's sari, waving his fists at her shining earrings. As she drew him to her all her bracelets fell and tinkled down her brown, slender arms.

'India is a wonderful place for babies,' Mona said.

Only now, at sunset, in lipstick and a silk blouson dress, did Mona seem truly awake. Her cuffs were tailored, and in this land of vivid colours, her silks were fawn or dove or sage. She no longer wore white, she whispered to Maisie, because since the baby was born she had never really stopped bleeding.

Mona never rose until tiffin and rested again in the afternoon. In her new heavy rings even her hands looked frail. 'It's this wretched climate,' said Mrs Black. She herself still wore her fawn lisle stockings and her lace-up bunion-moulded shoes. 'I wish you'd let me order in a case of stout . . .' Her voice trailed away. Mrs Black, so bold in ports and railways stations, now seemed to think of little else but Mona's health.

Standing, the ayah was hardly taller than a child herself, yet she might have been as old as Mrs Black. She wore her white muslin sari cowled nun-like over her forehead: slim as a girl, she glided on bare feet. If she saw you watching her she said, 'God bless you, darling.' When she smiled you saw her missing teeth and her face cracked like a sun-baked riverbed.

In the photograph of you as a tiny girl in Broome you are smiling in a big cane chair. Two Aboriginal women in high-necked Edwardian dresses, their hair pulled back, are standing behind you. Their hands rest on your chair, graceful and protective. You are smiling, but they are very grave.

'The trouble is,' said Mona, as the ayah held out Gordon for her to kiss goodnight, 'I don't really believe in babies.' She pecked him on each fat white cheek, like a lady at a reception. 'I can't help thinking they're just people pretending to be helpless.' She looked to Maisie to see if she would laugh.

Only sometimes now, when Mrs Black insisted that they learnt to cook plain English food for instance, did she and Mona laugh in the old way. Mona, in her after-noon wrapper, her hair in strings across her shiny face, had to cut her blancmange with a knife!

Mrs Black looked pleased then. 'I knew Maisie would cheer you up.'

They had one gin and tonic each as the evening deep-ened. Everything had become normal and yet there was a moment when the colours of the sunset, saffron, pur-ple, scarlet, became alarming, as if the sky might catch fire. And the English flowers that Mona had planted, the daisies, stocks and roses in their pottery borders, glowed lurid in the red dust, on the point of turning wild.

Everything was normal and yet Mona never held her baby. How did Maisie know this was not normal, she who could not even remember her mother? Once a flock of little brown birds swooped in through an arch and beat around them, whistling loudly, as if carrying an urgent message. It seemed to Maisie then that all this was familiar to her, that she had sat like this amongst women on a shadowy verandah, some time long before.

Why didn't you ask about her?

You didn't, in those days. You were told what you were meant to hear, no more. My father lived in Broome, my little brothers were boarded out. I never saw them. For some reason

my grandmother didn't want to talk about my mother: per-
haps she was not of 'good family'. I didn't dare ask my
grandmother. I was already enough of a nuisance.

Where was the snake in this Eden? The sheikh in this
harem? Look! An old Ford with canvas sides is bumping into the compound. Two bearers ride on the
running board, the tails of their turbans waving in the
livid light. A khaki elbow projects from either window. The men are coming! On the verandah the
women rise to their feet. But it's all right, one is a
clergyman, and one is Mona's husband. And both are
English, and of *good family*.

Noel, Mona's husband was much the more handsome
of the two. Padre Lewis's neck was scraggy above his
dog collar and his face was that tender, boiled shade of
pink that only Englishmen could have. He was, however, very gallant. 'Three beautiful Australian women!'
he said. 'How did you arrange this, Noel old boy?' He
escorted Mrs Black into dinner. Noel offered Mona
and Maisie each an arm.

Noel was hardly taller than they were, as if he'd
stepped in scale straight out of the little snapshots
Mona used to show around in the office. What you
didn't see in the photos was that in profile his nose was
very sharp. He was quite old, in his thirties, and had
lived most of his life in India. He was so tanned that in

the light of the lamp on the table he looked as dark and smooth-skinned as an Indian himself.

'Let me guess,' he said to Maisie, 'your mother is Irish. Eyes like that can only go one generation back.'

'Yes. But my mother is dead now.'

'Not while you're on earth, I would say.'

Dinner was late because Noel insisted that they eat the peacocks he had shot himself.

'I must introduce you to the joys of hunting,' he said to Maisie.

'And the quite delicious results,' said Padre Lewis, who never lost an opportunity to praise.

'No, hunting is the heat of the chase. The result is – only game.'

Noel clapped his hands and spoke in Hindi. His bearers, Mukhal and Ajib, rushed to clear away the plates.

Padre Lewis and Noel retired to the verandah for port and cigars. In the darkness of the night there were drumbeats from the village, distant chants and the tinkle of bells. A wedding, most likely, Noel said. Noel and the Padre looked contented, their plumes of smoke intertwining above their heads. Englishmen were at home anywhere.

Before Mona became pregnant, she used to go everywhere with Noel. Now every morning, between hasri and tiffin, Maisie and Noel went hunting in the local jungle while Mona was sleeping. Every morning they took the road outside the compound, while Mukhal and Ajib, carrying the rifles, disappeared into the mist ahead. White hoarfrost cracked beneath their footsteps and Noel took Maisie's arm so she would not slip.

Full soon thy Soul shall have her earthly freight, Noel quoted.

And custom lie upon thee with a weight.

Heavy as frost, and deep almost as life!

'Wordsworth,' he said. There was nothing like an English public school education. In distant fields Indians were sweeping off the frost with boughs.

The mud brick village seemed to grow out of the road, as if the earth had been swept up and sculpted into walls and doorways by one giant pair of hands. Along the walls women with pitchers on their shoulders turned their faces as they passed. You saw the flash of silver on their gleaming arms, and the billowing hems of their saris dust-stained red.

'Why are they so shy?'

'Because they know they are beautiful,' Noel said.

Maisie was wearing a pair of Noel's riding breeches, and riding boots, and one of his topees on her bobbed head. She felt like an honorary boy, a good sport, a father's mate, as if she belonged not only to another race but to another sex.

Across the clearing a peacock rushed, the golden eyes in its tail feathers as brilliant as fireworks, its lapis lazuli breast iridescent against the shade. Noel took aim and fired but the peacock escaped. A hare dashed out of some ferns in a panic and zigzagged back again. A flock of birds rose, shrieking, while their wings flapped like aprons in dismay. The agile bearers ran into the jungle, their turbans bright for a moment in the darkness. 'You go on,' Maisie said to Noel. 'I'll stay.' It was not, of course, that hunting wasn't terribly exciting, though this was a mild jungle really, without elephants or tigers. But the shots and shrieks and smoke had put her into a sort of daze. And the peacocks were such lovely birds, though, as she told herself, they numbered in the thousands and she liked their flavour as much as anyone else.

Across the clearing was a little shrine to Krishna, mighty hero, flute player and lover of cowgirls. Tree creepers covered its arches like curtains. When Maisie parted them she saw, seated cross-legged on a floor of fallen leaves, a woman in an apricot-coloured sari with a sleeping baby on her knees. Beneath the silver links strung across her forehead she stared at Maisie, her eyes blackened with kohl. Perhaps she had come to make an offering to Krishna. Or perhaps she was seeking shelter. Outside there was a volley of shots and a sudden terrible howling, but within the sun-flecked darkness the women slowly smiled.

Noel had shot a jackal. Mukhal and Ajib carried it strung on a pole between them in a procession through the village. Children mustering goats stopped to watch them, their impossibly thin legs blending in with those of their herd. In the midday sun the thatch shone golden on the village roofs. Wheatfields wound through trees like a river. A camel turned a water-wheel with a slow and graceful tread.

'If there is Paradise on earth,' said Noel, 'it is here, it is here, it is here.'

On Christmas Day they were woken to strains of 'God Save The King' as Mukhal and Ajib marched up and down the verandah, Mukhal on the trumpet, Ajib on the drum. At tiffin there was turkey and pudding, mince pies, paper hats and bonbons. Noel, said Mona, must have everything just so. It could have been a table in England, except for the scent of jasmine through the windows, and the way Mukhal and Ajib stood to attention, too stiffly, a piece of holly in each turban, like children playing a game.

'The Indians will never change,' said Noel. 'It's their religion. They call their time on earth their karma. The earth is a place of cruelty and sorrow. Each time the aim is to become a little more free. The lighter one becomes the happier one is.'

'Until it's paradise on earth,' said Maisie to him.

'Paradise is when one doesn't come back at all.'

'But who wants to leave?' cried Padre Lewis. 'Paradise is when a chap is surrounded by members of the fairer sex.'

'Earthly pleasures, Padre!'

'Mere appreciation of God's beauty in the world, dear boy.' His paper crown had slipped over one ear.

'Paradise is what you think might happen,' said Mona, 'and never does.'

'Paradise,' said Noel, 'is when you're satisfied.'

It was in the year of Mona's engagement that she and Maisie had stopped laughing. It used to be enough for them to look in a mirror together at a dance. 'What's so funny?' everyone would ask them when they were seventeen. They didn't have to explain to one another. It was their shiny noses, fat arms, slipping straps, the corsages limp across their bound-up breasts: the way they'd ended up so far from the ideal. But when she showed Maisie the photos of her tea-planter, and the ten-page letters in his tiny scrawl, Mona did not laugh. Even when they took their sandwiches to the river in their lunch hour, Mona was dreamy and self-absorbed. The ideal had happened. There was no need to laugh any more.

At sunset there were cocktails on the flat roof of the house. If she was lucky, Noel promised Maisie, she would see the Himalayas, sixty miles away. When she glimpsed them, whiter and higher than all the clouds, it was like seeing a castle in a fairytale. As if fairytales, like the afterlife, were just a matter of belief.

When the moon rose the dancing began. There were guests, neighbours, Dr Ram Shad, Colonel and Mrs

Orbison from the mission, and a young Anglo-Indian, Miss Dutter, who taught at the mission school. They shook hands all round. Mukhal and Ajib rolled back the carpet and wound up the gramophone. Miss Dutter did not dance. She wore a dark-green sari and spectacles and her only jewellery was a little gold cross around her sallow neck. She was very shy, but with a crisp speaking voice. 'I prefer to watch proceedings,' she told Padre Lewis when he bowed before her, 'as a general rule.'

What were the proceedings Miss Dutter saw and heard? When Padre Lewis danced 'The Black Bottom' with Mona he had to wipe his boiling face and mutter, 'Oh you naughty, naughty girl.' Mona wore a peacock feather in a thin gold band around her forehead, and earrings made of gold and brown striped stones called *tiger's eyes*. 'Oh why does everything have to finish so soon?' she cried, as the gramophone wound down.

'The waltz, Mukhal, look sharp.' Noel clapped his hands.

'Oh, not the waltz!' said Mona. 'Let's have "The Honolulu Moon!"' She was in a state of heated, fluttery anticipation between each dance.

'You heard me, Mukhal,' said Noel. He and Mona had not danced once together. Mona sat down next to her mother and did not dance again. 'You can be too proud, girlie,' Maisie heard Mrs Black say.

Meanwhile Maisie felt Padre Lewis's breath in her ear. 'What did Daddy Christmas put into your stocking?'

he was murmuring. 'Was he kind to you? Did Daddy Christmas kiss your baby brow?' His eyes were watering. Maisie turned away.

Dr Ram Shad, his white eyebrows knitted beneath his huge red turban, could not stop laughing. He said he was too fat to dance. But he was, he said, tickled to death by them all.

But never mind the Doctor's laugh, or the Padre's breath, or Mona's sulk, or Miss Dutter's steady gaze. When Maisie danced the Emperor Waltz with Noel, everything seemed forgiven. All the others seemed to draw back into a swaying ring around them. They might have been figures in a ballroom at any time in history, in any empire's outpost. *Da da dadadada.* Tempting to think that only she could dance like this with Noel. They swept across the floor and out onto the verandah. The tempo followed them, restoring order, a rising note of triumph across the moonlit compound, the fire-lit plains, the secret jungles, the winding river, the dark Mughal hills.

Every evening now as she dressed for dinner in her new rustling Indian silks, azure, cream, rose, Maisie saw that something had happened to her face. All her imperfect features, once so anxiously examined, for a moment came together. It was as if a woman looked out through a girl's face.

Did you look like her?

Nobody said. Each time I saw my father, I waited for him to say, 'You're the spitting image of her.' But he never did.

What did she look like?

She was beautiful.

How did you know?

From the way my father was. He grew very fat and red. From his silence about her. From the silence all around her, from what people did not say.

With the deepening heat came a rumour of an out-break of smallpox across the hazy plains of the Punjab. Although old Dr Shad still chuckled as he swabbed and stabbed the soft white arms of Mrs Black and Maisie in the dining-room, ten deaths in Hoshiapur had been definitely confirmed.

Maisie was on horseback when she felt the fever start, as if a current of cold air had spun across the windless plain and found her, set her shivering. But she did not say: 'I must turn back.' She and Noel were going hunt-ing for panther by the river, an expedition that would last all day. And Noel was preoccupied with his horse, which was so reluctant to carry him that he had to use the whip at every step. As it nuzzled at imaginary grass beside the road, Noel bounced on the saddle, his arms and legs flailing, his topee sliding over his face. Mukhal and Ajib were laughing as, barefoot, they ran ahead.

Maisie's head was drumming. The day had become overcast, or else her eyes had blurred.

In the distance vultures wheeled above a row of platforms on long spindly legs. They were, said Noel, the Towers of Silence, where the corpses of Parsees were left for the vultures to pick the flesh and the sun to bleach the bones. In this way the soul left its location in the body. Across the plain the wheeling birds could be seen for several miles.

Maisie and Noel rode in silence through archways of bamboo along the riverbed. It was here that panthers came at this time of the year looking for pools of water, but they never saw a panther. Noel shot a Brahmini duck instead. Maisie had not known he was going to shoot the duck. They had gone much further than they intended when they came upon the duck and drake alone together in a pool. Brahminis were very devoted, Noel said, they mated for life. Suddenly he fired his rifle and the duck fell dead. The drake flew up and circled her, crying. Noel took aim but missed.

The drumming seemed to break in Maisie's head. 'How could you *do* that?'

'Practice.' Noel said. Then as she turned her horse for home he called out after her: 'Aren't your qualms a little late in the day?'

Everything had darkened by the time she reached the plains. The horse knew its own way home. She let the reins drop and clutched the rolling muscle of its sides. Where were the Towers of Silence now with their preying birds and eyeless corpses? Where was the soul located? In the treacherous heart? In the milling static of the brain?

Hoofbeats pursued her, Noel bolted past. Now his horse was on the home run he could not stop her wide-hipped gallop. He called out some joke about being late for tea. Tea. Toast with fishpaste, mango jam, fruit cake: the silver teapot that the servants had to polish daily in this climate, the powdered milk in the jug, the vase of roses on the tarnished silver tray. They laid their rituals like a web across this country, and the bare white country she had left: but all the time drums beat and the songs rose in the village. The brides were children, the camels blinded, the vultures fed on human flesh. Mukhal and Ajib's feet were bleeding. Paradise was cruel.

She was looking now for the fires of the village, the lamps of the compound. Not even the evening stars had risen. Just the total neutrality of darkness.

They put her in a room she had never seen before. The nursery. She heard the word 'quarantine'. A bed, a rectangle of light, an open door. Somewhere close by birds call, leaves rustle in free air. In the end all you could ask for.

Somebody wipes her forehead, whispers, 'God bless you, darling,' disappears into the shadows. Come back! You're the one who knows I'm here, lying in the darkness. She hears her footsteps and imagines her growing smaller down an arcade of infinitely multiplying arches.

She doesn't belong to her body any more. Is it her wrist that is held so gently? 'Very unusual reaction. Occasionally seen in children. Rarely fatal.' A half-chuckle, 'Hardly more than a child herself.'

Why do people die young?
Who knows? She had four children in four years. Perhaps she was tired. Perhaps you die when your life's work is done.

There wasn't time for her to be anything but an angel or martyr. They whisper about her youth, as they come and go into this room, as if this is all she has left. She's always been told she looks young. But she's so tired she can hardly do more than open her eyes now. They don't know how quickly you grow old.

It must be early morning. There's a hush in the rooms around her. Only she is awake. The air is light, sounds carry very clearly. A bird on a tree by the verandah is preening its feathers and chirping, preening and chirping, as if it has plenty of time to get ready for an engagement. Or is the bird in her room? Outside a mass of greenery is rippling. Something extraordinary is going to happen.

It has been raining. In the Wet, all the women and children in Broome go south. Otherwise they grow long and pale and sprawling like plants in a cupboard. But the baby was too young. She had just put him back under his net when she heard the rain start. She stepped across the verandah and felt the spray splash from the leaves onto her bare shoulder and breast. She wiped at them with the baby's little shawl, and at the perspiration beneath her heavy plait.

Come back! Come back! they said. This isn't her country. She remembers another room in early morning, cows lowing outside in the mist, a candle by the wash-stand, her sisters sighing and bending, turning their backs to one another, *here, will you do me up?*

The web of light between the leaves reminds her of lace. In this climate her lace veil disintegrated after one season. On the verandah strange plants are bursting out of old china washbasins and chamberpots. By afternoon all the women and children are sleeping. Mrs Rodriguez arranges her veil for her. Only Mrs Rodriguez, with her waist like a girl's and her wonderful hat, like a tropical flower, blooms on and on.

He doesn't know about her nights. He keeps gentleman's hours, doesn't make an early start. He takes a long time to get dressed: he finishes with cologne, slapped onto his neck. Slap, slap. Since he married his neck has grown tight against his collar. She follows him down the hall in her bare feet, holds his jacket out for him. He moves the damp hair at her ear, kisses her. 'It's hot. I'll be home for a sleep.' He never dreamt of the violence he was doing her. He only knows how to look after himself. He smells very fresh, innocent.

There's someone by the bed in a nest of white muslin, black fingers draped where they fell from holding hers. She's leaving them all sleeping. So this

was it, after all, the tumbled bed, the cradle in the corner, a child's battered toy. A comb with a thread of
black hair running through it. The comb will make him
weep. All along she'd sensed it, this golden light within
things, waiting to be released. It holds them all. She
crosses the verandah. The bird chatters on, too casually. But it's keeping an eye on things. Now she's
stepping onto the grass, she can feel its wetness. She
has just lost sight of her white feet and the white hem
of her nightgown. She lifts up her arms to the rustling
leaves. It's beautiful. She can see the darkness shimmer
as it fades.

Do you remember when she died?

*Everything changed. I couldn't think of it for years. And
when I did it had gone.*

Don't you remember anything at all?

*Only the sound of leaves in rain. And a big white bird out-
side my window sang to me so loudly it was as if it was angry.*

Mukhal and Ajib took turns to crank the Ford and now
it was rumbling by the front steps, weighed down
under their trunks. A puff of red dust lifted with the
exhaust and spun across the compound. Mona's English flowers went frantic for a moment as if they too
were part of the farewell.

Mona had asked the Orbisons and Dr Ram and Miss
Dutter for tiffin, and for support in what she called

her hour of need. 'Plenty of rest. And a glass of porter before dinner.' Mrs Black, overheated in her furs, was on the point of departing down the steps when she remembered something else to tell Mona. Noel sat with his elbow out the window, invisible in the driver's seat. Padre Lewis had just remarked how calm Maisie seemed when suddenly she turned and ran up the verandah calling out that she had forgotten to kiss Baby Gordon. Her legs felt longer since her illness, her clothes looser, as if she were further from the ground. At the threshold of the nursery she stopped. Shadows seemed to move about the cradle. But she could only hear the lonely flutters of his breath. There was no one watching over him. The ayah had gone with her sisters on a pilgrimage to Benares, where chastely, in their saris, the women plunged into the waters of the Ganges, to purify themselves.

Noel blew the horn, Mukhal and Ajib salaamed, Dr Ram waved his handkerchief before offering it to Mona. Even Miss Dutter waved. In the middle of the compound, Padre Lewis blessed them with his hand. Noel pretended to run him over, so realistically that in their last view of the Padre he was tottering back-wards, his pink face suddenly aghast.

There remained only the letter to say thank you. And she was good at that.

In fact there remained years of letters with Mona, who became that rare exotic creature, a divorcee. During the war she lived in a hill station, sustained by an unnamed friend who was, she said, terribly kind. Gordon went to boarding school. When they came to live in Australia, all the mothers were impressed by Gordon's beautiful manners.

Did you want to go back?
    Not in the end. It was no place to bring up children.

On their way home Maisie and Mrs Black made their own pilgrimage, to the Taj Mahal, which Dr Ram Shad called 'a tear on the cheek of time'. Both rather tired now, both subdued, they shuffled across inlaid marble courtyards, with canvas coverings on their shoes. Shah Jahan had commissioned the building when his Empress, the mother of his fourteen children, died. Twenty thousand men had worked for twenty years to build it. They looked upwards. It was a wonder of the world. It was a monument to grief which had struck awe into the hearts of beholders for three hundred years.

In an end is a beginning. Let us return to Maisie at the beginning of her journey, to the ship that has not quite left, and the widening gap between us. The SS *Naloja* has at last gathered steam and is moving quite fast now. Fremantle's roofs, the Town Hall clock, the pine trees on the Esplanade, the distant shallow hills, have formed a single line that is sliding swiftly past her. The further out she goes, the more she'll see of the flat white coast she's leaving, that stretches north and south for thousands of empty miles. On this coastline there's no need to reach upward.

'*No doubt you'll find us all very ordinary back here,*' George has written in his farewell letter.

George has been watching the tugs nudge the *Naloja* into her proper channel. By golly those fellows know their stuff! He's always thinking about work, about ways of making the world work. For a moment he forgets everything else.

When he looks around he sees the ship following its own course as smoothly as a bath toy pulled on a string. Already it looks smaller, frailer, on its way to becoming a paper cut-out against the horizon. Setting off into a childish map of the world. Has he lost her? No, he's taken his bearings from the funnel, she's directly beneath it, a brightness he can sense more than see next to the dark hump of Mrs Black.

There is suddenly a lot of water, a lot of sky. Lights flash, red to the left, green to the right, on the lighthouse. Breakers dash about its walls.

The freedom of the open sea is terrifying.

From the moment he met her, took her in his arms on the dance floor, he felt responsible for her. He can't see how that will ever end.

But people cross the oceans every day. And there's that dashed puncture . . . he's going to miss the 6.15. He hopes they'll keep his tea warm. He's actually rather hungry. He has started to enter time again. This is the true farewell.

But Maisie isn't thinking about farewells now. She's being carried out, as swift as a river into the ocean. A wind blows, she's alone, on course. Clouds fill the sky with domes and turrets. Already she sees the women in bright saris coming down the dawn-lit hill. Suddenly it's heaven. This is something she already knew and had forgotten. She would have to learn it again and again.

Are you afraid of dying?
    Yes.

A horn sounds, a ship is leaving. A real ship, a real quay, a real time, sixty years ago. But did George and Maisie really think like this?

It's your story now. I've forgotten.

This is the angle of vision I've inherited. This is everything I know.

She leans out suddenly and waves.

He sees her. Or thinks he does. He doesn't know if anybody else can, but he lifts his hat up, as high as he can reach.

NEW STORIES

THE PHOTOGRAPHER

Oh, my dear — where is that country?
Edith Wharton, *The Age of Innocence*

It was no more than a stick, hacked to a fork, left to strike root in the rail yard at Pittsburgh. One lettuce-coloured leaf waved from the fork as if to fulfil an expectation. It was the only growing thing in a wasteland of gravel and tracks, smoke and telegraph poles. For some reason I thought of Australia. As my train moved out I looked back.

Why do I make these journeys, if not to live in every moment? Yet that day all the way from Pittsburgh to Cleveland, I did not notice my companions nor the grey towns and fragile spring fields outside my window. I was travelling once again across the desert to Kalgoorlie, rocking across a sea of red dust and mulga, saltpans and clumps of that bush which looked dusted with ash. All the windows were open for the heat, my veil was cast back so I could drink in the liquid golden light. My boys called out at a scattering flock of emus. It was late afternoon, the train was accompanied by its own long black shadow.

You felt surprise here too to see a tree growing, its sun-splashed white trunk rising above the scrub. The rest had all been felled for the camp fires of the prospectors, Claude told me, and later, when companies like his moved in, to drive the machinery of the mines.

We left Kalgoorlie in September 1913, nearly twenty years ago. I would have said that my memories of that time were shadowy and inconsequential to the course of my life since then. Yet in a flash I could trace it all back to that stump and leaf in the Pittsburgh station.

As soon as I reached Cleveland I caught the train back to Pittsburgh again.

Of course there was no purpose for the trip to Cleveland. Winters I spend with my sister Minnie in Baltimore. In early spring I pack up and take the first train out, from one day to the next. Min only knows I'll turn up again for Christmas. The rest of the year is for myself.

I started this way of life on 24 October 1929. The Crash, and we went with it. Everything, my dowry and Claude's mines all over the world. Without it I guess we would have gone on as we had from the beginning of our marriage. Behind our fences and our guards and our acres, we had become untouchable. I'd hardly caught a streetcar alone, although I often wanted to. When Claude came with the news, it was as if we were alone together for the first time in years. We were staying in our house in New York. The boys were

still in college and all the staff and friends had somehow disappeared. It was the first time I ever saw doubt
in his face. He thought it was Nature, that some men,
the smart brave ones, should conquer and accumulate.
Now Nature itself was defeated. Or else, after all, he
wasn't really smart and brave. He packed his own bag
with shaking hands and waited for the dark so he could
slip past his creditors. There was no question of going
together. Our sons, he said, like us, like all Americans,
would have to look after themselves. I've never seen
him again.

Where is he now? Did he manage at the last minute
to pull some strings, take a boat to South America, dig
up some long lost project? He looked puffy in the face,
yellow-eyed, when he left. He may be dead. Who
knows? In extremity we incline to our oldest beliefs,
and the God of his childhood was a vengeful God. He
may have taken this as punishment for his sins! But I
don't have to think about Claude any more. Of all the
things I've shed — corsets, visiting cards, the rings on
my hand — perhaps this gives me the greatest pleasure. To be free at last of Claude's thoughts.

I left at dawn. A man was sleeping on the porch and
I threw him the key to the house. The only way to
escape is to have nothing to escape from. The autumn
air was alive on my cheeks, the city was sleeping
amongst its tattered newspapers, yesterday's headlines
trampled by panicking feet. I caught my first streetcar
then to Grand Central Station.

I had a small bequest left to me by an aunt, in my

maiden name, Stroud, as she'd insisted. I used to use the interest for donations to feminist societies, Marie Stopes, the wives of strikers, causes that Claude would have no sympathy for. As if by God's judgement this tiny virtuous sum had survived the 24th. I took the whole lot out that day and stowed it . . . somewhere safe. It's just enough now for third-class trains and the cheapest rooming houses if I winter with Minnie. I don't know how long it will last. I'm not a freight car rider, I haven't joined the soup lines – not yet. But I sometimes sleep in waiting rooms and fields. All that matters in life, honey, I told a young woman who was crying in a station one night, is to find rest.

I eat onions as if they are apples, hang around reading rooms in libraries, breakfast at drugstore counters. There's always plenty of company. I talk with laid-off shoe salesmen, waitresses, bankers, fruit pickers, university professors, actresses, thieves. I talk too damn much. Sometimes I'm sitting by myself and I realise my lips are still moving. I've been from coast to coast, from north to south. I haven't yet met up with any other ex-millionaire's wives, but I've no doubt they're around.

When I returned to Pittsburgh I took a bed in a dormitory opposite the station. Every day I bought a paper cup of coffee at the station diner – I always buy coffee when I can find it – and then I drank it on a bench on the platform from where I could see the tree. Trains pulled in and out, crowds swelled and cleared. Whistles blew, steam filled the platform and dispersed. The leaf kept on fluttering. And every time I saw it I felt that same drop, that tug deep inside that you feel after somebody's death. Who or what was I mourning?

In Kalgoorlie everyone came and left on trains. Alice, Eddie, even Dwyer years before, had made their entrances and exits that way. At every beginning and end there was a train.

We arrived at night. In the last stretch we made our way through great white dumps like hills from the mines and camels grazing in moonlight bright as day. After thirty hours on the hard bench the boys' heads were heavy on my shoulders and my maid Louise was biting her lip to hold back tears. But Claude leapt from the train as it hissed to a halt and strode down the platform, calling for a porter, not crushed nor tired nor dusty, already looking ahead. At such a time I thought of the word 'husband', and I said it to myself as if it were a password, a key to delivery.

We married late. I was nearly thirty and Claude was thirty-five. He was a cousin of the McCurdeys, another old Presbyterian family in Baltimore so close to mine they were almost kin. Claude was a geologist recently returned from years abroad. He came to pay a visit to the Baltimore McCurdeys. I could hardly believe it when he started to call. But being Claude he soon made his suit unmistakeable. He was capable of heart-stopping gestures – the flowers, the little notes, signed confidingly, C. We were married in three months. Our first son was born within the year. In the first years of our marriage I was always a little dazed.

Why me? I used to ask Claude. He laughed – I always made him laugh. Because I trust you, he said. He was short and tautly built with white teeth and fine, receding black hair and blue eyes that went dark when he was watchful. He was the intellectual in the family, with a geologist's daring theories of evolution, and a distrust of human nature. In the end I believe trust was the reason for his marriage. I was rich and well-connected, but also – because there never had been anything I wanted enough to lie for – without guile.

I knew we were incongruous together, he so dapper and purposeful, me with my books always falling from my arms, my frizzy hair, my reading groups and salons, my vague promises to myself that I would do something with my life. I sensed that we were also different in a fundamental way, but I named it Male and Female, or Science and Art.

Claude was away a great deal in our marriage and it sometimes crossed my mind that this was a contract with a stranger for which you paid with your life.

I dismissed this thought the moment he returned.

When he told me he had bought a goldmine in Western Australia and that he wished me and the boys to spend a year there with him, I never thought to refuse. It was 1912.

There had been a dust storm the week before we arrived. Someone had left the windows open in the big dark verandahed bungalow Claude brought us to. There was red grit dusting the mirrors, in the beds and spoons and cups, in the warm rusty water. Flies on our faces woke us in the morning. Crows circled above the wide red roads. The little houses were made of timber and corrugated iron. There was no green grass anywhere. Like a giant factory, all day the city echoed with hoots and blasts, train whistles and the rhythm of the stamps. Without hills or forests to contain it, it trailed away into the desert, where camels roamed and men still died of thirst.

Our house had stables and a dusty piano and three palm trees on a yellow lawn. It was called *Waverley*. I had a maid (who couldn't stop crying) and twelve steamer trunks and a college education. But that first day, like a woman arriving to a tent in the scrub or a shack by a mine, I wanted to sit down and cry: *What have you brought me to? Why have you brought me here?*

Dear Min, I have resigned myself. There is no cultural or artistic society of any kind here. I am resolved to read and play the piano and improve my mind.

I employed a cook, Dulcie Feathers, and a groom and a woman to scrub. I tried to comfort Louise by playing the piano to her but it sounded desolate, out of tune. I took my sons to the nearby school. Strange birds laughed at us from the trees by the gate, as if we were on the threshold of a new, savage world. Soon my boys were playing cricket every day on a red gravel pitch amongst yellow grass. They were scrambling over the great white dumps, the children's secret territory. At every spare moment they slipped across the back fence of *Waverley*. At supper they were secretive, abstracted. They fell asleep at once, like little dogs.

'What will I do with myself?' I said to Claude as I saw him off at the door in my wrapper. It was early morning, those birds were laughing again. He would not reappear until nine or ten at night. He generally dined with colleagues at a hotel or even in his little tin office at the Blue Star mine.

'My dear Marian,' he said, 'I am sure you will find a way to spend that marvellous vitality of yours.' He was always at his best in the morning, his eyes dark and alert, his thin black hair combed sleek against his head. He loved anything new, a new project, a new day. He disapproved of anything that might hold him back. He was as humorous and strict as a father, and as impervious to complaint.

I dressed for town and had myself driven down Hannan Street. Someone had made great plans. It was a huge avenue, treeless, with grand two-storeyed facades and a clock in a town hall tower. The immense white glare of the sky bore down upon it. Each bar and store had a verandah so that the sidewalks were in shade. Men in soft felt hats sat talking together at the roadside. The dusty tram poles down the centre of the street disappeared into the horizon. It was the Wild West grown tame.

I bought stamps at the Post Office, and asked the clerk if it was possible to order American newspapers. He told me promptly that there was always a copy of the *New York Times* in the reading room of the Mechanics' Institute. I went straight there. The latest copy was six months old of course, and I was suddenly aware of the swish of my skirts across the polished boards. I could see no other woman there. I went outside onto the verandah. Men were lying back in deck chairs, reading. There were no spare chairs. I stood a little while at the balustrade, and watched a tram rattle down Hannan Street. I saw a sign, DWYER'S STUDIO, outlined in unlit bulbs on the roof opposite. Upstairs at the Palace Hotel someone was playing a piano. *Dear Min, The women here have had the vote since 1899! But it's a man's world.*

Pianos here were affected by the desert climate, the piano tuner said. The strings were pulled taut by dryness. A little linseed oil and beeswax could be applied to the surface — he swept his big-knuckled hand gently over the curve of the lid — but the strings were best left to him. He was a large young man, oddly built, with sloping shoulders and a softly protruberant belly. His name was Eddie Allum.

He said that he was kept very busy attending to the

pianos of Kalgoorlie. Most folk bought one as soon as they could afford it. All the young ladies were taking lessons. In Kalgoorlie they loved their music. They were as devoted to their singers as they were to their liquor and their good times! He was so shy he looked away to smile.

I asked him how long he'd lived in Kalgoorlie. He'd only recently arrived, he said, although he'd always wanted to come here. As a child in Perth he used to watch the trainloads of miners pass on their way from the ships of Fremantle. His mother told him they were going to the Golden Mile. His eyes shone in his long grave face. I could see he was an idealist.

The first night that Alice sang in Kalgoorlie was my introduction also to the city's social life. The Blue Star mine held its Annual Dinner that night at the Palace Hotel. There were bowls of ferns and roses on the tables beneath an enormous crystal chandelier. The Palace dining-room was apparently the acme of grandeur here, but it all looked a little overdone and provincial to me. I knew my plumpness and the plainness of my dress would be a disappointment for the other mine owners' wives, turned out in all their finery, their hair fussily dressed. The menu was English, a brown soup, a joint with Yorkshire pudding, a treacle tart. There was wine or ale for the gentlemen but Claude of course was a teetotaller all his life.

Port was served and Mr Spencer Cook of the Palace introduced a young woman standing in front of the

grand piano in the corner. Miss Alice Farrar, soprano
from Perth, on her very first engagement here.

Or anywhere, I thought. The young singer nodded
rapidly at the piano, gripped her hands together, rolled
her eyes to the ceiling and began. Her voice was
tremulous at first but by the time she steered the song
to completion, it had found its resonance, with a
purity that seemed to go beyond ordinary sweetness.
The audience sat very still. She was like a child in a
matron's dress, her slim neck rising out of folds of
grey tulle clasped by roses at her breast. Her eyebrows
were fine and arched in her round face. Her cheeks
were flushed. I heard later that before she sang she
always drank a glass of port brought to her room by
the kitchen staff. That night they were all watching
her, their faces around the kitchen door. The applause
was surprised and warm: we had all momentarily
adopted her. Her very shyness attracted speculation.
Without a word she bowed and fled. The accompanist
stood up and I saw that it was Eddie Allum, his big
hands dangling from the sleeves of his dinner jacket,
his eyes shining again. As the gentlemen retired for
whisky and cigars I looked around for Claude, but he
was nowhere to be seen.

The room to which Alice fled was at the dark end of
the hotel's upstairs corridor, overlooking the Palace
courtyard with its stables and pump and woodpile. You
could read the time from the Town Hall clock there.

When at last I paid my call on her, I saw how easy it was to duck into the courtyard from Egan Street and slip up the back stairs. At the top was Alice's room, with its little verandah enclosed in latticework. She lived between the maids' world and the guests'.

I used to picture her here at night, pacing up and down in her rustling dress, sipping port that the little red-haired maid brought her, while she waited for nine o'clock to strike, and the clattering of dessert plates in the kitchen. Her room was sweet with the scent of honeysuckle and roses. The delivery boys brought the bouquets straight up the back stairs.

Eddie Allum and Miss Farrar used to practise together at the upstairs piano at the Palace. It was said that you could sometimes hear Alice singing if you passed down Hannan Street at the quiet time of the afternoon. Already she was making quite a name for herself as Spencer Cook's little songbird.

I saw them walking together one sunset in Victoria Park. Louise and I were fanning off flies in the oriental rotunda. I recognised the young singer beneath a large flowery hat: in that dusty park she was the only fresh pretty thing to be seen. They were walking along a row of scrappy rose bushes, not arm in arm, but idly, half indifferent, like brother and sister. Eddie touched his cap but we did not speak.

In December I thought to have some photographs made to send as *cartes postales* to America, likenesses of my family prospering in its new venture. By now my life had taken on a rhythm, like the pounding of the stamps, or the crunch of buggy wheels across our gravel drive. All the respectable ladies in Kalgoorlie had come to call. At first I did not know quite what to speak to them about. They all complained about the heat and isolation, but if I ventured any criticism they stiffened and raised their eyebrows. So I served them coffee on the verandah and praised the birds and the clarity of the light. I made vague hints at some larger study I was engaged in, and thus avoided invitations to join card afternoons, amateur theatricals or charitable organisations. They suspected I was pretentious and eccentric. At heart of course, I was one of them.

I found the tomes I had brought with me to study, *A History of the Civil War, Great Religions of the World* etc were too heavy to hold in the heat. They started to look dusty and marooned, like old men whose day was past. I acquired a bicycle, and for the first time since childhood felt an exuberance for no good reason apart from physical space. I felt boisterous, hedonistic, reckless. I wondered if I had been affected by the spirit of the place.

One afternoon late I cycled to Jack Dwyer's studio on Hannan Street. I wanted to inspect his work, and if it pleased me to make an appointment for a sitting. Jack Dwyer was the best-known photographer in Kalgoorlie. His studio was said to be as up-to-date as any in Perth or Melbourne or even London. It occupied the whole top floor next door to the Palace and its glass roof had been specially designed. I had noticed Dwyer on Hannan Street, tall and slim in a white suit and Panama hat, an unusual dandyish figure.

I parked my bicycle in the courtyard, climbed the stairs and pushed through a set of heavy black curtains in the doorway. The blinds that covered the glass ceiling had been drawn back. Full in the hazy light stood Alice Farrar, against a canvas backdrop of a moonlit woodland scene. Dwyer had his back to me, bent into his camera, his head beneath a black cloth, one arm in shirt sleeves raised to signal. To the side, watching the proceedings was Eddie Allum. As I came through the doorway Alice's eyes met mine. Down came Dwyer's arm. Alice had to keep still. For some immeasurable little time our eyes were locked together, on and on. There was a click. Dwyer emerged from beneath the black hood. Alice and I removed our gaze from one another. Everybody breathed again.

Dwyer put his coat on, and offered us Chinese tea. He said he had no more appointments for the day and lit a spirit stove behind a screen. Eddie went in search of seats for us. He drew cane settees and rustic benches into a circle amongst the plaster Grecian pillars, vases of ostrich feathers, fur rugs and decorated screens. It was like sitting in a stage set, a simulated parlour. Far below in Hannan Street we could hear the evening trams.

Dwyer served our tea in pale green bowls patterned

with dragons. Close up his hands, his face, even his ears were dusted with freckles. He had spent years in the Goldfields as a young travelling photographer.

'This is all so *different*,' Alice Farrar said. She was wearing her flowery hat again, an absurd hat like an upturned garden plot of mauve petunias and ivy, a hat that only a young woman could be forgiven for choosing – in which only a young woman could still look charming. I think now about how young she was – twenty – and how that day she was quite bold and confidential, after the intimacy of being photographed.

'Different from what, may I ask?' Of course Dwyer knew very well. This tea-party had as little to do with the social rituals of Kalgoorlie as an attic in Paris. His blue eyes with reddened lids surveyed the young woman keenly. He had a reputation as a canny if cautious businessman.

'Oh, from everything else! From my entire past!'

'Did you come alone, Miss Farrar?' I asked. I felt an intimacy with her after our curious moment of exchange. She, on the other hand, now that we had been introduced, avoided my eye.

'Yes. But it was all arranged. Mr Huxtable, who's a boarder in my mother's house, wrote to Mrs Violet Cook at the Palace. She's an old friend of his. I do some clerical duties as well as the singing, and I have board at the hotel.'

We were all turned to her. I remember how the presence of a young woman can dominate a room. For a moment we were all transfixed by the mildness of her eyes, the softness of her mouth, the luxurious hair . . . *Somebody loves her*, I thought suddenly. Or had she too been affected by the freedom of this town?

'I have always wanted to sing,' she went on, confidential, trusting as a cherished child. 'Mr Huxtable paid for lessons. This is the first step in my career.'

Before we left, Dwyer took us on a tour of the studio, the dressing-rooms, the darkroom, the retoucher's bench. He showed us boxes of glass plates, portraits, row after row of them, families, weddings, sweethearts, all in their Sunday best.

A few prints were framed to show prospective clients. A view of Hannan Street from Mount Charlotte. The Annual General Meeting of the Chamber of Mines. His photographs were sharply focused, evenly lit, factual, confident. They were conventional. But there was one print of a tree in a dust storm that seemed to shimmer, hold a light that he just held back from. I asked him if he had seen prints from the latest salons in the photographic magazines, prints of landscapes which expressed a mood or frame of mind.

Dwyer said that the subjective was something he detested in his profession. He despised all tricks. He said his job was to record, and to satisfy his client, that a photographer had a duty to things as they are.

I muttered something about 'mystery'.

'Is "mystery" being out of focus? Smudging with lampblack, putting chiffon over the lens?'

Oh well, I said to myself, everything in this outpost

is at least a decade out of date. And after all, didn't the sturdy poses, the uncomplicated compositions, the very clarity of the light, express the spirit of the town?

The Town Hall clock was striking seven, Alice hurried down the stairs and made her way towards the Palace, Eddie following.

On Christmas Eve, Spencer Cook and Mrs Violet Cook gave a soiree at the Palace. A pine tree had been especially brought in on the train from Perth. This time, perhaps because of the smell of pine and the sight of the slender tree shining with little lamps, I was more disposed to enjoy myself. I had to admit that this was happening quite often now. Where once I had seen gaucherie, provincialism, I now saw frankness and good cheer. It was as if my eyes had become acclimatised to these faces in this light: I believed this occurred after I had viewed Dwyer's photographs.

When I told Dwyer of his genius he did not seem to understand. He was at the buffet, shy without his camera, in a freshly-pressed white suit, helping himself to sherry trifle.

'I only photograph what is there,' he said, in his impassive way.

'Exactly.' I felt curiously at home with him. I couldn't leave him alone. I didn't quite believe in his disingenuousness. I wanted to strike up against the flinty watchfulness I knew was there. 'I am talking about vision, Mr Dwyer.'

There was a string quartet from Perth, and a reading from Dickens' *A Christmas Carol* by Spencer Cook himself. A log fire was simulated with red paper and the room was decorated with paper chains, sprigs of holly and cottonwool snow. Yet it was so hot that all the windows were open on to the verandah. Wasn't the Christ child himself born in a hot country?

Alice Farrar was ushered in to conclude the evening's program. I looked around for Claude. He was standing at the back of the room with an air of listening intensely to his companions, which he adopted when most pre-occupied with something else. He had been offhand about this party, rushing in late to change and shave. These past few weeks he had been working so hard that he did not get home until well after I was asleep.

I saw at once that Miss Farrar had changed. She was wearing a new gown of moss-green satin, from which emerged her compact white shoulders and neck. Diamond eardrops swung beneath her lush brown hair, swept up pompadour style. It was said that Mrs Violet Cook had taken her under her wing. She no longer looked like a Sunday school teacher at a concert, nor quite like a singer in a mining town. Her voice bloomed straight from her throat. When she sang '*Ah, may the red rose live always*', her voice expressed so much longing and anticipation, it verged on breaking point. She finished with '*Silent Night*'. A bouquet of lily-of-the-valley was presented amongst much applause, and she was persuaded by Mrs Cook to accept a glass of punch.

As I approached I heard her tell the ladies sur-
rounding her that this was the first Christmas she had
ever spent away from her mother. Again our eyes met
but she seemed distracted as I complimented her, and
excusing herself to Mrs Cook, she left.

Christmas Eve. No night sky could ever be more omi-
nously spangled than that of the desert. I heard the
crickets in the silence outside my open bedroom window. Claude had stayed on with the men in the smoking
room of the Palace. In the parlour two bulging schoolboy socks were propped up in the unused fireplace: I
had played Santa Claus, but I could not conjure up any
nostalgia. Strange in this flat dull place to feel such a
quickening, a longing like the edge of sweetness in Alice
Farrar's voice. I watched myself undress in my mirror. I
let my straps slip down my shoulders, saw the moonlight full on my low white breasts.

Alice's mother was a widow, a pretty woman faded
from work and worry. Her husband left her a solid
cottage near the sea in Fremantle. The young widow
took in boarders, never more than three at a time,
clerks and businessmen in the port. One, old Mr
Huxtable, lived with them for years.

She never forgot to mention her husband's name at
least once a day. All her duties were in devotion to his
memory, she told her daughter. She taught Alice to be

devoted, modest and hard-working. To keep her heart ever ready for service. Once as she kneaded dough she spoke of love, what every woman must have, she said, her floury face smiling as her ruined red hands shaped the bread. Alice felt sick with embarrassment and pity.

All this I invented out of years of speculation.

I elected not to spend the summer on the coast, unlike the other mine managers' wives. I had just begun to grow accustomed to my new life. The boys were on vacation, gone from dawn till dark. Sometimes I glimpsed them running beside the railway track in ragged breeches and straw hats. Or in a pack of boys around a tap, each taking his turn to put his mouth over the spout. Sometimes I wondered if I should rein them in, give them chores, insist on shoes: but the heat made me languorous, and at heart I was glad for them to experience such freedom.

The heat seemed to make no difference to Claude. I urged him to come home in the middle of the day to rest, but he laughed at that as something for the Champagne Charlies, the drinkers and poseurs. For a man who worked eighteen hours a day in a tin office on a minefield, he seemed remarkably unspent.

And Louise? Louise was courting, dabbing eau de Cologne on her neck, walking arm in arm around our garden with a young mining engineer who was besotted with my pale, melancholy little companion from Iowa. Her eyelashes were wet now from the thought of leaving him.

I grew restless. In the early evenings, as other women worked in their furnaces of kitchens and their husbands washed themselves in a tub on the back verandah, I cycled over the warm-baked crust of the earth. Past the barking dogs, the lively shabby children, the little houses by the wide red roads. I even rode down Brookman Street, where no respectable woman went (I saw nothing of the Ladies of the Night, only ordinary girls, bringing in washing, chopping wood). I liked to ride slowly down Hannan Street, where all the stores and pubs were open, and the odours of sawdust and hops and coffee hung in the warm air. All the citizens of Kalgoorlie seemed to be taking a walk. Young ladies emerged from the stores carrying parcels, frockcoated businessmen strolled like royalty up the sidewalks, hordes of weather-beaten men roamed in and out of the hotels. A woman of exotic beauty was escorted from a motor car into the Palace. Once I saw a woman ride in from the desert, leap from her horse, toss the reins over a rail, and disappear into Brennan Brothers' Drapery. Her bonnet dangled down her back, her arms and face were brown as leather, she walked bow-legged like a man. None of the clerks in Brennans' would have dreamt of being rude to her.

A black man and two women and some children walked slowly up to the end of Hannan Street and disappeared into the bush around Mount Charlotte.

I parked my bicycle in Dwyer's courtyard.

'Well Mr Dwyer, what have you got for me to see?'
I prowled around his studio in a bold way that I couldn't
resist with him. I'd bought two or three prints from
him and intended to build up a collection to take back
with me to the States. I let him know what pleased
me. I paid handsomely.

I came upon a portrait hung to dry in the darkroom. It was a profile of Alice Farrar. Her chin was
lifted, her eyes lowered in serene composure. Her lacy
gown was pulled off her shoulders, her gleaming hair
tumbled down her neck. A strong black silhouette
traced her brow and throat and breast. And beyond it
was another, paler shadow as if the woman's image was
in the process of infinite duplication. It was artful,
intimate, unlike any other portrait by Dwyer.

'Is this for sale?'

'Between you and me, someone else has paid for it.
An admirer I believe.'

In summer the corrugated iron roof and walls of the
Hippodrome on Hannan Street made roller-skating
out of the question, but once the summer had moved
on it opened its doors again. As a girl I had skated
every day in winter, and now it became one of my
eccentric pleasures to cruise around the Hippodrome's great wooden floor, with – if I say so myself
– an ease and expertise rare in that part of the world.

The roller-skating season opened officially with a

Fancy Dress Ball. I decided to attend. The idea of circulating free and alone in the social whirl appealed to me – and yes, just a little, the chance to show off my unexpected grace. In a gesture to costume, I set off in Claude's cowboy hat and his holster hanging on his belt which just met around my waist. Everybody had returned from the coast and almost a thousand crowded into the galleries or around the rink, laughing and stumbling to the strains of the Kalgoorlie String Band.

Dwyer had set up lights and his second-best camera in a cloak room off the vestibule. He was doing a roaring trade. In front of his backcloth passed clowns and gypsies, a muleteer, an Indian chief, a shepherdess and the Queen of Night, all standing solemn for a moment on their roller-skates. At his age and level of success Dwyer could surely have afforded to send an assistant, but he appeared to be enjoying himself, ducking in and out from under his black cloth, calm and courteous, dressed as himself, all in white.

A huge Butterfly took up position in the glaring lights. It was Eddie Allum. His costume was most painstakingly contrived. He wore a tunic of grey worsted material daubed in curlicues, and thick black hose. His wings were made of gauze painted in radiant sunbursts, stretched across an intricate structure of wire. His coronet of generously curled antennae waved over his long grave face. How trustingly he stood there in his skates, slouched and stolid as a boxer, his potbelly straining his tunic, his big-knuckled hands dangling by his shapely legs. He was the very opposite, I would have thought, of everything a butterfly represents. Why had he agreed to this? What irony, if any, was intended?

A Spanish Lady was adjusting his wings and antennae. It was Miss Farrar, in a high comb and lace mantilla, a red rose pinned behind her ear. She was preoccupied, she did not seem to recognise me when I waved. She was thinner, her cheeks were not as round. She was pale and elegant and rather stern, as if she had been ill, frowning as she adjusted Eddie's costume. My guess was that she had dreamed it up for him. The butterfly which hovers around the flower . . . What vision had she had?

I did not stay long amongst the crowd. There was no room for real skating. Couples, families, groups of friends, hooked their arms around each other, falling and joking. Claude would have been impatient if he'd come. He preferred to work. I thought as I rode home in my cowboy hat that our marriage had become as flattened and spare as the country around us.

Our year in Kalgoorlie was nearly over. Louise began to pack the steamer trunks, red-eyed about what she called the Decision.

'It boils down to this,' I reported to Claude in one of the rare times he dined with me. 'The Love of One's Life or of the Country of One's Birth.'

'Oh spare me Louise's dilemmas,' he said. He was

so busy that he slept in his study now, and was not even sure that he could leave when we did.

One afternoon the palms by the verandah started rustling, and great flocks of cockatoos cried overhead. The air became bronze and heavy. Dogs barked and the horses swished their tails. Dulcie Feathers ran to bring in the washing, and the groom to fetch the horses into the stables. Down the road the school bell rang loudly to summon the children. Louise and I closed the windows and doors.

I lay on my bed as the dust blew around the verandahs, sprayed my window, threw the world into darkness. The roof creaked and the floors rocked and the pictures tilted on the walls. I felt myself to be in another room, high up over the darkened city, and on the bed in this room I saw or rather *felt* two bodies lying together. Far below a barrel rolled, a branch crashed, somebody shouted, but on this bed they could only hear each other. The man was whispering, telling her how he felt when he was away from her. How her voice sounded, the first time they met. The man's voice was familiar and yet hoarse, strange. Faintly through the storm a clock struck.

The wind dropped, the darkness lightened into a sort of sunset and I left my bed and picked my way down the street. Children were streaming out of the school gate carrying broken branches, running to play amongst the fallen telegraph poles.

It was soon after the dust storm that Alice Farrar went missing. Dwyer gave me the news. We met on Hannan Street mid-morning: Dwyer confessed that he could not properly attend to his work. She had sung at the Palace one evening, looking ill. She had missed some notes and left a song unfinished, fleeing the room. That was four days ago. She had not been seen since, in the town or at the railway station. A search-party had been organised with an Aboriginal tracker. Dwyer promised to keep me informed.

Some Afghan cameleers brought her into the town. A camel train passed down Maritana Street, and stopped a moment by the verandah of the Palace. After they had resumed their stately pace and disappeared down Hannan Street, Miss Farrar was found slumped over a bench on the verandah, shoeless, hatless, still in a satin evening gown, her arms and face crimson, her lips swollen, her eyes closed.

A doctor had been called and she was being attended in her room by Mrs Violet Cook herself, Dwyer told me.

She was recovering from dehydration: she was intent on going home, but was not yet well enough to travel.

She would see nobody.

We were to leave in a week. I heard the whispers at my dutiful farewell tea-party. Of course she was expecting a child. To a married man. It was, after all, a common story on the Golden Mile. The men with two families . . . everybody had a story to tell. But a girl like that! They spoke reluctantly, furtively in front of me. Perhaps it was a measure of her former charm that she was spoken of now with pity, not disgust, but a pity that had something grim and irrevocable to it, as if she was consigned forever to a different caste.

On the day of our departure, I took the fifty pound note I had ready for the journey and thrust it in my bosom and cycled hatless down the streets to the back entrance of the Palace. I saw a little red-haired maid I recognised from the dining room hanging out table-cloths in the courtyard. I threw my bicycle down and hurried up to her and even remembered her name.

'Millie, do you know where Alice Farrar is?' Millie stared at me from behind her mask of freckles. 'Would you give her this?' I thrust my card at her with shaking hands. *Mrs Marian Stroud McCurdey*. She ran up the staircase leading from the courtyard, then clattered down again and bent over her washbasket. 'She says you can go up,' she said. I noticed that she had blushed, that she was flaming beneath her freckles, as only red-heads do, as if they are more honest than other people.

I knocked at the door at the top of the stairs. Alice Farrar called 'Come in.' She was sitting in an armchair on her verandah enclosed with latticework. I sat down on the other side of a little cane table. You could hear pigeons cooing in the roof and down below the clatter and voices of the kitchen. For a while we said nothing but watched the shadows of birds swoop over the courtyard wall. I was reminded of a harem within those wooden lattices, of seeing but being unseen.

Alice was in a wrapper, her hair in a tousled plait. She looked like a sick child, or a very old woman. Her eyes were sunken and there were shiny red patches on her face where the skin had peeled away.

'Oh my dear,' I said.

'Don't call me dear.' She kept watching the birds.

'My poor girl.'

'I'm not your girl. I don't wish to be anyone's "girl" any more.'

'I'm sorry.'

'Don't be sorry. *I* should be sorry! Guilty – I used to break out in guilt all over, like sweat. But it's all sweated away now.' She passed her hand across her forehead. I could see that she was not much past fever, and that I should not stay long. Through the lattice I could read two of the four huge faces of the Town Hall clock. Ten to ten.

'And yet you know,' she went on, reaching over the table, touching my sleeve, 'at heart I can't get past the belief that I was innocent. As if that matters!'

'Well, you can sing about it.'

'I only sang for love; that was the trouble.'

We were silent for a little. She seemed deep in thought. 'But his beautiful white teeth are yellowing at the roots,' she said.

I put my fifty pound note on the table. 'I'm leaving Kalgoorlie today,' I whispered. 'I'm going back to the States. I just wanted to say . . . I wish you well . . .'

I'll tell Claude the wind blew it out of my hand, I thought, even then, the wife.

She threw the note back at me. 'I'd give *you* money if I could! Money to run away . . . I ran away because I heard a woman's voice crying out in the desert. I couldn't stop hearing it, even when I was trying to sing myself. I ran and ran until I came upon an old Afghan shouting at his camel. Do you know what he was shouting? *Liar! Liar!*' She laughed until the tears ran down her face.

The clock struck ten, I let myself out. The note fluttered from the table behind me like a falling leaf.

I am sitting on the bench in the station at Pittsburgh. It's early evening, I am waiting for the train to Cleveland again. My little tree has lost its leaf and its power to move me has all but worn off. Time to move on.

There were rumours of trouble in Europe when we left, the gold market was jumpy, the whole town restless. There was quite a little send-off party for us at the station, some mine managers and their wives, Dulcie Feathers, the Blue Star office staff. At the back, tall Jack Dwyer. He did not have his camera, but even so I wondered what he was seeing. Claude and I stood side by side on the little platform outside the guard's van, while the boys hung out of the carriage window and Louise sat sobbing her heart out behind them. (Soon after our return she paid a visit to her folks in Iowa, married her second cousin and stayed there all her life.)

'Do you have any regrets?' I asked Claude out the corner of my mouth as we waved and smiled.

He said that he did not, that he felt he had done his best.

The whistle blew and I whispered in his ear, *Liar*.

As the train left the city, he turned to go into the carriage and without looking at me he said, 'I do not think I can change.'

I didn't know then that for a long time after we left Kalgoorlie all other landscapes would look pallid and crowded. That for years I would be restless for the freedom I found there. It was just past noon. In that white light all I could see were the great dumps and craters, the distant poppet heads, the smoke and red dust rising across the plains. I pulled my veil down and went inside.

If I met Claude on the road, would we even recognise each other? My hair is wild, my face is weather-beaten, I've cut the corners off my sneakers for my toes. I'm still fat, in spite of all the walking and the shortage of meals. When I have a loaf of bread I tear into it with both hands.

Or perhaps we would fall into step together for a while. After all, are our stories so different from all the others on the road?

After all, is what happened so very important?

———

In 1927, Dwyer visited me in Baltimore. He had come to America on a tour around the world, a box brownie over his shoulder. His hair was snow white, his face splotched with sun spots. Dry skin covered his hands like rime. He was still slim, immaculate in a white suit, seated in my study. Later he would take a first-class sleeper to New York. He had retired from business, left Kalgoorlie in 1916, a rich man. He had become engaged to a young lady in Perth, but – here he coughed – it had come to nothing. He did not enjoy good health. I sat him beneath the photographs I had bought from him all those years ago, of the dust storm, and the prospector, and the family riding down Hannan Street on the back of the camel. I told him how glad I was now for their detail and clarity. He nodded and smiled but his eyes were distant, he was a tired man.

He told me that Alice Farrar had married Eddie Allum, he had visited them once, in Fremantle where they lived with her mother. There was a child, a girl.

'Was Alice happy when you saw her?'

He said she was not as pretty as she had been and had a rather serious way of talking. But Eddie was very happy. Eddie was just the sort to rush off and volunteer when war was declared, he said.

Eddie had got his head blown off on a beach in Gallipoli.

Dwyer heard later that Alice and her daughter had gone East. He had lost all trace of her.

A train pulls in and people pour out of it. Strangers brush past my legs, pause to turn up a collar, light a cigarette. I climb aboard, find a seat in the warm smoky carriage. The tree is lit from the train window, framed in darkness, shadowless.

THE NEW DARK AGE

Now that the long winter was over, and all the clues to his convalescence, the little table by the couch for his books and remote controls, the earthenware pot for Chinese herbs, the meditation tapes, had been packed away, now that he'd resumed his place in the world, George was conscious more and more of a twinge of misgiving, like guilt or nostalgia, as if for something or someone he missed.

In the shop, old customers and friends congratulated him on his recovery, with eyes that followed his to avoid looking at the thinness of his body. He said *cancer* whenever necessary, not 'sick' or 'unwell', in the same way that he'd said *die*, refusing 'pass away'. Back from the brink, he discovered that he had an urge to bear testimony. What was his message? What did he have to tell them?

Every time he tried to collect his thoughts, someone interrupted him. Of course he was tired. The lunchtime rush made him dizzy. There was also the Rip Van Winkle effect: he had just installed the computer when he left for hospital, leaving Ulla to wage a single-handed battle with its teething problems, and she was now very much the expert. She'd even fed a 'Welcome Back George' logo onto their receipts, though he soon put a stop to that. In a return to their old sparring form, she accused George of being a Luddite. Not at all, he told her gravely, modern pharmacology had saved his life.

It was his tenth day back, but still the shop did not look like his. There was a subtle change of direction in the stock. Ulla, not having strong musical tastes herself, always responded to the market. They now sold a lot of pop and rock, Alanis Morissette and Nirvana, and compilations of World Music, and more well-known classical pieces, especially if they'd become a movie theme. Meanwhile Country and Western, contemporary jazz, the avant-garde, had dwindled, gone ragged, lost their edge. Some of these he found in a newly labelled bin, 'Discount Discs'. Ulla had the print-outs to justify her decisions, but he noted that some of his favourite customers, the ones for whom he put aside new recordings if he thought they'd like them, had trickled away.

All this of course he could turn around in a few weeks. The thought made him weary. Although he'd always said that *George's* was just a way of making money to support his music habit, there was a time when he'd been happy to feed it all his energy and creativity, and taken pride in its success, but that seemed long ago. Now he wondered if he was really suited to being a businessman. Out the window the newly renovated arcade with its little trickling fountain looked like a film set. People ambled past, licking ice-creams, bathed in a kind of cathedral twilight. It all looked false to him, temporary, unreal. He'd preferred the old premises, between *Perretti Tailors* and the *Wing Lo Deli*. Perhaps the rot had started to set in a couple of years ago, when they moved into the smarter end of town.

But what would he rather be doing?

Late in the afternoon, on impulse, he put on the little Brahms intermezzo which he had listened to all through the winter. At once he was taken back, so intensely that he felt exposed, and went to listen in the office. What an austere, intense winter it had been, his season of reckoning. Day after day he lay on the couch as the leaves fell in the courtyard and his life unravelled before him. He was like a monk, in loose clothes, his bald head covered by the dark red Tibetan beanie Kristina had found for him. There seemed to be a ring of silence around him. Chaste, isolated, engrossed, he was cut off from everyone except Kristina. His daughter Grace sent him loving postcards from South America where she was travelling with her boyfriend. He had Kristina to himself. He waited all day for the sound of her key in the door and the sight of her tired, pale face with its new anxiety and kindness. He couldn't have survived without her.

In the cruel, colourless twilights he saw that all his time had been spent in accommodating people, keeping the show on the road, in compromise and self-deception. So here you are, the little melody seemed to say, this after all is how it is. He felt as if the most innocent part of him had sat down and wouldn't go on.

Before the piece had ended he realised that the shop was empty; no browser could bear too much of Brahms's penetrating sadness. Ulla had turned to look at him through the glass partition of the office. Their eyes met as she peered over the top of her tortoise-shell glasses and he saw the sharp, watchful query in them.

He watched her moving on along the shelves, with her cropped grey hair and her habitual white shirt and black slacks, her diligence like a reproach to him. She felt his distance, sensed that everything had changed. He knew her ethics, her sense of fitness. She had not received her due. Not that there hadn't been lavish thanks, and a generous bonus. But she deserved to share, however symbolically, in his recovery. She had contributed to it. She expected a gesture of acknowledgement.

Still affected by the spirit of the music, he walked out of the office and asked her home to dinner.

As soon as he issued the invitation, he regretted it. Ulla pulled out a bus timetable from her bag and pushing on her glasses, consulted it. She announced she would have to catch two buses. He'd forgotten the whole painful ritual. Ulla, for reasons of her own, did not drive, but utilised very ingeniously the scanty public transport system. She tackled travelling arrangements with an air of moral challenge. She was skilled at arranging lifts from neighbours, friends, even customers. Also she walked great distances. She was solid and fit with tanned sandalled feet and a healthy flush on her cheeks.

Years ago, when he first opened *George's*, she often used to come to dinner with Grace and him. She always arrived early, sometimes hours early, so that she ended up chopping parsley, walking the dog, reading bedtime stories to Grace.

He'd just come from a bad divorce and knew nothing of business. In that first year there was no detail of his new life, from invoices to child-rearing, that he did not discuss with Ulla. That was twelve years ago, long before Kristina. When he was about Kristina's age.

He went back in to the office to stop himself offering her a lift. Because he wanted to go home by himself. He wanted to shower, put on some music, cook slowly, without talking. Spend a little time alone with Kristina.

Kristina said: 'Why tonight?' George was ringing her from the car on his way home.

'Why not?'

'Jerzy is coming, don't you remember?'

'They might like each other.' At least he wouldn't be alone with Ulla and Kristina.

'They might *not*.'

'Ulla really held the fort, you know. For all those months.'

'Well, you're the cook,' Kristina said. 'You can ask who you want.'

He'd noticed that Kristina was very sensitive to any reference to last winter. It always softened her, she immediately gave way. He tried not to take advantage of this. He should have rung earlier, but he didn't want Ulla to hear him deal with Kristina's prevarications. She would consider that he was asking Kristina's permission. Even if he shut the office door Ulla had the knack of barging in at the wrong moment. She doesn't even knock, Kristina said. Sometimes he caught himself believing that Ulla read his thoughts.

He turned off the highway onto the ocean road. The black shore was crusted with swimmers, the sky above the horizon was watermelon red. He was playing Theodorakis's *Canto General* and ought to have been uplifted – the summer night, the sensual people, the heroic landscape . . . The triumph of survival. What had he thought he'd learnt from his ordeal? Life was becoming the same old dutiful, half-hearted scramble. Already he'd forgotten what he'd been so certain about. And with it the old question resurfaced: Why? Why me? Medical opinion shrugged its shoulders, but he couldn't help recalling his old suspicion that in his life there was some chronic underlying lie.

Kristina said that she would only come to live with him and Grace if she had a space of her own. The house was very small, a two-bedroomed worker's cottage, one of eight identical houses all joined up in a row. So he converted the old shed at the back fence into a studio for her. It would be a place where she could draw – she liked botanical drawing – or study or simply be by herself. She made it clear that she wasn't going to make any concessions to family life. She had a horror of doing what she didn't want to. But when she started her research at the hospital, she worked so hard that most nights she fell asleep in front of television and on the weekends she napped and read the newspapers. She lived like the daughter of the house, while Grace had always acted like a little wife.

In the end Kristina never used the studio. They started to dump broken chairs there, old bike helmets, collections of *Gramophone* going back ten years, things they no longer needed but were too lazy to throw out. Last winter George cleared himself a path from the door to the desk. It became the place where he went to focus, to attempt to still his mind. He'd been trying to practise this every evening after work.

Something in the room's damp smell and shadowy light seemed to be waiting for him when he opened the door. He sat down, positioned himself. He closed his eyes and saw himself straight-backed at the desk under the window. Beyond the window was the courtyard, the last in the row of courtyards that ran up the street to Monument Hill. He breathed in deeply, and out. He soared above the palm trees and the War Memorial, circled the rising sun of the giant AIF badge . . .

The kitchen flywire door slammed. He opened his

eyes. Kristina came into the courtyard. She stood with one hand cradling the elbow of the other, which held a cigarette. Two crows were sitting among the sticky leaves of the fig tree. Normally she would have paid them a little scientific attention, but tonight she just kept staring into the twilight. If she were happy she wouldn't be smoking. She kept a packet of Drum for emergencies in a tin on the kitchen shelf.

He might as well give up now. His meditation sessions became shorter every day. Although she refused to look at the studio, something about the way she stood seemed like an appeal. Besides he couldn't stop watching her. He loved the look of her standing in the greenish light, her shoulders high with tension, her hair pinned up for the heat, her vulnerable collar-bones, her shining narrow arms. Whenever he saw her he had a feeling of wellbeing.

She wasn't going to tell him about it. In the kitchen he poured a small glass of white wine for them both and put on Ella Fitzgerald. As he prepared to cook he discovered they were nearly out of olive oil. At once Kristina snatched up the car keys and said she felt like a drive. Surely it wasn't the prospect of Ulla that was upsetting her so much? He looked into her face. He'd noticed recently that she looked older. Her long eyes had become more deep-set, as if she'd gone further inside her own head. There were frown lines in the fine weave of her forehead. These past six months had been as hard on her as him. He thought these signs of care ennobled her. Besides, he liked to think that she was catching up with him, that their age difference wouldn't be so marked. He heard the car roar off up the street. She was in the grip of something. He knew how easily she became obsessed. She might park by the ocean for a while, or at the Monument and look down over the city.

'Where's the mobile?' Grace had come into the kitchen in her red silk kimono, her hair in a towel. 'Can I borrow it tonight?' Wafts of flower scents followed her from the shower. He could hear the thud of House music coming from her room.

'In the car. Kristina has taken it.'

Grace came to his elbow at the chopping board. He braced himself, a reflex action. Once she would have said something like: 'I see. And left you to do the cooking. Typical.' She would have used this moment alone with him to warn him that Kristina was selfish and he didn't see it. That she wasn't to be trusted and would let him down one day. But Grace was altogether gentler since she returned from South America. She had left her father in Kristina's care and Kristina had proved her colours. Like a miracle, like sun after rain, there was peace at last in his household.

Grace puzzled up her beautiful plucked eyebrows at George. 'What do you think this means? Denny had a dream last night that he was being unfaithful to me and he was *devastated*.'

'He's afraid of losing you.'

'Why?'

'He's fallen in love with you.'

She half-laughed, pleased. 'Wasn't he before, in the beginning?'

'That was only the beginning.'

It was so long since they'd had guests that George and Kristina were shy and out of practice. Suddenly their small, hot rooms seemed cluttered, on display. They bumped into each other in the hallway as they each rushed to answer the door. In the doorway Jerzy's eyes flicked over George, to make his own prognosis. He'd just come back from long-service leave, six months travelling the world. All winter long his sardonic post-cards, ignorant of George's drama, had dropped through the door. *Travelling is like death*, he'd written, *you see your old life with new affection* . . . Now he surprised George with a bear hug, hampered by an armful of beer.

Ulla arrived loaded with gifts, though it was a long walk from the bus stop. She and George allowed themselves a peck on the cheek. She offered him a large bunch of orange zinnias – the colour of life, she murmured, to no one in particular. Also some bottles of cider – she was now a teetotaller – and a Swedish crispbread for which Kristina had once expressed a liking. Later Kristina would realise she'd forgotten to thank Ulla for this.

Jerzy's hair was longer and greyer, slicked back from his sallow face. He strode through the house to the courtyard, like a Polish cowboy bringing news home to the ranch. Old Perth wasn't so different from other places, he said, opening one of his cans at the courtyard table, there was mediocrity and complacency all over the world.

'But the air isn't as clear,' said Ulla, smiling primly across the table. When feeling shy she often adopted a contrary stance. She was wearing evening glasses with a rhinestone in each corner and a Nordic-looking embroidered shirt. Ulla always looked a little at a loss away from the workplace, sitting still, her hands idle.

Jerzy ignored her. George could see that he didn't warm to Ulla. He would sum her up as bossy: he suspected all middle-aged women of being bossy. George remembered that Jerzy, eternal bachelor, liked women with leather miniskirts and blonde tousled hair. He leaned across to Ulla and asked her to select some dinner music.

Grace stood in the doorway to say goodbye. She kissed George and told him she'd stay the night at Denny's. Soon she would move out with him. She kissed Ulla and for a moment Ulla came alive, beaming, her brown eyes moist behind her glasses. They were all silent for a moment after this vision of radiant youth had disappeared. The fragrance of George's char-grilled capsicum and eggplant wafted over the table like a consolation for the middle-aged. From within the house came the rich strains of *Les Nuits d'été*. A three-star disc. George signalled his approval to Ulla. Was this her taste, or did she know he'd planned to select it?

In the dark courtyard next door he could hear lushly flowing water. Connie was watering. A year ago her husband Sam had died of Alzheimer's and Connie had not yet lost the habit of nurture. She could be heard watering Sam's garden at all hours of the day.

What they had to understand, Jerzy was saying, was that the whole world had entered a new epoch. That this was just the beginning. In these last days of the millennium they were in the grip of historic change. The forces of pragmatism had finally taken over. It was the end of history, the end of knowledge. Knowledge had been replaced with information.

'One thing never changes,' Ulla said. 'Human nature.' She meant: like half-drunk men who hold forth.

After dinner, Kristina had muttered something about making coffee and wandered off into the house. Long ago she had given up on Jerzy, had pronounced him sexist, irredeemable, Polish, like her father, the worst kind. He was a colleague of hers in the laboratory, and used to be a mate, but she had handed him over to George. George and Jerzy used to meet for drinks on Friday night.

Jerzy propped his boots up on Kristina's empty

chair and addressed himself entirely to George. He had visited laboratories in hospitals and universities all over the world. All you needed now were networks and publicists, he said. It was global. He'd visited his cousins in Poland and they had given him their name for it. The new Dark Age.

'I've heard that before,' Ulla said. She was less and less discreetly slapping at the mosquitoes that loved her healthy flesh. George felt achingly tired. Kristina was probably asleep. Ulla was not appeased. The evening was a dud. A bore, a waste of time. As all things were which didn't come from the heart.

When Ulla gathered up her bag for the last bus, George rose at once and insisted he would drive her home. Jerzy could stay and wait for his return if he liked. But Jerzy, taken aback, took his boots off the chair and said he'd find a late-night bar.

Jerzy would have travelled the world from bar to bar. George envied him that careless trust of his own body. They used to talk of going to Cuba together. Now George knew he would never make a trip like that, whisky and cigars and reeling down crumbling avenues at dawn. He had lost the necessary bravado, the necessary romantic belief. Some quota of his mortal energy had been used up. What was left he needed for something else.

Kristina was lying on the bed, a dark shape washed up beneath the fan, as George ushered Ulla out.

He and Jerzy would grow apart, George thought as he drove away from the house. Jerzy would think that George had had the stuffing knocked out of him: the stoic response was to carry on as if nothing had happened. And in some ways he was right. But what George wanted, more than anything else, was to change. George had never quite understood why Jerzy persisted in liking him. He would miss him more because of that.

It was pleasant bowling through the night streets. Ulla was relaxed, looking out the window with her own thoughts, a little smile on her lips. The old ease was back between them. She was pleased with him again.

Over the years he'd probably spent more waking hours with Ulla than with Grace or Kristina, but there were many things he did not know about her. Ulla did not give reasons. Why she'd migrated to Australia, for instance – he suspected a love affair. Why, with her energy and acumen, she continued to work for him.

For a moment he felt nostalgic for their friendship too as it used to be. When he had been raw and lost, the shop a desperate gamble, only Ulla had believed in him. When the sight of Ulla, in her neat black and white, had been pleasing to him every morning. The customers had commented on the good vibe in the shop. On *George's* first anniversary there was champagne for everyone at closing time. Afterwards he and Ulla allowed themselves a little sentimental self-congratulation and finished off the bottles. For some reason, Ulla pulled out from her bag a photograph of herself at seventeen and showed it to him, and he remembered being touched to see how soft her eyes were then, in the round face of a mid-sixties European schoolgirl. It was very late and somehow they ended up on the floor of the office. There had been laughter, an upturned wastepaper basket, carpet burn. George had blotted out most of the details. A last-minute intimation of danger on his part. Ulla's patience. A subdued brushing down. They must never drink again at work! they said the next day. He was relieved they both felt the same. After all, he told himself, he and Ulla came from the same generation. Those were rough-and-ready, more forgiving days.

When did he understand the grip that some people's love could have on you? Its weight, even its peril. In the hospital, Ulla's bunch of wattle had a scent of such virulent sweetness that it seemed to penetrate his brain. He couldn't have peace until, dragging his post-operative drip with him on its trolley, he carried the vase out of his room down the corridor and left it on the reception desk. But back in bed the scent found its way to him. Off he trundled again, this time to dump the flowers in a bin marked 'Hospital Waste'. It took a night for the scent to drift away.

'Of course you'll have to live differently,' Ulla said when she sat by his bed. 'Diet, exercise. No drinking or smoking. A more natural life.' *You caused this. You did this to yourself.* He didn't look at her. 'Does Kristina understand this?' she said.

'I'm re-thinking everything at the moment,' he said suddenly to Ulla when they were a few blocks from her place. 'About my involvement in the shop. The sort of hours I want to put in, the sort of commitment. Even whether to close the shop and turn the whole business into mail order, work alone from home, have a catalogue on the Web, that sort of thing.'

'What aren't you happy with?'

'Nothing. I just want to simplify my life.'

'You're good with customers, George. Much better than with computers. You need people.'

'Maybe,' he said as he pulled up. 'Anyway, I'm giving it some thought.'

As usual, Ulla offered him a crumpled five dollar bill to pay for the lift, though she knew this annoyed him. He shook his head at her and pushed her hand away. She walked slowly up the pathway to her dark-brick home unit through its drab bush garden.

He knew as he drove off how cruel he'd been. She didn't deserve this. For years her first thoughts had been for the shop. She really deserved to be made a partner. Or perhaps she'd known all along how it would end. On the freeway he opened his window to a rush of weedy river breeze. He felt cool and hard and savagely light-hearted.

It was clear at last that it must happen. Ulla would have to go.

Kristina was sitting on the front steps of the verandah, her bare feet on the footpath. The road was awash with the yellow light of the streetlamps. Behind her the black zig-zag roofline of the row of houses ran like a spine up the hill.

Kristina said she felt stifled in the house. She couldn't sleep. He sat down next to her. How unhappy she was, hugging her knees, not able to look at him, her mouth too set to speak. He wished she would tell him what was wrong. They were often at their closest when Kristina had a problem. An insult at work. What a colleague had said. She seemed to attract jealousy. He was very good at helping her.

'Did Jerzy say goodbye?'

'Yes. By the way, he wants to invite you to a game of squash.'

'Good God. I didn't know Jerzy played squash.'

'He doesn't. But he thought it might be good for you. Build you up a bit.'

In spite of herself Kristina laughed. George laughed too, warmed by Jerzy's loyalty.

They heard a trickle of water on the verandah next door and looked at each other: Connie, giving her rubber plant its late-night drink.

Connie had lived in her house all her life. She had seen many occupants come and go in the row. George would be one of the oldest residents now. When he first moved in, Des, in the furthest house, used to organise street Christmas parties, but nine years ago he died of AIDS. In the next house down, a couple of academics, Clare and James, had moved out to a serviced apartment when Clare became crippled with arthritis. Ted, of Ted and Mavis, had a stroke and died in a nursing home. Sweet Mary Van Beem died three years ago of breast cancer. After she died, Kristina had seen a white heron circling over the roofs of the terrace. Then Connie's Sam. Then George.

Every two years. You had to wonder if it was higher than the national average. Or if there was a reason why this row of houses had attracted the attention of a particularly vengeful angel. Death Row, George privately called it. One night last winter he asked Kristina if she ever thought of this. 'It's coming our way,' he said.

'No it's not,' Kristina said instantly. 'It jumps around. Ted and Mavis lived further down than the Van Beems, remember?'

So she had thought of it. She was surprisingly superstitious for a scientist.

When he opened his eyes from the anaesthetic, the first thing he saw was Kristina picking out the corned beef from a hospital sandwich, looking haggard and exasperated. She was wearing the little gold cross from her long-repudiated Catholic childhood, which she'd always worn to interviews and exams.

His mood had turned sombre. He felt his limbs

grow heavier by the moment. He touched her shoulder. 'I'm off to bed.'

Before he left, Jerzy had stood at the bedroom door and called into the darkness: 'Is he going to be all right?'

Kristina said that no one knew. If he made it through five years, his chances were good. He was in remission for the time being.

'Don't do anything to upset him,' Jerzy said suddenly.

In one bound Kristina rose up from the bed and stood blinking in the hall. She didn't dare ask Jerzy what he meant. They talked about George.

She'd been sitting on the steps since Jerzy drove off. From down the hill came the distant static of Fremantle on Friday night, shouts and crashes, feral drumbeats, the pulse of car radios. Her stomach hurt.

This afternoon, the man who used to be her lover had phoned her at work. He was a doctor at the same hospital. They'd had a long infrequent affair that she ended when George was diagnosed with cancer. No contact at all, she had said. She didn't tell him about the pact she'd made, giving him up for George's survival.

The doctor said today that he'd heard George had recovered. He wanted to see her again. Just for a walk or a drink, to see how she was. He said he missed her. In fact – his voice broke and he whispered – he was beginning to think he couldn't live without her. And Kristina croaked back that she never stopped thinking about him either. A hoarse craving voice seemed to be speaking through her. At the same time she was filled with foreboding.

Later she rang him from the car at the Monument to tell him she wouldn't meet him. They agreed to try not to meet.

The more they denied themselves, the more they desired. Kristina knew this. She also knew that the doctor wasn't as nice as he was charming. When she first met him she thought he would be funny, with his long upper lip and ironic hang-dog look. But he wasn't funny, in fact he turned out not to have much of a sense of humour. He didn't like her to cry, or even to dress carelessly. He could have a whining tone when he talked about his colleagues. He had a capacity to sneer. For all his height and authority, it sometimes crossed her mind he was a sleaze.

The one person whose advice she'd trust she could not tell. Her lover was not half the man George was, she knew. And yet her thoughts returned to him, over and over, like a mantra.

One seagull circled silently over the street, lit up white in the darkness.

The angel had got it wrong. *It should have been her, not George.*

She had kept her pact and the angel had flown off again. But it was watching. It had left its mark on the door.

Her lover said on the phone at the Monument that he was leaving it up to her. How had it got to this point, so quickly? She didn't know if she could find the conviction not to see him. She didn't know how much longer she could bear it.

God how tired he was. He had just enough energy to slide a disc into the player by his bedside, pull his clothes off and fall naked onto the bed. But still his eyes remained open.

He'd put on Kancheli's *Abii Me Viderem*. He'd been longing for it all evening. He was listening these days to composers from small, almost forgotten countries on the outskirts of the old Soviet Union. Countries which had known great suffering. Kancheli was Georgian. There was something pure and unsparing about this music, like walking over a strange harsh landscape. *I turned away so as not to see*, that was what *Abii Me Viderem* meant.

He saw suddenly the garden around the hospital, pretend bushland that had probably once been landscaped, stunted banksias and eucalypts, forlorn paths of grey sand, a picnic table and benches that nobody ever sat on. Still, it had a certain delicate, unassuming serenity. After rain you could smell the eucalypts. Freesias appeared in early spring and magpies chortled around the car park.

Inside was its own world, a lonely place, and yet there was no face which did not smile at him. You sometimes glimpsed children in pyjamas running down the corridors, bald-headed sprites surrounded by a sort of hush as all the adults held their breath for them. Once he walked into a waiting room full of women, old and young, in pastel floral gowns, and it seemed to him as they looked up that their faces were like flowers. Strangers told each other their stories, sitting together in gowns. They went very deep, very fast. Cancer had humbled them. Nothing had protected them, not virtue or intelligence or good looks. There was nothing left to separate them, nothing left to protect. A young Chinese woman called Mrs Cheng, sitting next to George, told him she had the Lord and that was all she needed. When she received her diagnosis, she'd reached into her handbag for a tissue to wipe her eyes and pulled out a little handcard, nicely printed, which said *The Lord Will Save You*. She had no idea how it got there. It was like a blinding flash, she said.

Sometimes he felt he *had* died and woken up.

How could he tell Ulla that to the end of his days (an end on which he now reflected daily), he would never pass a bus stop without looking for her, waiting in her dusty sandals?

He was growing sleepy. He reached out one arm and switched Kancheli off. Out of music comes silence. Once he fell asleep (after listening to one of the Russians) and dreamt that he was walking down a snowy street at night, lit by glowing, old-fashioned lanterns. How could he tell them that what he remembered most was the pull he felt, strong as love or nostalgia, to give up, lie down in the snow, and close his eyes.